A SNAKE AND A FEATHERED BIRD

A SNAKE AND A FEATHERED BIRD

by Angie Ellis

Thistledown Press Ltd.
Unit 222, 220 20th Street W
Saskatoon, SK
S7M 0W9
www.thistledownpress.com

Library and Archives Canada Cataloguing in Publication
Title: A snake and a feathered bird / by Angie Ellis.
Names: Ellis, Angie, author.
Identifiers: Canadiana (print) 20250192969 | Canadiana (ebook) 20250192977 | ISBN 9781771872812 (softcover) | ISBN 9781771872829 (EPUB)
Subjects: LCGFT: Novels.
Classification: LCC PS8609.L5553 S63 2025 | DDC C813/.6—dc23

Edited by Fred Stenson
Cover and book design by Michel Vrana
Cover image: Vintage oranges illustration. Digitally enhanced illustration from U.S. Department of Agriculture Pomological Watercolor Collection. Rare and Special Collections, National Agricultural Library (Rawpixel); Study of Clouds with a Sunset near Rome (1786–1801) painting in high resolution by Simon Alexandre Clément Denis. Original from Getty Museum. (Rawpixel)

Printed and bound in Canada

Canada Council for the Arts
Conseil des arts du Canada

Canada

Saskatchewan

Thistledown Press gratefully acknowledges the financial assistance of SK Arts, The Canada Council for the Arts, and the Government of Canada for its publishing program.

*For John, who bought me a laptop
and told me to write*

"To an ordinary observer there would seem but little in common between a scaled lizard or snake, a cuirassed crocodile, and a carapaced tortoise, on the one hand, and a feathered bird on the other. Nevertheless, the connection between Reptiles and Birds is exceedingly intimate..."

—Richard Lydekker, *The Royal Natural History, vol. V (1896)*

BEN

1875

HE SAT IN FRONT OF THE FIERY-HAIRED WOMAN ON HER horse. She clutched the reins with pale hands, blue veins lying flat beneath her skin as if painted there. When he squirmed, she patted him and whispered words he didn't understand.

They rode in the shade of a treed mountain and past a lake, where glimpses of silver water flashed through the branches. The woods became deeper. Here it was cool and still, and smelled of mud. A flash of black and the quick *whoosh-whoosh* of birds' wings. He looked up to where the tops of the wide trees disappeared in thick piney boughs. There was no sky here.

"It is good, this place, yes?" the woman said.

But he was afraid of the rustling, creaking sounds of the forest. And though the woman seemed kind, he was afraid of her too.

They came to a small clearing, chickens about the yard and a low grey cabin in the middle. The woman lifted him down and led him to the door, where his too-big shoes caught on the step and he fell, skinning his knee. She covered her mouth, tsking and clucking, and brought him inside. It was a small room with a bed in the corner and walls made from trees stacked one on top of the other. The woman hummed as she dabbed beeswax on his scraped knee. It smelled like pine trees and honey.

They sat at a small table, where she set a slice of bread and molasses in front of him. He watched her and she watched him, smiling and nodding and motioning to her own lips until he began to eat.

When he finished, she took his hand and showed him around the cabin, teaching him the French words for things. *Chair, chaise. Window, fenêtre. Hand, main. Heart, cœur.*

Mother, Mère.

She smiled and he smiled back.

Then a man walked into the yard and the woman went out to meet him. Through the window, they looked small—she holding her arms tight by the elbows and he waving wildly.

When they came inside, the man crossed the room and looked down. The lobe of his ear was chewed up, mangled and purple.

"Why doesn't he say anything?"

He thunked his finger on the side of the boy's head.

"See? What'd I tell you?"

The woman shushed and smiled and brought the boy to the sofa. She said it would be his bed. She slipped a nightshirt over his head. *Pillow, oreiller. Moon, lune.*

"Silent boy, *garçon silencieux.*"

She named him Benjamin.

BEN

1880

THE SUN WAS LOW AND COOL BUT THE SOIL WAS STILL WARM. He dug a finger around the root of a prickly weed, then grabbed the stalk and pulled, tossing it into the basket next to his mother. Tipping back his hat, he looked to the trail that left the yard and asked again where his father went so often and for so long.

His mother was still. Then she looked at him over her shoulder in mock reproach. "Are you not happy here with your mother, *mon chou*?"

"I'm happy."

"Ah. Good."

She turned away, her face hidden in the shadow of her wide straw hat. Her orange braid was thin like a mouse's tail. He picked weed after weed, and she sang.

À la claire fontaine
M'en allant promener
J'ai trouvé l'eau si belle
Que je m'y suis baigné

He knew this song to be about clear water, a place to swim. A bird. A sad woman. His mother's voice was high and strained, as if she was crying. He leaned forward, trying to peek at her face under her hat. She wasn't sad at all, she was smiling.

Soon, the evening fell silent and so did his mother's singing. She rubbed a carrot on her skirts and handed it to him, then took one for herself. Crouched in the garden, they ate. The carrots were crisp and gritty, and tasted like dirt.

The next morning was for washing, so they put on old clothes that were too small or worn out. Their noses were sunburned and their hands rough. While shirts flapped on the line, Ben practised his letters with the old seed catalogue.

Burpee's Seeds are warranted first class in every respect—few equal, none better! French Breakfast Radish. Montreal Green Nutmeg Melon. Giant Yellow Rocca Onion.

When his tongue tripped up, his mother leaned over his shoulder.

"It's a strange word that you will never use. Skip to the next."

And when his eyes were sleepy, she closed the book.

"I think we are done, yes? We should make tea."

And so they drank from tin cups as the sun beat its way through the tiny window next to them.

"I will tell you this about your father," she said. "Maybe you already know."

Ben held his cup and didn't drink.

"There is no virtue in him. He has been too long away from it." She waved her hand and shrugged. "It is not in his nature to love. It is not in his nature to be a father."

Ben looked again to the trail. He had thought nature meant trees. Or rain. Sun and wind and thunder. He imagined all of that fighting inside his father, making his eyeballs jump and hard words fly like bats from his mouth.

"But Benjamin," his mother said as she leaned forward and placed her hand on his cheek, "who cares about that? I wanted you before you were born. I loved you even then."

* * *

That night, his mind was heavy with sleep, and the sounds in his half dreams were as real as the forest sounds outside. He drifted and dreamed of his mother, kneeling in the garden in the moonlight. She peeked into the ground where all the unborn babies lay curled and damp in the earth with the soft worms and the clicking beetles. Her hands moved soil until she found him—*Je t'aimais même alors*—and lifted him, all dark in the night and purple with dirt. *I loved you even then, mon chou.*

The weather turned to rain and his father came home in shining boots. He dropped his bag on the floor and said, "Look inside."

Ben found an orange and a paper packet. It smelled like honey and pepper. Warm milk.

"Come on then. Open it."

In the folded paper, he found three dry sticks.

"Cinnamon bark," his father said. He nodded to Ben's mother, who stood quietly near the table. "See if she'll make a cake or something."

Then he took the orange and broke it open, the inside a glistening pulp. He handed Ben a piece. Clear juice ran down his dirty hand.

Ben bit into it. The brightest thing he'd ever tasted.

His father stayed until the rains eased up. When his bag was again by the door, Ben knew he would leave.

That night, he picked at the rough log wall behind the sofa as his father huffed and grunted on the other side of the curtain. Small bits of bark lodged under his fingernails and larger bits fell on the floor.

In the winter, the little window was as wet on the inside as out, blurring the moon to a smudge of light, but tonight there was no rain and the view was clear. He thought of the ink picture Will Stenhouse had shown him in his schoolbook—the moon distant from the earth, two marbles in darkness. Ben had imagined standing on one and yelling to Will on the other, but Will shook his head and said, "Too far. I'd never hear you. I wouldn't even see you."

The cabin went quiet, then three heavy steps and the curtain whipped open. Ben remained still and silent on the sofa, feeling the uncomfortable weight of his father watching, the broad, black shape of him.

"Tomorrow, we go the city," his father said. "We leave early. All right?"

Behind him, next to their bed, Ben's mother stood, pale in the lantern's low flicker, her nightgown hanging on her thin shoulders.

"Yes, sir," said Ben, and the curtain fell shut.

He couldn't sleep. He wondered what the city was. A sweet-smelling place where cinnamon bark grew? A forest of orange trees? The moon slowly rose to the corner of his window then disappeared.

When morning came, his father polished his new boots and his mother fried eggs. Ben brought in the bucket of milk and set it on the chair.

Bending to his ear, his mother said, "*Écoute-moi.* Tell him you are ill." She held Ben's gaze, the blue vein at her temple beating.

At the table, Ben stared at his bowl. Each time his mother caught his eye, he said nothing.

"Ben is unwell today," she finally said.

His father took a bite of egg, and the yolk dripped down his stubbled chin.

"He's fine."

"Benjamin." His mother placed her dry hand on his forehead. "How do you feel?"

But his mother had never been to the city. She didn't get to taste the orange. Ben shrugged. "I feel good."

"See, he's fine. For Chrissake, Agda."

And his mother stood and collected the dishes.

* * *

He had trouble keeping up with his father along the path, with its roots and dips and boggy areas. They reached the narrow road that ran around the lake, one way leading to the Stenhouse farm, the other to the city. Branches reached wide over their heads and fat roots spread under their feet.

Without slowing his stride, his father pulled a piece of bread from the pack and handed it to Ben, who hurried behind him.

"Watch for that Howland dog," he said over his shoulder. "He's hungry."

Chewing the sour bread, Ben watched the trees, saving a piece of crust in his pocket just in case.

The sun was high when they stopped at the grey-timbered store. It was so close to the road, the door nearly opened onto it. Ben had been here with his mother when he was a lot smaller, but now he could read the letters on the sign and sound them out—*Petrenko's Dry Goods & Post.* He followed his father inside.

The place was cluttered. The air felt heavy with warm-smelling things—dusty grain, dried fish, burlap, coffee beans, pickled vegetables.

In the corner by the woodstove was a man slumped in a wheeled chair. Mr. Petrenko, with his fringe of grey hair and long nose. Ben knew him to be a smiling man who had given his mother a jar of spongy bread starter. Sometimes he came out and helped them with the garden or small repairs, but now he was withered up like a squash left too long on the vine.

Ben's father smacked the bell on the counter and a woman appeared from the back room with a cup of tea.

"Oh hello, James," she said. "You brought a visitor!"

Mrs. Petrenko was built like a fir tree, and her voice was loud and friendly. Ben wondered if she ever hit her head on the ceiling and if her feet stuck out the end of her bed at night. She went to Mr. Petrenko and rubbed his back, then held the cup to his lips.

"Our young Benjamin is growing up," she told him.

"How many bottles you want?" Ben's father asked. "We'll be coming back through in a couple weeks."

"Three, but I won't pay more than a dollar and a half."

She straightened, hands on her hips. Ben waited for his father's temper, but he only ground his boot on the floor as if he was squishing a bug.

Mrs. Petrenko went over to a glass jar on the counter and pulled out a pink candy.

"These came all the way from San Francisco," she said, handing it to Ben.

He looked at his father, who was busy studying Mrs. Petrenko, so he popped the candy in his mouth. It sat hard and strange like a pebble on his tongue. When he bit down, his teeth stuck and his mouth filled with sweetness.

"You taste one of those before?"

He shook his head.

"You see that, Ed?" She turned to Mr. Petrenko. "Ben is having his first candy in our very own store."

But Mr. Petrenko's eyes remained fixed on the air in front of him.

His father bought little sacks of coffee, flour, cornmeal, porridge oats, bacon. No oranges that Ben could see.

"You'll pay what I charge," he said, then stormed out, letting the door slam behind him.

As they walked away from the store, Ben saw a flash of fur in the trees. A minute later, he saw it again. His father saw nothing. He was still muttering about Mrs. Petrenko—*cheap bitch!*—swinging his arm like it was a twitchy cow tail.

The dog stayed alongside them for a while. Ben got used to its rustle and swish, the glimpses of its long face. He stopped and held out his last piece of bread to the dark trees.

"What are you doing?" his father called. "Let's go, let's go!"

Ben tossed the bread and the dog lunged for it.

Again the road broke in two. One led away from the lake and the other went to the school—a small log building tucked into the woods. Ben had only ever seen the school from the Stenhouse farm across the water. Now, he saw its windows, glossy and black, and the silver bell that hung above the door. Will and Effie would be inside, maybe reading a seed catalogue. He stopped and looked across the lake to their farm, their fields dotted with sheep and cows.

The last time he visited the Stenhouse farm with his mother, he'd waited at the lake's reedy edge while the teacher rowed the children home. The boat was just a little red spot on the black-green water, but he could hear their voices.

"Not so close," his mother yelled from near the house, "or I will have you come up here and make a quilt with us old ladies."

Ben was near enough to see the yellow pollen dusting the water's slick surface, the tiny fish darting among the stones at the bottom.

"Benjamin. Not so close or you will fall in. You will breathe water and drown."

And he imagined breathing that cool water, growing silvery scales and eyes that bulged.

Later, when Ben helped the Stenhouse children with their chores, he asked Will and Effie about school. Effie said it was terrible. Will said it was easy.

And Ben wondered. *What was terrible? What was easy?*

And how did it feel to be on top of the water in a little red boat?

Ben's father didn't turn toward the school or continue on the road to the city. Instead, he cut onto an overgrown trail through the trees.

Ben ran after him. They climbed over shrubs and fallen branches and around fat fir trunks and bushes. He smelled woodsmoke but didn't see a cabin until his father called out to it—*Hallo there!* Wild, leafy shrubs surrounded the tiny shack, and ferns grew from the chinks between the logs. The man who opened the door looked first at his father, then at Ben. He was small and unwashed, and his face was soft, hanging loosely as if it wasn't properly attached. He wore murky spectacles that made his eyes large. Each man said the name of the other with a short nod of the head. *James. Connie.*

Connie stood aside and waved them in.

Inside, the cabin smelled of old smoke and ash. There was no window. Light came from a fire in the stove and a lamp dangling from the ceiling, its chimney black with soot. The cabin was much smaller than their own, with room only for a cot and a chair. Hanging on the walls were full sacks, tin dishes, an oilskin coat, an axe, a gun, a shelf of sticky jars, and every other thing.

"I brought the boy," his father said, setting his bag on the bed.

Connie watched Ben, then looked away into the fire. One of his hands shook in his lap, a slow rocking from the wrist. His head swivelled too. Ben wondered if all of him was loose and needed one more twist of the screw.

"You bring tobacco?"

"Next time I will."

Ben looked again at the jars. Five of them, grimy and part full.

"How old is he?" Connie asked.

"I'm eight," said Ben, and both men turned and looked at him. Ben's toes curled in his boots. "I haven't been to school yet."

His father held up his hand. "Why you talking so much?"

Ben hugged his arms close. It was hard to breathe in the smoky room, and he had the urge to fling the door open to the air outside.

"Well?" said Connie.

His father opened his bag and took out all the things he'd bought at Petrenko's, plus the bread Ben's mother had sent. Connie looked it over, opening packages and sniffing the contents. He unwrapped the bacon and ran his jerking finger along it.

"Next time bring tobacco."

They stayed for a long while. Ben sat next to his father on the bed as the two men discussed things. Whisky and islands. Weather and tides. Connie spoke like the one in charge, the one who knew things, while Ben's father nodded and listened. *Oh yes, I sure will, Con. Uh-huh. You're right about that.* His eyes were focused on the hat in his lap. His mangled ear shone darkly. Ben looked from one man to the other, but mostly at his father, who seemed like a stranger in this place.

"Merritt's back," Connie said. "I left him in charge until you get there. He can accompany you on the run."

At this, Ben felt his father stiffen, as if he'd stopped breathing.

"I don't need—"

"You don't? You plan to guard the whisky *and* deliver it? Be in two places at once?"

"I'll bring Oland."

"He's running the place, you idiot."

"Well, I brought the boy."

Connie stared at Ben with pale eyes, large as an owl's behind the smudged glass. "It's too bad you're still so stupid."

The words stung like a slap, but then Connie's eyes shifted to his father and stayed there.

"Never known anyone so stupid as you, James. How are we brothers?"

Ben braced for his father's anger, but instead his father looked down and spoke quietly.

"He's a thief. Merritt. There's no good in that man."

"Last time," Connie said, "you told me he was a dullard and a quitter. Perhaps you only describe yourself."

He poked at a dark tooth on one side of his mouth, then wiped his shaking finger on his shirt.

"Go on then. Bring the money here when you're done. And keep your hands off Merritt. You know I'll be asking him how you fared."

Connie twisted his neck and looked into the fire.

"Don't know why you brought this boy."

Outside, it was growing dark, but not as dark as Connie's cabin. As they walked, words erupted from his father.

"Fecking *Merritt*. No good thief and abandoner. *Never again*, I said."

They didn't go far. When they came to a clearing, his father dropped his bag on the ground. Ben gathered sticks and his father built a small fire, then they lay down beside it, shivering under a shared blanket.

The Howland dog sat at the edge of the clearing and watched until his father shooed it off. But later, when his father was asleep, Ben whispered to it. The dog came out of the trees and sat, its eyes gleaming black in the fire's light.

In the morning, it was gone.

His father shook him awake early. It was barely light, and the rotting leaves on the ground were frosted. They drank handfuls of creek water, then followed the trail back to the road, where Ben stepped into his father's long-striding footprints.

The road was bendy and well treed. Gulls called and the air smelled strong—a cold iron-pan smell that his father said was the sea.

When they were near the city, the road opened up to partly cleared land. They walked on planks set in the mud, past half-built homes, piles of timber, fat stumps, and slow-moving wagons loaded with stones or bricks. Men stood guard over brush fires as big as houses, while children played around them. The crackling heat warmed Ben's face as he tripped after his father.

Then the road turned sharply and the city came into view. Down at the bottom was the harbour, and between here and there, a slope full of houses with a few old black firs left standing. Some feeling shook Ben, a pebble rolling down the hollow of his bones.

"Will we see the water?" he asked.

"It's right there in front of you."

"But will we go near it?"

"Of course we'll go near it."

The harbour was like a lake that the city cupped around, but unlike a lake, a piece of the far shore was missing. The water went on and on until it disappeared. Boats sat motionless and narrow canoes glided from one side to the other, and above it all, the sky opened up, wide and grey.

As they walked down toward the sea, the buildings became taller, the road firmer, and the trees sparse. Everything was unusual. So many kinds of people—some dirty and ragged, some finely dressed, hurrying, limping, laughing, coughing. Faces of different colours with different expressions. Hats of all kinds.

They passed a group of men, all wearing red shirts and blue caps, chopping at logs, their feet chained one to the next. Then they turned a corner and passed a group of women in short woollen capes, each holding a black book. They were singing, but it sounded funny and out of rhythm with the men's chopping. One of the women looked at Ben straight and stern, like he'd done something wrong.

They passed shops with swinging signs and giant windows. Shining brass lamps. Tall doors of polished wood and glass. The shops sold cigars, boots, dead chickens, gloves, bread. A herd of squealing pigs was fenced between two painted buildings, one blue and one red. A tiny wooden church stood right across from a giant stone church that towered cooly over them like a hollow mountain. Sounds rose up through the bottoms of Ben's shoes—the crunching of iron wheels on cobbles, horses clopping, voices shouting, gulls calling.

His father pushed on, looking nowhere but ahead, then suddenly he turned and went through a door. Ben read the sign above. The Brown Jug.

Inside, it smelled like fresh firewood and something else, old and sour. The planks on the walls and floors were still yellow, like they had been cut from a tree that day. All the chairs were turned upside down on the tables, except one in the corner where a young woman slept, her sand-coloured braids wrapped around her head in a ring.

Ben's father walked over and kicked her chair three times before she opened her eyes. She smiled.

"Uncle," she said, a soft rasp to her voice. "How funny."

Ben's eyes darted to his father. He'd never once mentioned a brother or a niece. Now Ben had met both.

"I was dreaming of you just now." She motioned to the top of her head. "You wore a feathered hat."

"Where is he?"

"Merritt? Out back. Loading the wagon." She tilted the chair onto its back legs and leaned against the wall behind her. "I was going to help today."

"There's no need." His father pointed. "I brought the boy."

She turned to look at Ben, her head still against the wall. Her eyes were pale green in the light from the window.

"So you did." Her smile was sleepy but wide. "Agda's baby."

"I'm eight," said Ben.

"Are you really?" She let the chair fall forward, then set her elbow on the table and her chin in her hand. "Hmm. What is it eight-year-old boys do, anyway? Scuffle, I suppose. Kill birds?"

Again he looked at his father, a nick in his chest. Why would he kill a bird?

His father whistled and Ben followed him out through a back door to a yard, where a man in a checkered vest was loading small milk cans into a wagon. He was loose-limbed and tall, with chin-length black hair tucked behind large ears. When he walked by with a can in each hand, his eyes flashed from Ben to his father.

"You're lucky I allowed this," his father called after the man, face red and voice booming. "Eh, Merritt? You're lucky I let you work here at all!"

The man acted as though he didn't hear it. He swung the two cans into the wagon bed and turned back for more.

"Merritt," said the niece, who had come outside. She leaned against the doorframe. "I believe my uncle extends an olive branch."

Merritt grabbed two more cans and crossed the yard.

"Uncle, Merritt understands your feelings, and he's grateful for the job." She plucked a stem of grass and held it between her teeth.

Ben's father drew in a long breath, his chest expanding and holding. Ben thought they'd leave right then, march back out of this place as quickly as they'd come into it. But instead, his father nodded to the wagon and they got to work.

Ben hefted one can and followed his father, who carried two. It sloshed heavily in his arms, throwing his weight so that he staggered. He struggled to lift it onto the wagon bed.

"You're scrawny," his father said, slamming his two cans down hard enough to bounce the wheels.

"Sometimes small is strong," said the niece.

"Not with this one."

"Like a little ant." She leaned her head against the doorframe. "Or a mouse. I've seen a mouse carry another mouse like it was nothing at all."

When they were done, his father nodded to the back of the wagon and Ben hopped up and sat among the cans. His father climbed onto the front seat, and Merritt sat tall and silent beside him. As they pulled out of the yard, Ben held up his hand and his father's niece did the same. Her smile was very pretty.

It started to drizzle as they went along beside the harbour, a misty wet that hung in the air. Ben wedged his shoulders against the cans and rested his arms on top. His legs stuck out straight and bounced on the wagon's bed.

They left the shops behind, then the houses, then passed by a row of Kanaka shacks sitting along the wide, empty mudflats. Neither man said a word the whole way, but still it was a noisy ride—seagulls calling, wheels squealing, and crunching stones. The sloshing and rattling of the cans, and the horse's hooves striking packed earth. After a while, they turned onto an overgrown road, two ruts barely showing in the weeds. The track led through a wild tunnel of bush and trees to a small beach.

Fog hovered over the water and crept through the tangled growth at its edges. Across the channel sat an island of spiky black firs. It didn't seem far at all, and Ben wondered if Will could swim it. He stood in the wagon so he could better see the cluster of low houses at the island's end, smoke rising from each flat roof, pale against the dark forest.

Merritt dragged a canoe from the bushes and pushed it into the water. Twisted trees stretched over the lapping waves, their glossy leaves dipping low and almost touching the water's surface. The trees' red bark curled off like paper, revealing smooth golden trunks underneath, which is how Ben imagined cinnamon bark would look.

"Load up," said his father, so they carried cans from the wagon to the canoe, splashing knee-deep. The water was so icy cold it burned.

His father angled his head toward the village. "We paddle there, sell what we can, then come back. Merritt stays here and guards the wagon. Then we'll go to two other places close by. Tomorrow, we hit two more islands, a couple of homes, and another Indian village. Got it?"

Ben was trying to imagine so many villages, so many islands.

"What will I do?"

"Get in."

His father held the canoe steady while Ben crawled from the back to the front. The canoe rocked and Ben froze, one hand on either side.

"Sit, sit." His father splashed up next to him and handed him a paddle. He clamped Ben's hands in the right spots and showed him a long, dragging motion. "If you're a quick learner, I'll get you another orange. How's that?"

Ben nodded and his father climbed in behind him. Then Merritt pushed them out, a smooth and quiet glide that flipped Ben's stomach. The water stretched wide all around them, mist hanging over but not touching. Strange things floated—part animal, part plant, with hairy spines and bulbous heads. Clear, round ghost-animals pulsed like small hearts beating. Shimmering black ribbons clung to his paddle.

"Not like that," his father said. "Long and steady. See?"

It was quiet on the water, only the splash of paddles dipping and his father's wheezing breath behind him. If the canoe tipped, he would fall to the invisible bottom. He would walk the ocean floor where sea creatures lived. *Breathe in water and drown.* He nearly dropped the paddle.

He looked back at his father.

"Keep going. You're no help to me like that."

Will had told him about whales—monsters in the deep, as big as a barn. He looked over the side. Maybe this boat was a speck to a whale below, like seeing the belly of a bird when he looked up in the sky. He felt dizzy.

"Now on your left."

His father thwacked the side of the canoe with his paddle. Ben worked on that side and the boat began to turn.

"See? Now do one side, then the other."

They moved sluggish and tipsy.

"Weaker than I thought. That's Agda's doing."

Ben paddled harder, then stopped.

"Are there whales here?"

"Whales? Too shallow for that. Too narrow. Keep paddling."

But Ben wasn't sure. The water was black beneath the boat. How could anyone know how deep it went?

They were quick to reach the shore, where the fog had settled, fading the village down the beach to a soft haze. They jumped out and, splashing and gasping at the cold, dragged the canoe over the pebbles.

"See those arbutus?" His father handed Ben a can and nodded up the hill to a patch of peeling red trees. "Past those is the shipwright's shack. Lengnick, that good-for-nothing. Make sure he pays first. He's wily. If he's laid flat out, you kick him. He sleeps like the dead. And don't let his squaw see you. All right? She keeps a tight rein." His father grabbed two more cans, one in each thick, purple hand. "Go on now."

Ben looked up the rise, where a path led through the trees, then back to his father, who walked along the beach, shoulders weighed down by the swaying cans.

"Where will you be?" he called, but his father was fading in the mist and didn't turn.

Ben struggled up the trail, his feet slipping in the leaves and mud, the can like a wriggling pig in his arms. It sloshed and threatened to knock him off balance, and twice it fell to the ground.

It was slow going but finally Ben found the cabin, small and grey in an open patch of scrubby grass, surrounded by twisty oaks. He heard the man's wet snoring before he saw him—sprawled long-legged on the porch, a big wet patch on the front of his trousers. Ben was embarrassed at a grown man peeing himself and tried not to look. He quietly went up the steps and peeked in the window for the woman who didn't want him there. Nothing could be seen through the smudgy glass, so he took a step closer to Lengnick. Close enough to smell him, rank and mouldy. Close enough to see the warts on his pale skin, and the stubby wet of his eyelashes.

"This is for you," Ben whispered.

Lengnick didn't move and his breathing didn't change. Ben took another step forward and spoke louder.

"I have your milk."

As Ben tapped the bottom of Lengnick's bare foot with his boot, two things happened. The man opened one bloodshot eye, and someone shouted from somewhere in the trees. Ben jumped back to see a Songhees woman running toward him, thrashing through the woods with a baby on her hip. He stepped back again as she came closer, his heart thumping against the can in his arms. The woman stopped just in front of him, pointing back to the trail.

Ben shook from the inside, like he'd done something horribly wrong. He looked over to Lengnick, who was struggling to get up, then back to the woman. Her baby sucked noisily on a strand of her hair as she jabbed her finger again, first at Ben and then at the trail.

"Go!"

So Ben ran, quick-footed into the trees and down the trail, the can sloshing in his arms. He was halfway to the beach when Lengnick roared somewhere behind him—an animal sound from deep in the woods. Ben hurried and Lengnick kept coming, his words lost in all the crashing through brush, the whipping branches and skidding boots.

Finally, he broke onto the beach, searching the fog for his father. But there was no sign of anyone, so he ran to the canoe and dropped the can in with the others. With a quick look behind, he caught a glimpse of Lengnick tearing through the trees, mouth gaping as he hollered. Ben shoved the canoe into the water, splashing in up to his knees. When he clambered in, the boat tipped so far, he soaked the cuff of his sleeve, so he made himself be still, carefully knelt, then jammed his paddle into the silty ground and pushed. He did this again and again until he could no longer feel the bottom, then he paddled. One side and then the other. Lengnick still hollered behind him, but Ben didn't want to look until he was at a safe distance.

He was careful when he stopped paddling, careful as he turned to look over his shoulder. There he was. Lengnick. Pacing the foggy shore, his arms in the air, his long legs bending this way and that. Ben's father was nowhere and the village invisible. Ben turned back around and paddled harder. Everything inside him churned and trembled.

The further he went, the thicker the patches of fog, until he felt alone in the middle of the sea. But if he focused hard, he thought he could see the beach where Merritt waited—a wispy, barely there place. He tried to keep his eyes forward and not look back to the island where his father would be looking for him, or up where the gulls rode the air like ghosts—or down where the whale's eye watched from below, as big and dark as a washing kettle.

Somewhere behind him, Lengnick was like a sea creature himself, with his leaking, watery eye and barnacle skin.

Ben shook again, a violent spasm that sprung his hand open, and just like that, the paddle fell from his grip. A silent slip from his fingers, a gentle bobbing as it drifted away.

"No-o-o," Ben whispered, his voice close in the fog.

Quiet.

He reached out over the black water, feeling the chill beneath his palm. Would a whale flick its long grey tongue and snatch the paddle away? The canoe dipped near the water's surface, so he stilled, then carefully reached farther, but his fingertips only grazed the yellow wood of the handle, nudging it away. Desperate, he rose up onto his knees and leaned, his breath held tight.

Then, without a breath or a blink, the canoe flipped and Ben plunged into the icy water. He tumbled under and rolled up, then under and up and under, and under and under until there was no up at all.

He surfaced and gasped, mouth full of salt water.

Then under.

His legs moved in all directions, his clothes heavy and tight around him.

And up—he gasped.

Under, just as quick.

Down and rolling further into the dark until his mother spoke.

You will breathe water and drown.

He opened his eyes. Murky green, long, slick grasses, a forest of kelp. His mother's face showed pale in the weeds, as if sleeping. Slippery kelp fingers took hold of his ankle and she disappeared.

He kicked, wriggled, and fought the weeds as his lungs burned for air. Something took hold of him. He struggled harder as he was pulled by the back of his coat, fighting the strong arm that hooked around his chest. Finally, he burst through the surface, gasping and choking as he was carried over a strong bony shoulder, a checkered vest. Merritt.

Ben felt himself grow heavier as Merritt carried him out of the sea, through chest-deep water, then waist-deep, then splashing, then onto the beach. Back at the wagon, Merritt lifted Ben onto the seat. He bent forward with his hands on his knees, heaving and coughing. His hair hung in black ropes over his face.

"You would have died," he said through clamped teeth, his lips inky blue. "Where's James?"

But Ben was too cold to answer. Merritt shook his head like a wet dog, then rummaged in the back of the wagon. He came back with blankets, wrapping one around Ben and one around himself. Then he climbed onto the seat. Taking his hat from beside him, he placed it on Ben's head. It was large and low over his eyes, but warm.

"Where's James?" Merritt said again, his voice broken and raspy.

Ben's whole body rattled and his teeth were locked. He clutched the blanket to keep from shaking so violently, salt on his tongue and in his eyes.

Neither said anything more until they arrived at the Brown Jug. Merritt took back his hat and placed it on his own head. "Go find Lily," he said. "You'll be all right."

Then he left.

The pub was rowdy and warm, and lit by gas to a murky yellow. A fire blazed on the hearth on the far wall, and the familiar sour smell hung in the air, along with smoke and sweat, and something roasting. Ben left a wet trail as he wound his way through the tables, holding himself hard to stop his shivering, forcing his locked knees to bend.

He felt small in this place of men, the deep rumble of voices from every direction.

Finally, he saw his father's niece. Lily. She sat at the same table as earlier, but with two men now. When she looked Ben's way, she smiled and kicked a chair out for him.

"Little drowned mouse," she said, like he'd done something clever. "Where are the others?"

Ben's body stiffened. His jaw clamped tight.

"They leave you here?"

He nodded. He was beginning to feel warmth from the fire at his back. He wanted to crawl inside it, curl up in the coals.

"You tipped the canoe then?"

He nodded again.

She placed her chin in her hands.

"That happens. You can stay with me while they finish, all right?"

Tears spilled over onto Ben's cheeks. He rubbed at them with his sleeve.

"Lily, take the boy home," one of the men said. "Look at him."

She reached over with her own dry sleeve and wiped under each of his eyes.

"Is that what you want? To go to my place?"

Ben nodded.

"All right then." She finished her drink. With her head tilted back, Ben could see a long purple scar on the side of her neck, like a wrinkly worm. "It's not so festive at home, but we'll have each other for company."

She wavered when she stood, clutching the table. "Ha. Look how clumsy. And I wanted to give my speech."

"We don't need your speeches, Lily," said a second man. "Take the boy home." Then to Ben, he said, "Keep an eye on your valuables, boy."

It was darker and colder when they stepped outside, so Lily put her arm around his shoulders to warm him. She walked like he'd paddled—all twisty and turning. They went along the street, then down an alley, then up a narrow staircase on the outside of a tall building to her door. Inside, Lily's place was chilly and dark. It smelled rain-soaked, but when she lit the lamp, everything was dry.

Lily talked while she stacked kindling in the stove. Her words were raspy and strung together so that Ben had trouble sorting them. She struck a match with hands as small as his own, a quick flare of light on her face. Some of her hair had come loose from the circle of braids. It was pale gold in the firelight.

Ben hoped that Merritt had gone back and collected his father by now. He imagined them paddling back through the misty dark to the beach with the twisted trees. He imagined his father raging the whole way. He shivered again.

As the fire crackled and the room slowly warmed, Lily searched through a chest near the sofa.

"This belonged to a friend," she said, taking out a shirt. "He had orange hair and white eyelashes. He preferred dresses to shirts, so I traded him one of mine. Does it look nice to you?"

Ben nodded, so she tossed it to him. As he changed, his hands were cold and clumsy, his fingers like wooden pegs. The shirt hung down to his knees.

"You should keep it," she said. "It'll fit you one day."

She pulled a quilt from her bed and draped it around Ben's shoulders.

"My uncle pays for this place, you know." She moved to the corner of the room where it was dark. "He's like a father to me, as he is to you."

Lily hummed as she poured from a bottle, then handed him a glass of sparkling brown liquid. It sent a syrupy flame down his throat and into his belly. He drank more and, with each sip, the warmth spread like he'd swallowed the sun.

"Isn't this funny?" Lily said, but he didn't know what was funny. "A little mouse in my old house. No one would believe it."

She stretched, which lifted the hem of her dress enough to reveal men's work boots and long tights, boldly striped. Setting down her drink, she lay on the sofa with her arm draped over the side.

"You're quiet." She closed her eyes and smiled. "I tend to jabber on, so we may be a good pair."

Ben couldn't see her right. He was under the sea again, the room rolling over.

"Do you remember," she asked softly, "coming from the water? It must have been terribly dark."

His hands didn't move where he wanted them to, and his glass fell to the floor. He tried to look at Lily but she was all blurry on the sofa. He couldn't stop the hot sick that rushed up his throat and down the man's shirt.

"Poor Mouse. You don't like whisky?"

Lily gave him a rag for his face. She mopped the floor with another.

"No one ever told me about children," she said.

He bit the inside of his lip to keep from crying.

There were no more clothes in the chest, so he put his damp things back on. His shirt stuck as he pulled it over his head, and his hand caught on a tear in the sleeve and tore it farther. It was the shirt his mother had made.

"No one ever told me about children," Lily repeated as she pinned his shirt together. "I hardly remember being one myself. Maybe you'll forget one day too."

He lay on her sofa and she placed the blanket over him before adding more sticks to the fire. She gathered up the soiled rags and opened the door, tossing them off the side of her stairs.

"See?" she said. "Like it never happened."

Ben woke with a dry, sour mouth and an upset stomach. Lily was gone. He stood at the window, watching for his father as he picked the wood frame with his fingernail.

The street was busy, but he saw no sign of a short, broad man with long arms swinging. But he spotted Lily. She walked like a breeze was nudging her this way and that. She turned down the alley to her apartment, and soon he heard her on the outside stairs. When she opened the door, she smiled.

"You're still here," she said. "What a funny boy."

Ben told her he was hungry, and she sent him down the street with a penny for buns. He sat at the small table across from her and ate them, his cheeks full and his eyes nearly closed. He asked when his father would be back, and she said in a few days, since he had Merritt along to help—though of course they didn't get on. He looked out the window at a gull coasting by. A few days felt like forever. He looked back at Lily, who was resting her cheek in her palm, elbow on the table.

"Why don't they get on?" he asked.

"Well. Sometimes men get all caught up in one thing or another. Women do too, but differently." She leaned forward. "Here's a trick," she said. This close, Ben could see freckles on her nose and under her eyes. "When my uncle's angry, pretend there's a glass box around him. You can't hear anything! Go about your business and he'll tire himself out." She smiled and ate some of his bun. "He doesn't mean any of it. He doesn't care if anyone actually hears him."

"Does Merritt do that?"

"Merritt more than anyone."

She stood and looked out the window, then off she went again and Ben was left alone. Later, she came back with a drinking glass, criss-crossed in deep cuts.

"It's crystal. Listen."

She flicked it with her finger and a soft chime filled the room, then quieted. She let him hold it for a while, heavy in his palm and catching every colour as he turned it. He flicked it several times until she took it away and set it on a shelf that was cluttered with trinkets and tins and stacks of papers. She poured herself three careful drops of medicine in a glass of water, then slept for a while. When she woke, she gave him a kiss on the top of his head and left again.

Ben liked Lily, but he wondered if he should try to find his own way home without his father. In his mind, he traced the route—city, houses, farms, school, lake, Petrenko's store, the Stenhouses' drive, home.

But that night, while Lily dozed and Ben looked through an old book of songs, his father arrived.

For a long moment, James stood in the door with his eyes on Ben. Then he crossed the room and hit him hard on the side of the head. The thump knocked the thoughts out of Ben's mind and made his teeth rattle like pebbles in a jar. It hurt enough to make everything blurry and bright for a moment. The book fell to the floor, and this woke Lily.

"How'd you get here?" his father said to him. His clothes were damp and the icy night air hung around him like a fog. He turned to Lily. "When'd he get here?"

"Yesterday. Before Merritt went back to find you." She sat up. "Where is Merritt?"

His father turned back to Ben. "Did Merritt tell you to leave me there? Is he behind this?"

Ben shook his head and his father drew back his broad hand.

"You lying to me?"

"No, sir."

Ben braced for another thump, but none came because Lily spoke.

"Uncle," she said softly, "have a drink. Sit by the fire and warm yourself."

But his father didn't do either. Instead, he went to the window and pulled back the curtain. He studied the street below.

"When does Connie return?" he asked.

"When his twitches settle. But you know that."

"Tell him nothing."

"He won't be troubled over a few lost cans," said Lily. "Just pay for what was lost."

"No," his father said, his hand absently scratching his chest, which Ben knew meant hard thinking. "You tell your father we left early. Tell him everything was lost and Merritt called it off."

"Did Merritt call it off?" Lily tilted her head and watched him. "Where is Merritt, Uncle?"

"Do I look like his keeper?"

"You don't look like any kind of keeper. Did he leave you?"

His father stared at her, his eyes ticking like a skitchy old clock. "Yes, he left. I'll be blamed, no doubt."

Ben was sitting still in his chair, watching them. He pictured Merritt in the wagon, reaching the overgrown road that led to the beach, but instead of turning to get his father, passing by. On and on and out of sight, alone in that wagon full of milk. Ben opened and closed his jaw, touching the bruised bone. It made a clicking sound inside his head.

Lily and his father sat together on the sofa, drinking the same hot syrup that Ben and Lily had the night before. Lily's voice was soft and his father grunted in response to the things she said. He finished his drink and settled back with his hands behind his head. When he fell asleep, Ben whispered to Lily.

"Should I tell him I'm sorry?"

"For what, Mouse?"

"Tipping the canoe."

She shook her head. "No need for that. My uncle is often overburdened by small things." She smoothed the hair from his eyes, then yawned. "Canoes tip all the time. Whisky gets dumped. My uncle gets bothered, then settles."

Whisky. Ben had imagined clouds of white spilling in the water. Now he imagined the sparkling brown liquid, like honey, fish sipping at it and swimming upside down, bumping into seaweed and becoming ill.

Lily closed her eyes. "This is between two men at odds for a long while, little Mouse. Anyway, Merritt has his own way of coming and going. Perhaps he planned it this way."

So with the warm fire, and his father calmed, and the happy thought that they were going home soon, Ben fell asleep under his coat.

When he woke, the fire was cold and everything dark. His father snored on the sofa and Lily sat on the sill of the open window, parts of her showing in the moon's light—her braids, the edge of her cheek. An icy salt breeze filled the room and Ben pulled his knees to his chest and his blanket up to his chin. As he drifted off, he wondered if Lily always slept that way—sitting in the chilly window, facing the harbour where the drunken sea creatures thrashed about.

Ben woke to a kick on the sole of his boot. He jumped up. The window was closed and a faded pink light shone through.

Without a word, his father threw open the door and pounded down the outside stairs. Ben looked once at the small mound of Lily asleep under a blanket, then hurried after him.

They walked fast, his father muttering, shoulders rolling. The city looked soft in the early morning haze. Even the water slept, calm and glassy. But Ben wasn't fooled by it, now that he knew what was underneath. A chill ran through him from hair to boots.

"Come on then," his father called over his shoulder.

Up ahead, a few men were gathered near the docks. They spoke in low voices, shaking their heads and shifting their hats. They all looked at a long pier with small boats tied up to its side. Songhees men watched from their canoes.

Ben ran ahead and joined in the crowd. On the wet boards, a man lay sprawled in his long underwear, arms out oddly. His colourless face was turned toward Ben, ragged black holes where his eyes once were.

Everything stopped—sound, breeze, breath. Without meaning to, Ben grabbed the coat of a man next to him. The man looked down.

"You know that fellow?" he asked.

Ben jerked as a pale crab poked out between the open buttons of the long underwear, tugging at a rope of flesh.

"Who is he then?" the man said.

"It's Merritt."

"Merritt," the man muttered, like the word was new to him. He looked again. "You shouldn't be here, son."

Ben turned and ran up the steep street to catch his father.

"That's your friend," he said, out of breath. "On the dock."

His father grunted, his stride long and quick. "No friend of mine."

Ben stopped and turned. From here, Merritt looked like a doll, arms and legs off kilter. More people had gathered.

"I think he's dead." Ben's body felt full of bees. He caught up again, repeating it louder, "I think he's dead down there on the dock."

"Don't worry about it. He met his end and likely deserved it."

"Why? Why'd he deserve it?"

"Thieving or lying or doing what he shouldn't. Now that's enough."

"He thieved?"

His father stopped and put a finger to Ben's face. "I said enough. We're done talking about it. You understand?"

Ben nodded.

"And don't trouble Agda with it. She'll get all bothered."

His father stared him in the eyes until Ben nodded again.

On the long road home, his father spoke to himself in grunts and whispers. Nothing new to Ben, as he often talked out his troubles without need of a listening ear.

At West Cane Lake, they stopped at the trail to Connie's cabin. Instead of going down it, his father stood very still, looking at the ground. After a while, Ben leaned nearer to peek at his face. He was careful, expecting to see anger and perhaps be dealt another blow, but instead he saw the look of someone thinking hard, eyes moving without seeing.

Then his father raised his head and Ben took a step back. For a moment, they looked at each other, as if his father would speak, but something rustled in the trees and they both turned. A flash of some animal, then gone.

"Let's go," his father said, turning away. Ben hurried after him.

"Will he be mad we didn't come? Your brother?"

"Stop talking, boy."

Ben looked back once more before hurrying to keep up with his father.

"But will he be mad about what happened to Merritt?"

* * *

By the time they reached Petrenko's Dry Goods & Post, the sun was high and cold behind hazy clouds. Ben followed his father inside. They had no whisky for Mrs. Petrenko but bought some flour.

Ben watched her make a mark in the ledger with a stubby brown pencil. He wanted to tell her what he'd seen. He wanted her to say something good about it, that maybe Merritt was only hurt and he would be all right once a doctor tended to him. His eyes moved to his father's nicked hands gripping the counter, the veins fat and blue, then to the shelves behind Mrs. Petrenko, filled with labelled cans—pictures of yellow peaches, glossy red beans, and dark cherries dripping with syrup.

Mrs. Petrenko's voice was deep and it filled the room. "I expect three jugs on your next trip through, or I'll start ordering it myself. People like to warm their tea. I like to offer it."

"Do you have oranges?" Ben asked.

Mrs. Petrenko looked down at him and smiled. "No one has oranges around here. They only grow where the sun always shines, and the sun doesn't shine much around these parts, does it?"

Ben shook his head.

As his father left, she winked and handed him a candy. Ben popped the treat on his tongue and waited for his mouth to fill with sticky sweetness.

"For later," said Mrs. Petrenko, slipping another one in his pocket.

He thanked her, then ran out the door and down the road after his father. Again, the Howland dog moved fast in the trees alongside, but this time Ben paid it little attention. Instead, he watched his father walk bowlegged in front of him, with the sack of flour across his shoulders.

A cool mist had settled in their yard, and his mother was in the garden, digging ashes into the soil. She wore his father's shirt and an old pair of his trousers, cinched with string. Behind her on the line, her dress waved in the breeze like a headless woman.

"You're home early," she said, leaning on the shovel.

As his father took the bag of flour into the cabin, she placed her hand on the side of Ben's face and kissed his head. He smelled dirt.

"I will need to make you a new shirt," she said, touching the tear in Ben's sleeve, held together by Lily's pins. "This one is beyond mending."

"I'm sorry."

She waited for him to explain, but the words lodged in his throat.

"It's no matter," she said. "Anyway, you're too big for these clothes now."

They went inside, but Ben noticed his mother favoured one leg. Inside, she bent carefully to throw a log in the stove.

"What happened to you?" his father said from his chair.

"Just a bite."

"From what?"

She nodded toward the potato bin, so Ben grabbed three and began washing them in the basin while she sliced a fat cabbage.

"I disturbed a snake when I was milking the cow."

"And you're limping over it?" his father said. "Some garden snake?"

Ben looked out the window, then up at his mother, who didn't answer. He'd spotted plenty of small snakes in that shed—wriggly frightened things that slipped under the walls. Gone before he could catch them.

"And how was it then?" his mother asked him. "How was it in the city?"

Ben looked at his father, the potato in his hands dripping water onto the floor.

"The boy lost half the whisky. That's why we're back."

"That's good for me then. He's a help here at the cabin."

"Lost me a good job, he did."

Her hand stilled, the knife halfway through the cabbage.

"Over some lost whisky?" she said. "I'm sure it's not so bad."

"Ha. You don't know Con."

Ben cut a potato in half. What about the rest of it? The worst part? As he waited for his father to say it, he nicked his finger. Blood spread across the white flesh of the potato, fanning out along invisible veins.

"A man died," Ben said. "We saw it."

His mother turned toward him and his father shifted forward in his chair.

"You shut up now. Stop causing trouble."

"He had no eyes," said Ben, the words unstuck now. "A crab was eating him."

A knot of wood cracked in the stove, the flames licking the iron door.

His mother spread her hand on the table. "You saw this man die?"

Ben shook his head. He still held the potato, now smeared watery red. "We saw him after," he said. "It was Merritt. He came with us in the wagon."

He didn't look at his father, but his mother did.

"I don't know who it was," his father said. "This boy was nothing but trouble, start to finish. Who knows what he's on about." He leaned back in his chair and closed his eyes, his jaw working and his breath out of rhythm.

Ben's mother took the bloodstained potato and swished it in the basin, then dropped it into the pot. Her lips were pressed together. Her nostrils flared.

"Don't you worry about any of that," she said to Ben. "You can stay here with me from now on, yes?" She pulled him to her, whispering, "Your father does a bad work in the city, and you are good. You understand?"

He nodded, biting down on his tongue. The pain ran through his tender jaw.

* * *

Ben fell asleep early. In his dream it was himself who lay on the dock, splayed soundless and still as a picture, his hair spread slick around his face. Instead of eyes, two ragged black holes. He woke with a gasp, as though his body had forgotten to breathe while he dreamed.

His mother was talking from their bed on the other side of the curtain. Her voice was firm and cold, and Ben thought at first someone else was in the house. "I said not to take him to that place."

"Shut up, Agda. He's stronger for it."

"Do you see how simple you are? How stupid?"

Ben was careful not to creak the sofa. Maybe he was still dreaming.

"What did you do to that man? Merritt?" she said.

"I did nothing."

"I don't believe you."

"He drowned."

"In shallow water. You must think me a fool."

The night was still and silent and the moon had long moved past the view from his little window. Blankets shifted. The ropes under his parents' mattress creaked. When nothing more was said, Ben lay back and curled on his side. He pressed his forehead into the back of the sofa and breathed in the old velvet's musty smell. The air was cold on the nape of his neck. Pulling the blanket around his ears, he thought of Merritt, nearly blue, with holes for eyes.

Why was he so pale and blue? Because he was cold, tumbling under and under that icy sea. Ben still felt the salty chill he'd brought all the way home inside him. He took a long breath, trying to fill his shrivelled lungs.

But what happened to Merritt's eyes? Did the waves take them along with his clothes?

Waves can't do all that…

Maybe the eyes fell out, like acorns fall from trees, and rolled off the dock and into a whale's mouth.

Eyes don't fall like acorns.

Then what happened to them?

Maybe they dissolved in the salty water.

Or maybe the crabs ate them.

Or.

Maybe his father took them.

Ben imagined Merritt's eyes in his father's pocket. Rolling and knocking with each step he took. Catching a glimpse of the sky when they bounced near the pocket's opening.

Ben curled up tight.

"Don't you see?" his mother said, her whisper harsh and loud. "You have brought misery into our home. Now we all must suffer."

His father grunted and soon was snoring.

Over the following days, his mother's limp worsened. She wouldn't show Ben the bite, so he imagined it—pulsing, oozing, violent red. She spoke little and sat often. She nearly used up the small crock of salve on the table.

When Ben milked the cow, he made sure to watch for the snake. Twice he found his father in the cowshed, stuffing moss into gaps in the walls, sweeping out cobwebs and musty old straw.

"That woman's crazy or lying," he said.

Even the cow seemed bothered, with her ears pushed forward and her tail between her legs. Ben wondered what she had seen from under her long cow lashes.

Since returning, Ben had been busy hauling firewood. His father chopped all day and even at night, more than they needed and faster than Ben could carry. Ben fell asleep to the clear sound of steel on wood and in the early morning, he woke up to it.

By the third day, the shed was full, and Ben stacked the rest against the outside wall. He checked his mother often, peeking through the window to where she stirred soup with a trembling hand or sat by the fire, still as stone. When he saw that she'd moved to the bed and lay flushed and damp on top of the quilt, he hurried back to his father.

"She's lying down now," he said. "Should we get a doctor?"

His father let the axe fall, a clean split.

"You think I have money for that?" He nodded toward the woodpile, and Ben gathered another armload.

"We could trade something."

"You don't need a doctor over some little bite. He'd come all this way for nothing."

"A doctor helped Effie."

"Lot of good it did. Isn't she crippled?" He set another log on the stump. "And didn't the other one die?"

The wood was heavy, sticky with sap. Sharp-smelling like medicine.

"She'll be fine," his father said, lifting the axe. "Now get to work."

Ben took the wood to the pile and dropped it, then went inside, where his mother's breath was quick and shallow, her face shiny pink. He made her a cup of tea and, as he set it by the bed, she took hold of his hand. Her eyes were wild.

"This is punishment," she said, panic in her voice.

"Punishment?" Ben looked out the window to where his father chopped and chopped like a man who'd done wrong. His mother had her arm across her eyes. Ben leaned in and said, quietly, "I'll be right back."

And he left. He walked past his father, who didn't look up, and when he got to the trail, he ran.

He ran along the soggy path and through the snapping pine boughs. The sun was low and the woods dark, but he knew the path well enough to be quick. He jumped over fallen trees and slowed down through trenches. When he arrived at the Stenhouse farm, his hair was wet, and the sun had set behind Ash Mountain.

Mrs. Stenhouse answered the door, her apron stretched taut over her swollen belly. She listened and nodded briskly. After sending Will out to get Mr. Stenhouse, she quickly gathered small things into a basket, then hurried upstairs.

Ben waited in the kitchen, where Effie sat by the fire heating her leg under warm blankets.

"Are you scared?" she said.

Ben nodded.

"If she dies, you should live here. Not with mean Mr. Maclean."

"She's not dying. She's sick."

"I said *if*." Effie faced him, her eyes squinted. "*If* she dies, you should live here with us and we can play in the hayloft. I'll show you the baby mice. You can sleep on Will's trundle."

But Ben wasn't listening. He was thinking of his mother, punished and alone. He knew why too. He knew it so hard he felt a jolt through his body. He came closer to Effie, with a quick look up the stairs.

"My father did something," he whispered. "Something bad."

"Mr. Maclean did?" Effie watched him without a flicker in her face, without lowering her own voice. "What'd he do?"

But Mrs. Stenhouse came swiftly down the creaking stairs with two bottles, adding them to the basket. She wrapped a shawl around her shoulders and gave Ben a hard wedge of cheese from the table.

"Eat up. No sense going hungry."

Together, they went outside, where Mr. Stenhouse was waiting with two horses.

"Well?" Effie called after them. "What'd he do?"

And as they crossed the yard, she screamed it. "I *said*, what did Mr. Maclean *do*?"

The sky was deep green, but once they were in the black trees, they saw mostly by lantern light. The horses stepped quietly, a spattering of foxfire on either side so it seemed they walked a path among stars.

Ben didn't like sitting still: His legs wanted to run and the horses were slow and careful. The wedge of cheese softened in one hand, and with his other, he held the back of Mr. Stenhouse's shirt.

When they reached the clearing, the moon had risen large and pale over the treetops. The cabin was lit silver beneath it.

"You take the horses," said Mr. Stenhouse. "We'll go in and see Agda."

Ben tied the horses to the post. While he was filling the trough, he could see Mrs. Stenhouse through the small window, moving in the dim light.

Ben's feet felt stuck in the mud until he willed them to move again. He went inside.

It was warm, and everyone stood around the bed. Mrs. Stenhouse rushed over and held him by the shoulders, blocking his view. Her eyes shone like black glass.

"Agda has died," she said. "Do you want to see her?"

He stretched to look past Mrs. Stenhouse to the bed. His mother lay under the quilt, her neck tilted back like she was trying to see the wall behind her.

"I told you we didn't need help," his father said. His eyes ticked back and forth, and one hand pressed the top of his head like he meant to keep himself from floating off. "Now these nice people have to trek home in the dark."

"We'll stay till morning," Mr. Stenhouse said. "I can help with the burial and Mrs. Stenhouse can prepare the body."

Ben had only ever heard his mother use the word for cooking—prepare the chicken, prepare the crust, prepare the apples for baking.

"It's late," Mrs. Stenhouse said softly to Ben. "You go on to bed."

Through a gap in the curtain, Ben heard but didn't see much of Mr. and Mrs. Stenhouse's quiet work. They nailed a quilt to the ceiling next to his parents' bed, so his mother was hidden. For themselves, they put blankets on the floor beside the stove. Mr. Stenhouse helped Mrs. Stenhouse lower herself down.

Ben's father came into the lean-to and lay face up on the floor with his hands behind his head and a blanket pulled up. Ben watched his bulky form rise and fall. He watched till his own eyes turned wet and blurry, then he turned over and picked at the log wall.

Mr. and Mrs. Stenhouse began moving around at dawn. His father snored deeply, but Ben had been awake so long, he wondered if he had slept at all.

He sat up and leaned so he could get a better look into the kitchen. Mrs. Stenhouse was just stepping behind the hanging quilt with a bowl of water. A minute later she pulled it back and whispered harshly to her husband, "That was no snake that bit her. Come."

Mr. Stenhouse joined her and they whispered back and forth. Ben strained to hear what they said, but none of it was clear. When Mr. Stenhouse went outside, closing the door quietly behind him, Ben pulled his pants on over his long underwear, then stepped over his snoring father and into the kitchen, where porridge bubbled on the stove.

"Ben." Mrs. Stenhouse peeked out from the edge of the quilt. "You go and fetch the eggs. I'll make biscuits soon."

She smiled, a tight smile, then let the quilt fall back. From the other side came the swish of water and the dripping sound of a cloth being wrung.

He wanted to ask what had bit his mother, but his father began to cough and stir, so he put on his boots and went outside. It was foggy and everything damp. Mr. Stenhouse was nailing together the old grey planks that Ben's father had brought home the year before to repair the chicken coop. Ben understood that this was his mother's coffin. He thought of splinters and tight spaces, and his breath stopped as if he were the one crammed inside. Mr. Stenhouse nodded at him, and Ben went to milk the cow and collect the eggs.

By the time he finished, his father was sitting on the front step, scruffy and shirtless in just his overalls. He had a piece of wood across his knees and was carving into it with his skinning knife. Ben went past with the milk bucket and eggs in his pockets, and he saw an *A* and a *G,* and part of the *D.*

Inside, Mrs. Stenhouse had her hands in a bowl, crumbling butter and flour. While her back was turned, Ben pulled back the quilt, just enough to see.

His mother lay on her back in her dress with hands folded across her chest. The skin on her face looked dry and waxed. A blue pattern crept along her jaw and cheekbones, and her hands too, like the tea-stained cracks in the bottom of a cup. Her mouth was parted, and her teeth looked too large, as if her papery lips couldn't close over them.

Not his mother at all.

He pushed the blanket a bit farther so he could see the bite but her boots were on, all properly shined, and her skirts covered the tops. He took another step.

"Ben, come set the table."

Mrs. Stenhouse stood right behind him, her voice nearly at his ear. She drew him by the arm and shifted the quilt back.

After his mother was buried, Mrs. Stenhouse put a pie in the oven and scrubbed the floor, holding her pregnant belly with one hand. Ben helped Mr. Stenhouse saddle the horses, then he watched from the porch as the couple disappeared down the trail. He wished he'd thought of a way to go with them. To do as Effie said and stay at the farm for a while, now that his mother was gone.

During the next few days, Ben helped his father with their usual chores. He carried the slop to the pigs, filled the water trough, milked, checked for eggs. All the while, his father was grim-faced and twitchy, grumbling at Ben or to himself, as though some discussion were going on.

"Won't be any more of that around here, that's for damn sure… Don't know what she was thinking half the time— You'll be going to school now. You understand?"

Ben nodded and said, "Yes, sir," but he felt no thrill in the idea of school as he had before. Instead, he thought about the misery his mother spoke of. How his father had brought it home with him. He imagined it to be a wet, slithering thing that pulled Merritt under the water, that sunk its long teeth into his mother's ankle. This misery entered his dreams and woke him, cold and breathless, and he was sure it lay stinking and rotten under the sofa, or just beyond the curtain, its watery eyes peering through.

Three days after they'd buried his mother, as his father sat across the table slurping porridge, Ben's tears came quick and without warning. He wiped them with his sleeve, but they wouldn't quit, so he rested his forehead in one hand while his other held his spoon.

"What?" His father stared at him over his tilted bowl.

Ben shook his head, his face hot and his throat pinched tight.

"Well." His father drank his last bit of milk, then scraped his chair back. "That's enough of that. We're done with that, you hear?"

Leaving his bowl on the table, his father got up and went outside. Through the window, Ben saw him take a shovel to the garden. He knelt in the dirt with his back to the cabin and plucked a grub from the soil, flicking it to the chickens. Like it was any other day.

Ben gripped his spoon. He jumped up from his chair, swung open the door, and pulled back his arm. The spoon flipped over itself in a long, slow arc toward his father, while all Ben's insides dried to powder.

It landed in the dirt behind his boot. The boot remained still. His father remained still. Ben waited for him to jump up, but he reached forward instead and picked another grub. Flick. Then did it again and again. Flick. Flick.

Ben walked barefoot through the mud. He bent and grabbed the spoon and took it inside.

That night, Ben woke to the smell of smoke, the pop and crackle of a bonfire. He stood and opened the lean-to curtain and, through the cabin's window, saw a flickering orange light. In his long underwear, he went out on the porch. The fire raged, consuming the old cowshed and shooting sparks into the sky.

His father stood facing it, black against the flames, and beyond him was the silhouette of the old cow, tied to a tree, swaying its big head. Afraid he'd be seen, Ben went back inside and sat by the window to watch. The whole yard looked orange and wobbly through the glass. The shed's roof collapsed, then the walls, and his father just stood there. But Ben could hear him talking. He leaned closer to the window as his father's voice rose to a shout.

"See what you've done?"

JAMES

1864

JAMES KNEW WHEN SHE STEPPED OFF THE BOAT THAT SHE was past childbearing years. That was fine by him. He was on in years himself and only needed a woman as any man does—at his stove and in his bed. For how long had he been coming home to a cold cabin? With supper badly prepared and only his own hand to satisfy?

But God, she was homely.

He took her bag and led her to his horse, helping her onto it. She was frail. Under his hand he felt bone, not flesh, and he knew he would get little pleasure from this brittle woman. He knew it so hard he felt his anger flush—didn't life always play a joke on James Maclean? Luckily, he was a man with regular urges that came upon him quiet and easily fulfilled. Unlike his tyrant brother, Connie, a man of greedy thoughts and dark moods, whose lusts raged cold and brutal so that any woman near him had best hide herself.

James had spent the previous night at the Brown Jug, a pub owned by his brother. Con allowed James a cot next to his bed, on account of Agda coming. It was the first time he'd ever set foot in his brother's private rooms.

"Where's the girl?" James asked, meaning his little niece.

Connie was on his way out the door. He shrugged. "Around somewhere."

So James looked through the place, then went outside where the moon was high and bright. He walked until he found her—a young slip and unafraid. She was crouched knees to chest to pet an old bent dog. Lately, he'd only glimpsed the girl when he came to load the wagon—sticky-haired and skinny, peeking out windows or slipping out doors. When she was a toddler, he'd find her safe and well-fed by whores, being passed from soft arms to soft laps. He didn't have to concern himself about it then.

"It's too late for you to be out here," James said to her now.

She followed him, simply because he'd told her to. There were men that would take advantage of that, foul and wicked men out on these streets at night. The thought made his shoulders hunch, his tongue go sour.

He took her back to Connie's room. In the lamplight, he saw she wore a man's shirt, down past her knees.

"You should sleep."

"I'm not tired."

"What happened there?" He tapped his neck to indicate her own, where a fresh scab stretched like a long angry finger.

She shrugged and skittered to the window. "I watch the boats from here," she said, touching her dirty palm to the glass.

"Did you eat today?"

She thought about it but couldn't seem to remember.

So, with a huff and slamming the door behind him, James went downstairs and put together a plate of cold lamb, ignoring the women's calls as he carried it back upstairs.

"If he forgets to feed you, just go feed yourself, all right? What do you do all day?"

"I go to the docks. Or to the mudflats."

"You should be in school. Learning your letters."

She spoke around a mouthful of potato. "I go to school if I feel like. I can spell my name—L-I-L-Y."

As he watched her eat, his hatred for his brother filled him. Connie had always left James behind to care for the weak—first their mother, now this scamp. That was the way between them since they were sticky-faced scrappers.

Your mind is unfit, James, Connie would say. *It's better this way.*

And here she was, this girl. Clever enough to spell her name, and not a single person to give her so much as a wink about it.

"You go to sleep now," he said, then went outside. He walked hard along the harbour until he was needed back at The Jug.

On their way home, Agda and James rode together on the old mare, mostly in silence. Her wispy hair clung to his face and she smelled of soap, as good women do. Only once did she speak.

"Please, can I go into the trees for a moment?"

He got off, helped her down, and waited, grumbling at the darkening sky, wondering if he had the patience required for a wife. She emerged, shy, and he helped her back up. On they went.

They took their meals next to the small window that James had cut into the logs when he prepared for her arrival. His own mother, God rest her, had said a person needed sunlight to have any good feeling. He figured she meant women needed this as he didn't know of any man who would say such a thing.

Only his mother's one window had been so near the brick wall of the ironworks, no sunlight had entered. So she sat, frail and unwell, mind turning to sorrow while James fed and cared for his younger brother, Connie. He didn't like to think of it.

At these meals by the window, Agda often spoke of her brother's children.

"Maurice will be starting school now."

"Who?"

"My nephew, Maurice. The youngest." She picked up her fork, her small nostrils flaring. "He is too gentle for school."

"Who? This nephew?"

She nodded.

She said strange things, and James didn't question them. His own mother had been bullied all the years she lived with his father, up until her last day. So if Agda said that some boy was gentle or what have you, James just took another bite of potato, then chewed his words up and swallowed them altogether.

One night, they lay shoulder to shoulder, facing up into the dark.

"I would like to have a child," she whispered.

Agda being strange again. But he stopped himself before rolling over to sleep. One thing James knew was that people shared their deepest yearnings under cover of darkness.

"Aren't you too old for all that?"

She took in a shaky breath, and he felt her head turn away on her pillow.

"Well, what?" he said. "How old are you?"

"Forty-three. Still childbearing age."

He lifted his head from the pillow and looked at her. "I thought you were older than that."

And so he did his duty by her when she asked for it, more than his previous weekly restorative. But he had no conviction that anything would come to her in the womanly way.

And it didn't.

BEN

1890

THE COW WAS SICK AGAIN, BUT BEN KNEW BETTER THAN TO tell his father, who figured Mr. Stenhouse went out of his way to give them the worst of everything. Ben kicked the mud from his boots and poured the rain off his hat onto the porch step. When he opened the door, his father was already leaning forward in his chair by the stove, watching.

"Well? Let's see it."

Ben tilted the bucket, showing the scant amount of milk at the bottom. "I'll take her back tomorrow," he said.

"Old Stenhouse is stringing you along again."

Ben hung his coat on the wall, then peeled off his wet socks and draped them on the string by the stove. Salt pork cooled on the table by the window. He sat and ate directly from the iron pan, water dripping off him in tiny splatters and forming a puddle beneath his chair. He watched his father while he ate. From this spot, he saw only the edges of him, the strong nose, the hair lit brilliant white in the firelight. When they were small, Effie had shown him a book where angels had such hair.

"Angels live with God," she'd said. "Unless they're cast out."

Effie no longer believed in God.

"I'll take that milk now," his father said, his eyes on the fire, skipping over the flames in ticky little jumps. "And some little sweet. Some kind of cake or something."

Ben's fork stilled above his plate. "We've got nothing like that."

After his mother died, some illness crept up on his father and slowly claimed him, mind and body, year by year. Lately, he'd taken to making odd requests. Not in any loud or bullish way, but as a child would. Ben figured his brains had softened as the rest of him hardened. His body all sinew and bone, veins protruding like wintery branches. But his mind was full of holes and soft places, and his wish for cake was, to him, as real as the floor beneath him.

Ben scraped back his chair and emptied the milk bucket into a cup. He waited for his father to finish drinking, Adam's apple lurching sharply like the head of a pecking chicken. Ben shifted his jaw, *click-click,* then took the cup and rinsed it on the porch and sat to finish his own supper.

That night, he fell asleep to the sound of embers crackling in the stove and the soft drumming of rain on the mossy roof. He rarely dreamed, but when he did, they began as memories. His mother making bread in the grey morning light or picking mushrooms in the shade of old oaks. The orange cat stretched long on the step, its sun-warm fur smelling of trees and woodsmoke. The animals fat. His father away.

In these dreams he was always silent and stuck, feet rooted under the tree, a watcher in the doorway as his mother did all the usual things. And though she was his mother in every way, he waited, breath caught, for her to turn strange, and he wasn't afraid when it happened. A web of blue spreading just under the skin of her hands while she knitted. Her teeth falling out one by one and skittering across the floor as she swept. Her gaze moving up the wall while kneading a stiff ball of brown dough. Up to the ceiling and across it, as if watching a spider crawl, further and tilting, each little neck-bone cracking, until she stared pleasantly out the small window behind her where the sun shone.

And in these dreams, he always wanted to ask her, *Are you happy with me?*

In the dark morning, Ben lit a fire and set the iron pan on the stove. He had an old French song in his head about a sleeping miller in a pile of grain. Today he was going to the Stenhouse farm, so already it was a good day.

His father coughed from his bed. When he bent to spit into the chamber pot, his spine showed like a bony snake through his thin underwear.

"Who are you talking to?" he said.

"No one. I was humming."

"You're lying."

The pan smoked hot, so Ben grabbed two eggs from the basket. "You think everyone lies."

The first egg sputtered and popped when it hit the grease, but Ben froze looking at it, the shell held loosely in his hand. What should have been bright yellow was black and jellied, the white threaded with red like blood in spit.

"What now?" his father said. "What is it?"

"This egg's tainted, that's all."

Ben put on his boots and took the pan outside. The rain had quit and a heavy fog had moved in. His steps were loud in the mud as he walked to the back of the cabin and flung the egg into the trees. He breathed in the wet air, the smell like rotted grass and soil.

One of the chickens had followed him, hoping for a meal, so instead of going back inside, he set the pan on the porch, where it hissed on the wet boards. Grabbing the slop bucket, Ben crossed the yard. Spindly black firs stretched up from the fog, and Ash Mountain loomed darkly in the grey mist. He tossed some scraps to the chickens and more to the pig. He scratched its head, bristly and warm.

In the shed, baby barn owls shuffled in the rafters like wide-eyed spirits, pale and naked on two skinny legs. Beneath them, Mr. Stenhouse's old cow leaned against the wall, her eyes rolled back to see whose boots hit the mucky ground. Ben spoke softly. Her breath was shallow under his palm as he petted her.

When he pushed her out into the yard, she moved slow and protested, then slipped and dropped in the mud just outside the door, a heaving fall that splashed her hide and Ben's trousers. Nose to the ground, she exhaled, then rolled onto her side. Mud speckled her eyeball as she stared into nothing, taking shallow breaths.

Ben knelt behind her and pushed on the large jutting bones of her hip. She was solid and unmoving, so he shifted, his back firm against her ribs. He pushed up with his shoulders and his legs. His feet slipped and his face felt hot. He knew she'd die in this spot if he didn't raise her, so he tried again and again until he felt cruel. Then he sat, the heat from her large body against his back. He took off his hat as rain stippled the yard—the henhouse, the two wormy apple trees, the charred remains of the old shed, and the goat pen, which hadn't seen a healthy goat in years.

He tasted mud on his tongue and spit hard to the ground. This was a place for dying. Dying or leaving. He looked up to the cabin, where his father peered out the window, mouth going as he tapped the glass.

Before the trek to the Stenhouse farm, Ben covered the cow with dirt, a hilly grave that would greet them first thing upon opening the door each morning. The crows were already watching, hunched and ruffled, from the branches of the large oak.

Last thing before leaving, Ben grabbed his mother's bowl. He always brought something when he visited, like a bird building its nest elsewhere, piece by piece.

"Agda will groan in her grave to see you off with her things," his father called out from his chair.

But he was wrong. She'd be pleased to see it all placed safely at the Stenhouse farm. Ben, too, for that matter—he nearly felt her nudge him, wishing him tucked away into a new family, a better family, but still in the shade of Ash Mountain.

He hiked into the trees, where fog hung ragged in the soaring firs, twisted oaks, and old black-limbed maples. If it rained, he'd hardly feel it. Giant ferns covered the ground and slugs spotted the path. Water crept up from the soil and in through the broken seams of his boots. Mushrooms grew at the base of trees, or from their trunks like pale ears.

He was careful with the bowl, which had already broken once and was now held together with staples along three cracks. When he was young, his mother had used it for rising bread, or preparing fruit for canning. Now and then, she polished it with linseed oil to brighten the painted image in the bottom—a faceless man and woman in ochre and blue, their shapeless hands reaching for each other but not touching. The staples pressed into Ben's palm as he filled it with mushrooms along the way. Golden chanterelles, black morel, pine.

He hadn't been to the Stenhouse farm since he'd paid for the now-dead cow—three weeks' work at harvest was his usual deal with Mr. Stenhouse. In the spring, he worked the same for a young pig. He'd go more often if he could because the Stenhouse family lived well, and Ben lived well when he was with them. They worked past dark and ate big meals of fish stew or bacon or vegetable pie. Mrs. Stenhouse kept a large garden and Mr. Stenhouse grew tobacco in a patch under the eaves.

They were a big family with plenty to say to each other, and they shared bedrooms where they bickered and snored. They fished and hunted and had a hired man to help. They sold fat animals in the city and traded their butter, known to be sweet. They went to church and had company for dinner, and every week, they brought a copy of *The British Colonist* home from Petrenko's Dry Goods & Post.

Ben arrived at their farm, a big swath of stumpy land on West Cane Lake, in the cool afternoon, A gauzy fog hung over it this time of year, but in the summer, it was washed in greens and yellows. Blackberries grew like weeds then, and the trout were large and plentiful.

Like the family, the house had grown in stages. First, it had been a small log cabin, then a second floor was added. Later, a low timber kitchen. The kitchen door became the most used and the other was eventually blocked off by a tall cupboard, so close to the table that, at dinner, the thinnest one was given the chair that jutted up against it.

Mr. Stenhouse kept a chair on the porch, where he sat on late summer nights to view his property and the lake beyond. Next to this, the log wall was marked in the shape of a bear where a huge hide once hung.

Ben found Mr. Stenhouse at the water pump, splashing his face and the back of his leathery red neck. Ben told him the cow had died, and Mr. Stenhouse turned to face him with his moustache dripping.

"She wasn't sick when I gave her to you."

"I guess she was old."

"Not so old."

From behind Mr. Stenhouse, Ben caught sight of Effie limping through the muddy yard. She was swallowed up in her brother's old wool coat.

"If you're asking for another cow," Mr. Stenhouse said, "you'll have to work extra next spring."

"Yes, sir. I will."

"Stay the night and I'll have her ready in the morning. How's James?"

"Getting worse, I guess."

Mr. Stenhouse straightened his long spine.

"And when he passes?" he asked.

When his father died, Ben wanted to work here as a farmhand. Mr. Stenhouse always had a hired man—they came and went like the seasons. But as Ben was about to answer, Effie joined them.

"I thought you'd come by," she said to Ben. "It's that old cow, isn't it?"

At this, Mr. Stenhouse dipped his chin and headed for the porch, where he kicked his boots against the step, mud flying.

"Yeah," Ben said. "She died."

"I figured as much. Next time, get a better cow."

He watched the door close behind Mr. Stenhouse. "I didn't choose her," he said.

"That's what I'm saying, Ben. Next time you should."

He looked at Effie now—her hair wet, narrow eyes beneath low brows, thin and straight. "They're not my cows to choose from," he said. "Where's Will?"

She nodded toward the barn and they headed over slowly, on account of Effie's limp.

"Isn't it ugly?" she said, nodding to her boot, where a leg brace attached to the high wooden sole. "The other one broke, so my father made this."

"Is it better?"

"Don't I walk better?"

"I think so."

"I don't mind that it's ugly. Of course, Sarah's worked up about it. You can imagine."

In the barn, Will was pitching hay in the dusty light.

"Ben's cow died," Effie announced.

Will turned to them, straw dust in his hair. "Yeah?"

"She was old," Ben said.

"Ben wants to see you, not me, though he'll pretend otherwise." Effie went to a loose floorboard, where she kept a bottle of cooking brandy hidden. Dust puffed up as she pried it open.

"That's because I'm nicer than you," Will said.

"Well. Maybe you are." She looked at Ben with the bottle in her hand. "But there was a time you preferred me to him. Don't forget."

Ben smiled, but it wasn't true. Though she'd outgrown it years ago, Effie's tears and temper used to erupt without warning. He'd always been careful around her. *Ornery child*, Mrs. Stenhouse used to say. *Quarrelsome child.*

"I like you well enough now," he said.

"Say what you like. It's a wonder I share my brandy with either of you."

"Not your brandy," said Will.

"It's still a wonder I share it."

After passing it around, they all set back to work—the boys in the barn and Effie in the kitchen, where the women were preparing supper.

In the cramped and smoky kitchen, Mrs. Stenhouse stirred an iron pot with a wooden spoon. Her sleeves were rolled up, revealing small, muscled arms and hands scrubbed pink. The room was crowded with daughters, all sweaty-browed and working.

"Those are fine mushrooms, Ben," she said. "I'll make a gravy tomorrow." She dumped them in a wire basket and handed him back the bowl.

"I brought it for you," he said, "if you want it." It struck him then that this was what his father had said when he first brought the bowl home to his mother.

"You would give up something so fine?"

He lifted a shoulder. "We don't use it."

Mrs. Stenhouse tucked back her small chin, as if to argue, but reconsidered. She set the bowl above the stove. "I'll take care of it, then, until you wish it back. Bring the beans to the table, will you?"

It was dark when they sat down to eat. The edges of the room were in shadow, but the fire flickered an orange light on the table, where they sat so tight their knees touched underneath.

Will had four sisters: Sarah, the eldest, soon to be married; Effie, a year older than Will, who was Ben's age; then the twins, born much later, who squirmed and fidgeted, leaving muddy boot prints on Ben's pants. There had been another brother, Lee, who died years ago. Lee was Effie's twin, and no one spoke of him.

Girish, the farmhand, took his meals with them. He turbaned his hair, as was the custom in India, his homeland, where the sun always shone. So said Effie. He was so strongly built, the chair he sat on looked like a child's.

Dinner was the usual rush of ideas and goings-on—the price of pork declining; the new premier who stood his ground against the Americans; two wagons colliding on Fort Street in town. Mrs. Stenhouse tapped her knife on the side of her plate to stop Will arguing with his father. Will and Girish supported the development of a railway linking the island towns. Mr. Stenhouse said the idea clearly came from men who had more money than sense.

"Soft backs, soft brains," he said, his head bent over his plate and his voice low.

Mrs. Stenhouse didn't allow contentious opinions at her table, though Ben could tell she held them herself.

"Look at Ben." She pointed her knife at him, her mouth set in a firm line. "Not arguing with a soul."

"What would he argue about?" said Will. His eyes were quick and sharp, but just for a moment.

Ben knew what was meant. He wiped his mouth on his sleeve. "Not about trains, I guess."

"That's right," said Mrs. Stenhouse. "Leave that to the higher-ups who know what's what."

Sarah set down her fork. "Eli sent my poems to Toronto yesterday," she said. "I hope to be published soon."

Whenever Ben looked at Sarah, he thought of fullness. Round cheeks, plump arms. Around her neck, a pink crease, like a thread was pressed into its softness. All flesh, no bone. He tried not to look at Sarah too often.

"Perhaps," she said, "I'll write an entire book of poems. I already have a dozen."

"You won't have time to write anything once you're married," said Effie. "You'll be too busy plucking chickens. And growing fat with Eli's pink sons."

Mr. Stenhouse looked up sharply, and Mrs. Stenhouse tapped her plate twice.

"Effie! Don't be vulgar."

"You're wrong anyway," Sarah said. "Eli's building me a writing desk."

Ben hadn't met Eli Chadsey, but he knew that the family owned a cheese operation on the other side of the lake. Effie had nothing good to say of him, or his cheese.

"Without the railway," said Girish to Mr. Stenhouse, "my brother and I could not transport our lumber."

"By train? Costs too much."

Ben stopped chewing and looked at Will.

"Girish is leaving?" he whispered.

"They're starting a lumber mill up island. Him and his brother."

"When?"

But the twins were talking about a cougar seen nearby, and Effie was speaking over them both.

"Besides," she said, "I've read your poems and they're not that good."

"Effie, enough." Mrs. Stenhouse's voice cut sharp. "Be kind."

"Honesty is kind." Effie looked from her mother to Will, then around the table. "How am I wrong? If she wants to sell poems, she should write better ones."

"Eli loves my writing."

"Eli's a dolt."

"Effie!" Mr. Stenhouse shouted, sending the table into silence.

Mrs. Stenhouse dished out pieces of apple cake and they ate quietly. Then Girish pushed his empty plate aside. He stood and thanked Mrs. Stenhouse, nodded at the rest of the table, and walked out the kitchen door into the night.

Ben stuffed the rest of his cake into his pocket, then turned to the window, where his own warped reflection looked back. Sticking-out ears, black spots for eyes. He imagined Girish on the other side of the glass, heading to his room at the back of the barn. He'd build himself a fire in the small stove, stretch out on the bed, and rest up for another good day tomorrow. The thought of it turned warmly in Ben's chest as the women cleared the table and Will and his father sat in quiet.

Later, in the cold, Ben and Will fed the animals by lamplight, while Girish forked hay down from the loft. Ben could smell winter coming.

"He's tough on Effie," Will said, meaning his father. "She's difficult, but only because she doesn't lie like everyone else."

A cat hunched on top of a stall, watching with silver eyes as Ben set down pails of boiled turnips for the horses.

"All she has is this place," he continued. "A whole life of it."

"Maybe she wants that."

"Why would she?"

They carried their empty buckets to the pump. It was raining now, a smoky, dark rain that chilled the bones.

"I'll try to be back before Christmas," Ben said.

"You'll probably get my room to yourself, then, if I'm not home."

"Not home?"

"I started high school there in September. In the city."

Ben stopped. "You've already been to school."

"The school here? That doesn't count for anything. I knew more than the teacher."

Ben waited while Will filled his bucket, the icy water sloshing on his trousers. He felt strange, his face hot under the cold drizzle.

"Your parents are okay with it?"

"Not my father. But I come home to help on weekends."

"Your mother must not like it. Especially her, I'd think."

Will lifted his bucket with a glance at Ben. "You're being funny. It's common these days." He nodded toward the house. "I wish Effie would go. She's smart but she doesn't want it. Thinks the boarding house sounds terrible." He smiled at Ben. "We call it Lockwood's Lair. It really is terrible."

Ben looked to the house, where a light shone in the kitchen. He lifted his hat and let the rain cool his forehead. When he turned to speak, Will was on his way back to the barn.

Later, they sat around the fire, their hats and coats dripping from hooks on the mantle. In the past, Mr. Stenhouse had read from his Bible every evening, but now he smoked his pipe and jotted down figures in his leather book while Sarah read poems.

The fire spat and hissed as one of the twins made short braids in Ben's hair. She patted his head. "There. You look like an Indian now," she whispered.

The other twin was trying to do the same with Will, but his hair was too short. Effie smacked any hand that neared her head so no one would attempt it with her. Soon she was asleep anyway, her bad leg wrapped in hot blankets to ease the ache. Ben tapped his heel against her chair and she woke.

"It's this horrid poem," she whispered. "It has no end."

Sarah read louder, her arm lifted and her eyes shining darkly in the firelight. She probably imagined the poem was her own and the audience a finer one, as Sarah saw the best in everything and everyone, including herself. Different from Will, who saw things as they were but wanted more. Maybe Ben understood that after all. Something similar made him come here as often as he did.

He looked again at Effie, who chewed her thumbnail as she watched the flames jump in the hearth. He saw now what troubled Will: Effie was no dreamer. She saw what she had been given and didn't hope for anything else at all.

In the morning, while it was still dark, Ben folded the blankets and eased the trundle back under the bed where Will slept. He stepped out the creaky door, then felt his way down the cold, narrow stairs, his shoulders brushing the walls on either side. In the dark kitchen, he found Mr. Stenhouse crouched in front of the stove to light the fire.

"Off so early?"

"I have to get back to my father."

Mr. Stenhouse shut the iron door and straightened, joints cracking. "Go easy. Won't be light for an hour."

They walked to the barn. All the heavy clouds had vanished, revealing endless icy stars and a sharp sliver of moon.

Ben shifted his hat, his breath tight. "Who will replace Girish when he leaves?"

"Are you asking for work?"

"Yes, sir. After my father's gone."

"What about your place?"

"There's nothing there."

Mr. Stenhouse pulled his pipe from his pocket, already packed. "The Lamb boy was going to help fence the north field, but the job's yours if you want it. I'll need you before the rains quit."

Ben nodded. He knew what it meant—the timing of things—and he didn't feel too badly about it.

As Mr. Stenhouse went into the barn, Ben looked out to the lake, a black slick in the moonlight. Somewhere on the other side, near the school he never did set foot in, an owl called. He realized the sounds of this place would soon be familiar to him, ordinary comforts. And this view would be his whenever he wanted it. He could get up in the middle of the night, if he had the inclination, to look at that moon on that water.

Mr. Stenhouse came out of the barn leading the cow, warm breath puffing from her nostrils. Even in the dark, Ben could see she was a bony old thing. He ran his hand over sharp ribs.

"When you can pay real money, son, you'll get a younger one," said Mr. Stenhouse. "You understand?"

Ben took the rope.

"Yes, sir," he said.

Mr. Stenhouse headed to the house with long strides, pipe smoke lingering behind him.

The path was narrow and lumpy, with roots that troubled and tripped the cow. She planted her feet, so Ben had to switch between pulling her and letting her rest. When he finally led her into the yard in the cold morning light, she was slow and unhappy, stopping near the buried cow, where crows were pecking through the dirt with their strong beaks. Ben pulled her into the shed, her old bones jutting and swaying, then went back and swatted away the crows. He shovelled the dirt back over the dead cow, then fed the chickens and the pig. He gathered an armload of knobby potatoes from the cellar and carried them inside.

Pushing the door open, he saw his father sitting near the cold stove. His head drooped and his hands were purple on the arms of the chair.

Ben's heart thunked once against his ribs as he stood frozen in the doorway. He's dead, he thought, and a potato slipped from his arms and dropped to the floor with a bang. His father's head shot up.

"What took so long?"

Ben exhaled. He picked up the fallen potato and set everything on the table.

"The cow's slow," he said.

"I thought you'd run off with one of those Stenhouse kids."

"I wouldn't do that." He took the cake from his pocket—now in several soggy pieces—and put it in a tin cup.

"I thought you'd got held up in the woods or something."

From where he stood, Ben could only see the back of his father's head—a scrabble of wispy hair, flattened from sleeping. He imagined him waking alone in the cold cabin, mumbling to himself, looking out the window with his ticky eyes.

"Nothing like that." Ben brought him the cake. "Mr. Stenhouse waited till this morning to hand over the cow."

His father poked a finger in the cup. "And her all sick and slow."

"It's fair for three weeks' work."

"You watch," his father spoke around a mouthful of cake. "That Stenhouse is a greedy devil, up to all manner of thievery. It's how he got that good land."

"It's good because he worked it."

He threw two dry logs on the embers, then blew underneath until the coals glowed. When he had the fire going strong, he pulled his feet from his boots and set them by the door, his socks leaving wet prints on the floorboards. He'd heard plenty about the good land and didn't care to hear more.

He set the pan on the stove and cut up the potatoes, tossing them into the crackling grease. While the cabin warmed, his father swiped a finger around his cup to get the last of the cake crumbs.

As winter approached, the rains settled in, a constant battering against the roof, pelting the chickens, and turning the yard to mud. Dark arrived before supper and stayed long after the morning chores were done.

Death crept in slow steps, taking what was left of his father's strength, then his hunger. Finally, his mind. He asked questions with no possible answer. *Where's your mother? How'd the horse hold up? Where'd you come from, boy?*

Ben slaughtered the pig, a violent job he'd dreaded. He stunned it with a hammer, then slit its throat and collected the blood. He hung it head-down and sliced its belly. The innards spilled on the ground in hot, slippery coils. It was a smell he knew well—musk and blood and rotted hay. It stuck to him long after he was finished, though he stood outside and let the rain beat through his shirt. Later, after washing up, when he lay on the sofa to sleep he still smelled it.

The next day he salted the pork and packed the pieces into crocks. Before carrying them to the cellar, he topped them with brine and weighted each lid with a heavy stone.

He chopped wood and stacked it. He buried the dead cow again after the rains unburied it. He shooed away the crows. He milked the living cow, who held up fine. He cooked pigs' feet to make broth, and checked the cellar, where he found a half bucket of mealy apples, a couple dozen potatoes in the bin, and plenty of tough cabbages, wrapped in straw.

He had saved seeds in folded bits of paper laid out on the table. Each time he walked by, he shook a packet, just to hear it rattle.

"Who's that?" his father called from his chair. "Who's here?"

"No one's here," Ben said. "Just me."

Ben was knitting a sock, slowly and badly, when his father kicked his shin. They were sitting next to each other by the stove, quiet and reasonably contented except for the odd coughing spell that shook his father purple.

"Go on and get that tin," his father said.

"What tin?"

Again, he knocked Ben with his boot, waving his rag toward the cupboard in the corner.

It was dark, so Ben brought the lamp to the cupboard and opened its small door. It was full of whatever his father had crammed inside over the years, whatever he'd rather not have or think about. Rags, a Bible, empty bottles of liver tonic, an ancient Sears catalogue, a yellowed piece of paper. Ben unfolded it and read.

KNOW YE that WE do by these presents… the sum one hundred and sixty dollars… grant unto James Maclean… Lot of Land situate in the District of Ash Mountain…

At the very back was a tea tin. Farmen's Finest Tea.

Ben held it up and his father nodded just as his cough returned—an explosion that nearly threw him from his chair. Ben wished himself outside when these fits came, as there was nothing to do for it but watch. When his father finally settled, he brought him water.

"It's for Lily," his father said. "You remember her?"

"I remember." Ben turned the tin in his hand but didn't open it. "What is it?"

His father pressed the rag to his mouth and spit.

"You want me to take it to her?" Ben asked.

"If you can catch her. She's trouble, that one."

Ben only recalled Lily in flashes—hair lit gold, sand-coloured freckles, the warmth of her little fire. The hot burn of her whisky down his throat.

"She was nice to me," he said.

But the thought of going back there left him cold. He was about to ask when he should take her the tin but caught himself. He knew the answer, so he set it on the table and sat again by the fire to continue working on the sock. He was clumsier now, his mind distracted and his fingers gone stiff. The old memory of being pulled underwater, of ice in his bones.

That night Ben dreamed that his mother was chopping potatoes at the table while he stood in the doorway.

Écoute-moi, she whispered, looking at him with a twitch of her eyelid.

Reste.

Stay.

But his voice had left him, and his lips were glued shut.

The mound of potatoes grew higher. The twitch in her eye pulsed like a tiny heart. She smiled at him.

Why would you leave?

And again, his words were stuck, his mouth unmoving. He was forced to watch as her eye trembled and bulged, then slid from its socket, gently, like an egg being laid. It landed on the table and rolled. He heard the firm, wet turn of it against wood until it stopped at the table's edge, its pale gaze fixed on Ben. Still his mother chopped, a murky tear sliding down her cheek from the empty socket.

Tell him you are ill.

Ben woke, his throat dry, his forehead damp. He swung his feet to the floor and lit the lamp. When he blew out the match, the sulphur smell burned his nostrils. From his father's bed came a quiet strangling.

He grabbed the lamp and and pulled back the curtain, the flame casting light at odd angles. His father's dark face, eyes stretched so wide the whites were exposed. Ben set the lamp on the side table and poured whisky, then held his father up to drink. When he settled, Ben eased him down onto his pillow, but still something gurgled, as if a muddy creature resided deep in his throat.

Ben built up the fire, then sat by the bed.

"Do you need anything?" he asked.

His father didn't look at him, but his broad hand lifted, then landed heavily on Ben's knee. Ben resisted the urge to pull his leg away. Outside, the barn owl screeched its rusty-hinge call.

"It'll settle," Ben said. His father's grip tightened and his eyes grew wider—a panicked animal. Ben patted his hand and made to hold it, then instead, he moved his father's arm to his chest and patted it once more. "It'll settle," he said again, but it was a useless thing to say, and he wasn't sure his father heard anyway.

Ben took the last of the whisky and downed it himself, then leaned forward, elbows on his knees. His eyes were burning and his jaw felt tight. He let his head hang for a long moment.

"I know what you did," he said.

His father's look shifted past Ben to where the cabin was dark.

"I know why everything dies here."

He waited for a response. Some word or gesture, some catch in his eye. But he only stared at nothing and died before dawn.

In the grey morning light, Ben took the tin and sat with his back against the bed. The rusty lid scraped as he pushed it open, leaving orange powder on his fingers.

Inside was a thick roll of mildewed banknotes curled tight and faintly damp under his thumb. The smell was musty and nearly warm, as if the money breathed out at him.

And so much of it.

Ben's foot slid forward, the sole of his boot scraping the floorboards. How long had it been here, moulding and useless? While his mother needed a doctor? While the cupboards sat empty all those years since she died? Stranger still, why had his father kept it hidden while he himself was sick and in need?

Ben clicked his jaw and looked at his father, whose eyes had sunk beneath closed lids. Then he stood and went out in the rain. He grabbed a shovel, and walked past the hungry animals, past his mother's grave, and on to the property's edge, where he had butchered the pig.

The dense clay resisted his shovel, but he hammered it in with his boot, tossing the heavy clumps into a sloppy pile of earth. It was midday by the time the hole was big enough to fit his father. Ben was soaked through.

Back inside, he left muddy footprints from the door to the bed. He rolled his father in the thin blue quilt, pulled it up, and tied knots above his head and below his feet. He dragged the body along the floorboards, out onto the porch, and down the step with a sickening crack. His father's heels left a snaking trail from house to grave. Ben set him down and adjusted the quilt. It was wet now and clung to his father's shape—the strong nose, the wide arched ribs, the toes pointed skyward.

Muddy water had already pooled in the bottom of the hole. Broken roots and stones were exposed on the walls. Ben took a breath and, with no other way to do it, rolled his father into the narrow pit, where he landed solid, like a felled tree, splashing mud in Ben's face. He wiped it off and leaned forward.

The quilt had fallen open, revealing one side of his father—one eye cocked half open, one arm bent forward and the other behind.

Ben stepped back. His eyes were blurry with tears, angry and hot. Once more, he leaned over the grave.

How did it feel? To do the very worst thing to another person? To bring that home, clinging to your clothes, then sit with it for years?

Lowering himself onto his belly, Ben reached in and pulled the quilt closed. Then he began to fill the hole.

It was dark, but the chickens needed scraps and the cow had to be milked. Once done, Ben made a fire and sat while the potatoes boiled.

He opened the tin again and took out the fat roll of money. He counted fifty-four one-dollar banknotes, each reading Dominion of Canada in intricate green and black. His teeth worked the inside of his lip as he tapped the bills against the tabletop. He had seen Mr. Stenhouse count money after a day at the market, but he had never seen it in this cabin. Its value could be anything. A bag of flour, a horse, a barn.

Turning the lid over, he found a folded piece of notepaper pressed into the rim. He left it in place, but read his father's scratchy writing.

For Lilie. abov the Bucher on Warf str.

Ben thought of Lily—her hand on his cheek, the sick in his belly. "Do you remember?" she had said. "You came from the water. Was it terribly dark?"

In the morning, he stood leaning back against the cold stove, his hands in his armpits to warm them. His father's boots sat near the door, bent and crusted with mud. His own were beside them, too small and worn through the soles. Ben bit his thumbnail, his eyes on the better pair as if on an unpredictable animal. Finally, he tried them on, felt the shape of his father's wide foot, the dips where his toes had pressed into the leather. But they were roomy and the soles sturdy, so he tied the broken laces, and when he went out to feed the animals, frost crunching under each step, he threw his old boots into the trees behind the cabin.

After washing in icy water, he pushed the chickens into a crate and packed his bag—a candlestick to match one he'd already given Mrs. Stenhouse, the last of the dried beans, apples from the cellar, the packets of seed he'd saved. He rolled his blanket tight and tied it to the bottom, and in a secure place on top, he placed the tin for Lily.

Leading the cow, he stopped at his mother's grave, where old grass had grown so long the marker barely showed. He parted the grass and saw that rust-coloured moss had filled the letters of her name.

Not long after she was buried, he'd left one of Mrs. Petrenko's pink candies on top of the cross, imagining she would somehow receive it. But it had sat there through the rains, shrinking away until only a muddy-looking glaze remained on the wood. With his foot, he swept the grasses back into place and headed for the trail.

* * *

The Stenhouse yard was empty when he came into it, pulling the old cow. Ash Mountain was pale and frost-covered and the dark lake beneath was spotted with dull patches of ice. Footprints led to the barn, the chicken coop, the pump, and out to the field. Bundled in the old woollen coat and looking like a bear, Effie was walking to the house with two swinging buckets.

Ben opened his crate and let the chickens run free with the others, then he took the cow to the barn. Inside, Mr. Stenhouse sat on a stool next to the small window, a broken chair on the floor beside him. He was carving a new chair leg in the cold light. When he looked up, his gaze moved from Ben to the cow.

"How's your father then?"

"He died. Early yesterday."

Mr. Stenhouse ran his thumb and finger down his rusty moustache. "I'm sorry to hear it. Do you need help with the burial?"

"It's done." Ben looked past him to the room where Girish slept. The door was open and the mattress bare.

"He left a couple weeks ago," said Mr. Stenhouse. "Starting that sawmill with his brother." He spoke low, as if the decision was a poor one. "I told the Lamb boy I'd need him to help fence, but it looks like you're ready to start."

"Yes, sir. I only need a couple days to go to the city."

"Mm-hmm. Did James leave you the land?"

"I don't think so." Ben hadn't thought about the land, only that it would be reclaimed by forest in no time. He imagined strong oak arms breaking through the windows, raccoons nesting in cupboards. Bees swarming in the springs of the horsehair sofa.

"He left money for his niece," he said. "I have to deliver it."

Mr. Stenhouse stilled the knife blade.

"James had money?"

"Fifty-four dollars. Hid away."

Mr. Stenhouse turned the piece of wood in his hands. He found a rough spot and ran his knife along it, a fine peel curling off and landing on the floor.

"Well," he said, "that should be all right. I hope it won't be a habit, running off to town."

"No, sir. I don't much like it there anyway."

Mr. Stenhouse set down the chair leg. He stood and straightened his back, then came forward to take the cow.

"I'll wait till you get back before butchering her." He nodded outside. "Will's in the north field."

Ben held the rope a moment before he handed it over. The cow stared dumbly at the wall, not knowing that the long trek was all for this. And how could she? It was her nature to trust she'd be cared for, not harmed. Ben watched as she was led off, then he headed outside.

He found Will at the edge of the field, where two cedars lay on the ground like fallen giants. Together, they hacked off the branches, then piled the boughs in the field for burning. Their hands were plastered with needles and numb with cold.

Ben told Will about the tin.

"That's a month's wages, at least," Will said, bright red spots on his cheeks like burns. "Why should she get it? You were the one that took care of him."

"I think he took care of her."

"Isn't she a grown woman? She might be married now. She wouldn't need it."

"I don't know anything about that."

"Do what you want, I guess. Just seems you should have it."

Ben shook his head. "I met her once," he said. "She was nice."

"Well shit." Will straightened, looking past Ben toward the house.

Two horses were pulling a red delivery wagon up the drive. As they turned toward the barn, the side was revealed—*Chadsey Cheese,* in curling white letters. Eli Chadsey, set to marry Sarah.

Ben and Will headed across the field to the barn to help look after Eli's horses. By the time they reached him, he was bent over with a hoof flipped up, grumbling about stones.

Ben got a good look at the man when he stood—pink and nearing plumpness, thick yellow hair tamed with grease and combed to the side. Eli said a somber hello to Will, enquired after the cougar that had been killing chickens, then sniffed loudly of the biting air with only a brief glance at Ben.

"This is our neighbour, Ben," said Will. "He's replacing Girish."

Eli's hand was soft when they shook, his eyes fixed on the yard where Effie limped toward the house with a chicken perched on her shoulder.

Ben had heard about Eli's cheese farm, which he ran with his father, uncle, and brothers. Each round of cheese was aged a year before being wrapped in cloth and placed in birch-strip boxes, then taken up the foggy coast by steamboat. The whole venture thrilled Sarah and garnered Mr. and Mrs. Stenhouse's respect. But Eli himself was cold-mannered. He looked at a person in the way others counted potatoes in a cellar or read a ledger.

"Lucky I'm staying at a friend's place tonight," Will said as he and Ben watched Eli walk to the house. "I can't stand being in that man's company longer than a meal."

Inside, they brought their plates and forks from the kitchen to the table. Mrs. Stenhouse patted Ben's arm as she squeezed past him.

"Ben," said Sarah, "I feel just terrible about James's passing."

Mrs. Stenhouse and everyone else sat down, except Effie, who stood holding the back of her chair with both hands.

"Why do you feel terrible?" she said to her sister.

"Effie," Will said. "Sit down."

"He was cruel. And a criminal. Why pretend?"

"You say the most awful things, Effie," said Mrs. Stenhouse. "Go get the butter. Go on now."

"It's all right," said Ben, as Effie disappeared into the kitchen's dark, her brace clanking and rattling. "I don't mind."

When Effie returned with the plate of butter, she took her seat next to Ben. Her cheeks were flushed and her face set.

"I really don't mind," he whispered to her.

Mrs. Stenhouse said grace—bless this bread, bless this home—then Mr. Stenhouse carved the ham, glistening and oily in the firelight. Sarah spoke as everyone dished out, relaying a dream she'd had in which she laughed without ceasing in church. Ben was interested in this sort of dream, but Eli interrupted her and spoke of cheese. Sales were up by one-sixteenth, the new hotel in the city had ordered four rounds of cheddar to be delivered weekly, and an article Eli himself had written had been published in *The British Colonist*.

"Did anyone read it?" he asked. 'The Wondrous Health Benefits of Chadsey Cheese'?"

"I read it," said Will, but nothing more.

"You boys watch for that cougar tonight." Mrs. Stenhouse pointed her fork at the men. "Mrs. Byrne spotted him on her way to church, I heard. Looking all mangy and hungry."

"I said I'm taking care of it," said Mr. Stenhouse. Will had told Ben they went out with their rifles twice a day now, and had three traps set.

"It was a fine article," Sarah said, looking at Eli but speaking to everyone. "Well expressed."

Effie slipped a piece of ham into the napkin on her lap. "I read it too. Strengthen the liver and fight consumption. That's a wondrous cheese indeed."

"It's all true, Effie," said Sarah. "When I felt low yesterday, I ate a piece and was instantly revived."

Eli watched Effie. His face was calm, his middle finger circling a button on his shirt in a way that tightened Ben's scalp.

"Cheese is a known blood stimulant," he told her.

"Is that right? It's a shame we weren't acquainted when my brother was ill. Perhaps your cheese could have saved him."

"Effie!" Mrs. Stenhouse's head snapped up on her thin neck. She never spoke of Lee. No one did.

Mr. Stenhouse finished chewing before turning to Effie. He looked at her for a long, cold moment, then back to his supper.

"This is how she jokes," Sarah said to Eli. "Effie, I think we've had enough of your jests."

"If I was jesting, I'd laugh," Effie said with quiet firmness. "Nothing about miraculous cheese is funny."

Will groaned and set his elbows either side of his plate. He said something to his father about the upcoming election—Senator Pickering, young blood, another crash. Ben wasn't really listening. His plate was empty and his hands rested on his knees. Effie sat stiffly beside him.

She glanced at him, then slipped another slice of ham into her napkin. He shook his head slightly, already knowing what she was up to.

After supper, Effie walked with Ben to the barn. She carried his blankets, and he had an armload of firewood. In his room, she scratched at the frosted window with her nail, then looked around, rubbing her hands together.

"I wouldn't mind this myself," she said. "Sarah snores."

Ben dropped the wood next to the stove. "Maybe you do too."

"Maybe." She shrugged, then sat on the bed with a puff of icy breath.

"You should go back inside," he said, nodding at her legs. Mrs. Stenhouse would have a blanket warming in the drawer under the oven.

"You have something to tell me first, don't you? You've been odd all night."

"It's nothing much."

"Nothing much?"

Ben heard the tightness in her voice, the rise in pitch, and he thought it was something a person would grow weary of if they were too often in Effie's company. He took the tin out of his bag and handed it to her.

"This is for my father's niece. She lives in the city."

Effie opened it and ran her fingers along the edge of the banknotes.

"What a brute," she said. "To have money while you got skinny. Living off our chickens and cow's milk, like we had it to spare. Do you know how long he's had it?"

Ben put the tin back in his bag.

"I don't know."

"When your mother was sick?"

"I think so."

Biting her nail, she watched Ben. "I suppose you already told Will. I suppose he told you to keep it."

"I won't though." He leaned against the doorframe. "I met her once."

"What's she like?"

"She seemed nice."

Effie sighed. "Well, that tells me nothing. Anyway, look at Will. He went to the city and now he only comes back on Fridays."

"He likes it there, I guess."

"I don't know why. It's so fussy. The city. Everything there is just..." She shook her head, a seething little movement. "So damn fussy."

Before leaving, Will invited Ben to join him and Eli for a cigar. They stood on the porch next to the mark of the old bear hide. The moon lit the frosty fence posts and stumps, and the dead grass sloping down to the lake.

When they were small and Mr. Stenhouse more inclined to tell stories, he would tell them about hunting the bear.

Way up north, he'd say, *long before I built this cabin so Mrs. Stenhouse would marry me... When all my hair was atop my head instead of on my lip... When my arms were poker thin and my eyes razor sharp... See*—and here he would pause and hold your eye—*I was too young to know fear.*

All the children would shiver except Lee, who was his father's favourite. He would ask him to tell it again.

Eli pulled a cigar from his pocket. He expertly snipped it and lit it. On his first exhale, he leaned back against the porch railing and crossed one foot over the other.

Will stuck his cigar between his teeth, where it seemed large and out of place, then handed it to Ben. Ben took a draw and coughed.

"I didn't like them at first either."

Eli pointed his cigar at Will. "You find yourself a city girl yet?"

"I've met some nice girls."

"I didn't say *nice* girls."

Will turned slightly from Eli and spoke to Ben. "It's too bad you can't get a ride to town. I'm going halfway tonight and staying the night with a friend."

"Tell me," Eli said before Ben could respond, "what does Effie's leg look like anyway? Have you seen it?" He looked at the rafters and blew smoke. "What I mean is, is it just like the other leg, only smaller? Or is it withered?" He curled his hand like a twisty paw, his eyes dull and unblinking.

Will's lip twitched.

"I haven't seen her leg since we were small," he said.

"Perhaps it's still a child's leg," said Eli. "Dimpled and soft. She could be all right, you know, if she wasn't so..." He circled his cigar around his face. "She's rather like a ferret, isn't she? An angry little ferret."

He grinned and leaned his head against the post, looking at Will as if he was in on the joke. "What? Don't brothers poke fun at their sisters?"

"Not like that."

"Well." Eli shrugged. His eyes flicked over the outbuildings and fields, his tone easy and untroubled. "I meant no harm."

Ben looked through the kitchen window, where Effie sat near the stove, her leg on a chair, covered in blankets. She had a book in her lap, her finger marking the page, but her head was tilted with her ear toward the porch. When Eli stubbed out his cigar and went inside, she opened her book and bent as if reading.

Ben looked at Will, who was staring at the ground, face tight and eyes narrowed.

"I don't listen to most of what Eli says," Will said, then spit over the rail. "You shouldn't either. I have to pack."

Ben stayed outside on the porch, still tasting the cigar. He'd only asked Effie once about her illness, and she'd said she didn't remember much. But Ben did—the quiet secrecy, the family shrinking by one.

He considered heading to his room, but it felt good to be on the porch alone, on his first night here. He stuffed his hands in his pockets to warm them, and spotted Mr. Stenhouse out near the barn. A flick of a man beneath the stars, his own land stretched out on all sides and past the trees.

The door creaked open and Effie came outside, carrying a bundle. She held a finger to her lips and Ben nodded, having already guessed what she did at night.

She struggled out past the yard, where the stumps of ancient trees sat rotting in the ground and infant trees grew in and around them. Mr. Stenhouse had felled each one of those trees before Effie was born. Now she faltered out amongst them, small and blue in the moon's cool light. He killed the bear and she fed the cougar.

EFFIE

1881

WHEN EFFIE WAS EIGHT YEARS OLD, SHE WATCHED HER TWIN brother die next to her in the bed. As she got better, he got worse. His back arched, wild and bendy, like a sapling stretched tip to the ground. The doctor, who had a pickled smell and drooping bags under his eyes, bent over them both with droppers and scopes and pungent salves. Their mother scrubbed the floor and cooled their heads, and their father sat vigil with his Bible, his eyes fixed on the page unmoving.

When Lee died, their mother wailed and her chair crashed on its side. Their father stood quietly and set his Bible next to the lamp. Her parents stopped sitting bedside, so Effie spent her first night without Lee alone. He was moved to the kitchen table and she was too weak to go see him. The bed was empty and enormous with only her in it—like a field or a frozen lake. Too quiet with only her breathing, and too cold without her brother.

That night Will brought her a cup of broth.

"Mother's out of her head," he whispered, nodding at the window. "She's burning his clothes. I had to build the fire for it."

Effie looked outside. The night was black and moonless but she did smell the smoke.

In the following days, visitors came "to pay respects," which Effie thought was like paying money, but for what? She heard Mrs. Petrenko's voice above everyone's. Her own husband was weakened by a stroke, which Effie thought meant a hard slap—strike, struck, stroke.

Mrs. Petrenko's words carried up the stairwell.

"Mrs. Stenhouse, you must rest yourself. Grief waits no matter how hard you try to shut it out."

Then she came upstairs and sat with Effie—a tall woman on a small chair. She told Effie a story about a painter who lost his painting hand, so what did he do? He learned to paint with the other, and his landscapes were the better for it.

"I must see to Mr. Petrenko now," she said, grazing the backs of her fingers on Effie's cheek. "But I'll say hello to you in church soon, won't I?"

"Will Mr. Petrenko be at church?" said Effie.

"Yes. Mr. Karlsson has fashioned a ramp for the back of the wagon."

"Mother said his mind is gone to mush now."

Mrs. Petrenko looked at her hands, which were puffy on the tops, unlike Effie's mother's hands, which were bony and dry. "Well, he can't talk any more, but he listens, and I can talk enough for both of us."

She kissed Effie's forehead and left.

Many months later, as the rain beat like hooves on the barn roof, her father carried her up the ladder to the hayloft. He held her to his side with one strong arm while the other grasped the rungs and pulled their weight. This close, she smelled the hard musk of his oilskin and the sour heat from his hat. They followed Will, so she had a view of his boots from the bottom with the tiny nailheads around the edge. Will stepped off the ladder and pushed open the two halves of the loft door, but only a murky light entered as the rains were dark and angry.

Effie was with her father in the barn that day because she'd been underfoot in the kitchen and had made Sarah cry by gagging on her oatmeal pudding and spitting it across the table. But Sarah's pudding was terrible. It sat on the back of her scalded tongue like paste. Sarah cried at everything.

This wasn't much of a punishment—Effie preferred the barn. Will and her father worked in silence, each knowing what to do, and how, without wagging their tongues about it. Whenever she was in the kitchen, Sarah and her mother chattered about the obvious—*Put the pudding in now so it's warm for supper... Take these scraps to the pigs... Leftover ham for cold lunch tomorrow... Let's cream the peas... Father likes minced onion*. Sometimes, Effie felt so bunched up in that place that she'd say mean things, or throw an apple at the door, or scream into the blanket that warmed her leg.

The kitchen was small and stuffy and the barn wide and cool. Large things stomped and tiny things scurried. The barn smelled alive, but the kitchen held dead things in the hot oven.

Effie rarely had an appetite since Lee died.

While Will and her father forked hay into a manger below, Effie climbed around the mounds that lined the walls. She and Lee used to scurry like mice, but now she struggled alone. She went near the window and perched like an owl, her bad leg out straight in its wretched brace. When she heard a squeak, she moved through the hay, trying to be quiet. She liked the pathways and hollows that the hayloft provided.

Will went back down to the main floor to feed the animals, but her father continued—stab, rustle, drop—his boots scraping the dusty floor. She found a mouse and followed as it slipped through the straw. It might lead her to the entire mouse family. Once, she'd found a nest of babies, a mound of fleshy pink beans. She named them all. Celeste, Howard, Pork Pie, Pinky Pie.

Then she noticed the quiet—or rather the people-quiet, as the rain was still pelting and animals stepping and snorting below. She stood, her good leg sore from overuse, and limped to the edge of the loft. The ladder was removed and hung on the wall. She went to the window and saw the wagon driving away, two figures in floppy black hats on the wagon seat, one tall, one small. She called but the rain buried her voice. The wagon rounded the bend, off to sell fattened pigs without her.

She yelled at the house, but it sat quiet and still. She screamed at nothing, rageful at being forgotten, her face hot in the blowing rain.

For the rest of that day, Effie had a good view of her father's bear hide, blackest of black, on display for visitors and his own enjoyment. Her father used to read about the sin of pride from his Bible at night, but he'd hung the bear right out front where everyone who came into the yard would see it. He told the story of hunting that bear, but he didn't answer Effie's questions. Like, *Why was he so tall?* Or, *How do fish breathe in water?* Or, *Why did Lee die?* She used to be frightened of the bear, but now she watched it with a hard look, biting her nails and spitting into the rain.

E.B., the farmhand, came from the field near dark. He heard her yelling and carried her down, his beard scratching her neck. He set her on the floor, and she limped hard into the downpour and across to the house, mud splashing her stockings and skirts. Inside, her mother was scrubbing the blackened wall above the stove, and when she turned, she gasped. Effie burst into loud tears.

"Why aren't you with your father?"

At that time, her mother had been filled up with two babies in her belly. Her voice was tight and her fists jammed fast to her hips.

"Why are you not with them?"

That night, when her father came home with Will, Effie was still at the table, nodding sleepily over a bowl of Sarah's oatmeal pudding, a warm blanket over her leg. Her mother and Sarah were knitting by the hot stove.

"I'm sorry we left you," said Will. "I thought of it halfway to town."

"I suppose your brain's turned to mush like Mr. Petrenko's." Effie poked her spoon into the pudding.

"Hush now," said her mother.

"We knew E.B. would get you," said her father. "And did he?"

"Only at dark did he come."

"As he would." Her father placed his hand on her head, brief and purposeful like he would steady a horse.

Effie wanted to fling pudding across the room, but instead took a bite and swallowed hard, so it lodged in her throat like wet clay.

That night, Effie couldn't sleep. Her leg hurt and her insides burned. Before the sun came up, she snuck down the stairs, holding her hands against the walls to quiet her brace. She took the long knife from the kitchen and stood on the porch in the misty early morning, testing it against the bear. The hide was tough and the fur thick, so she jabbed it harder, and again. Finally, she was hitting the log wall on the other side, and pulling down. She did it over and over until she was winded. The hairs shed, long and sticky, as she worked, plastered to her face, hands, nightdress until she was itchy with them. She imagined she looked like a bear herself.

Her first Sunday back at church, Effie still had sore legs, both of them whipped clean by her father. Well, she had been especially terrible. People stared at her, some with side glances and others with sad looks. She glared back until her mother yanked at her sleeve. Mrs. Petrenko sat at the very back with Mr. Petrenko in his wheeled chair. She nodded at Effie, her smile warm and strong in a way that said *Well done, Effie!*

Effie followed the children to Sunday school, several paces behind. When they reached the class, they wanted to see her new brace.

"No," she said.

The teacher handed out the little Bibles, crisp and small.

"I can see part of it," said Aaron Drinkwater, pointing, and Effie ripped his Bible from his hands and threw it across the room.

"Your mother has a crossed eye," she said.

"Effie," said the teacher, her face hard but her voice measured. "To the corner."

When she returned to the little school across the lake, Effie didn't listen to Mrs. Balodis, who spoke mostly to the youngest children or the stupid ones. Effie liked numbers as much as Will did—puzzles that quickened her heart and made her chalk press too hard and fast on the board—but she hated reading.

I can hop, I can run, I can stop, fun, fun, fun.

What was fun about that? And she couldn't do any of it anyway!

Mrs. Balodis was a dull woman with a flat face, but if her mood was pleasant, she let Effie stay in at lunch. Effie did math problems or looked at encyclopedias where the birds were wild and bright and cats had stripes and trees stood like wide umbrellas. Sometimes she watched the kids playing out the window, and sometimes she broke their pencils or spilled their ink. They called her Awful Effie.

BEN

1890

HIS MOTHER STOOD ON THE PORCH, STILL AS A PAINTING BUT for the snake that curled, glossy black, around her ankle, disappearing beneath the gauzy linen of her nightdress. As he reached out, her mouth fell open and water gushed, ribbons of seagrass hanging from her teeth.

Ben woke shivering under his blanket, a point of pain behind each eye. His breath came in gasps and stutters as he cracked the frozen layer on the water jug. He splashed his face and dried it on his sleeve, then checked his bag to make sure the tin was safely inside.

The yard was dull with frost. A patchy string of clouds moved over the moon so that it seemed to sway, its silver light brightening and shrinking. Mr. Stenhouse was awake. Lamplight showed through the kitchen window, where he'd be building a fire in the stove.

With his bag over his shoulder, Ben headed down the long drive. His boots crunched the frozen grass between the ruts, and an owl called from somewhere far behind him.

As he followed the road around West Cane Lake, the sky slowly lightened to a watery green. Flashes of black water showed through frosted trees and brush where the Howland dog had once shadowed him and his father.

By the time he reached Petrenko's Dry Goods & Post, the sun was showing on the edge of Ash Mountain and the ache behind his eyes had spread like a slow leak to the back of his head. Mrs. Petrenko stood, feet apart, in the doorway, seeming unbothered by the cold. She was changed. Her hair was grey now, loose and wiry, her shoulders thin under her dress. But her voice was familiar when she called to him—full and deep with a tremor running through it.

"I know you," she said, holding up her pipe in a wave. "James and Agda's boy, all grown."

"Yes, ma'am. Ben."

"Ben. That's right. Come warm yourself. I have tea made."

"I can't stay," he said, but she had already moved inside, her walk slow and stiff.

"These old knees," she called back, her hand holding the counter, then the wall, then the windowsill until she sat by the stove.

Ben followed, breathing the familiar dry smells of grain and spices, the sacks and tins and barrels. But the shelves were only half full and dusty.

When she took a good look at him, her smile faded. "You look like death in boots. Are you ill?"

"Maybe a bit."

"Sit." She reached and squeezed his arm before nodding to a chair by the stove. Then she poured tea into two chipped cups. "And how is James?"

Ben's chair creaked beneath him. "He died. Last week."

"Oh dear." She pointed her pipe at the front window. It showed the trees on the other side of the road and the short trail to the dock. "My dear Mr. Petrenko is gone as well," she said, as if he'd simply walked down that trail and paddled away.

Ben had heard from the Stenhouses that he'd died and that Mrs. Petrenko continued to run the place on her own. This, they all agreed, is what she'd always done anyway, being a strong and robust woman, and Mr. Petrenko being afflicted with a sensitive nature, ill-suited to business.

"He visited your cabin on occasion, I believe?" she said.

"Yes. He brought us his yeast starter. And tomato seeds."

Ben sipped the tea, remembering their quiet work, the three of them in the garden. Mr. Petrenko's slow smile. *See here, Ben,* he'd said, holding out his hand. *These are the good insects, who eat the bad ones.*

Mrs. Petrenko looked at him closely. "He helped anyone who asked. Most around here have a piece of his yeast starter. It came all the way from the old country."

Ben didn't tell her theirs had turned black when he forgot to feed it after his mother died. His father chucked it into the woods, where it shattered on a tree trunk.

"And Agda gone. And James," Mrs. Petrenko said. "It appears we both of us walk alone now. I am not yet accustomed to it. How are you faring?"

"My father was sick for a long time."

"Yes, of course. And if I may say so, perhaps you aren't entirely grieved." She patted his knee and nodded firmly. "Well, that is perfectly fine."

He nodded, his eyes on his empty cup, his stomach bunched up. "I buried him without a coffin."

She shrugged. "And what would a coffin bring him?"

"I guess nothing."

Then she brightened and clapped her hands. "Are you hungry? I can open a can of peaches."

"No, thank you. I should go." Ben reached for his bag.

"And where do you head to now?"

"The city. To find my father's niece."

"Your cousin then."

He saw through the window that a wagon had pulled up alongside the door. The driver hopped down and stretched his back.

"I guess she is my cousin."

Mrs. Petrenko squeezed his hand and stood up. "That's lovely, Ben. Just lovely to have family to visit."

Later in the day, the clouds returned and the rains came, gentle and cool, melting the last of the frost. Ben followed the road that turned from the lake, away from the school and the trail to Connie's cabin, if it still stood. His head throbbed, as if his heart resided inside his skull, swollen and beating.

He stopped to knock pebbles out of the broken seams of his father's boots, then stopped farther along to be sick in the bushes. As he spit on the ground, a wagon approached, its wheels squealing and splattering mud. The driver was bundled in furs.

"You going to town?" the man asked. He was deeply lined and dark, his hair shaggy and streaked in silver.

"Yes, sir," answered Ben. "Wharf Street."

"Hop in."

Ben set his bag in the back, then hefted himself onto the wagon seat. The man introduced himself as Billy. He smelled of woodsmoke and animal grease—maybe a hunter. The jostling of the wagon and the smell of grease soured Ben's stomach and knocked his brain about like jelly in a jar.

Billy talked on and on, his voice scratchy and hoarse and his stories out of order. He'd lost his thumb, caught in the reins of a spooked horse, and he'd cured venison on a hanging rack he fashioned himself. He'd fished at sea in his childhood, but fish never did like him much. His mother once shot a man she mistook for a wolf. He built the cabin where his four children were born, where one of them died, and where his first wife's tooth festered until she, too, passed on. His father was a German and his mother Songhees. She'd taught him Lekwungen. *Hay'sxw'qa.* His youngest brother was born stained purple on the top half, like he'd been dipped in ink upside down. One of his wives was Kanaka and the other Irish, both good women, broadly built and strong. He made his currant bread even sweeter with bear fat, and he once saw a whore run down in the street by a runaway buggy.

"Did she live?" Ben asked.

Billy shook his head. "Three men carried her into the tavern, all limp and bloody."

It had started to rain again. The cool sea air and the drizzle helped settle Ben's stomach as he took in the changes since he'd come here with his father.

The half-built houses were now finished, painted and lived in, with small trees planted in muddy yards. Chickens pecked and cows chewed grass along the roadside. A woman hauled her laundry in from the rain while her children played and hollered. Then the road turned and the city and harbour came into view.

Ben's palms turned slick as he watched the water, dark and dull, and the slender dock where he'd seen Merritt. Now it was a busy place, with large and small boats and sleek canoes.

"Where are you from?" asked Billy.

"Ash Mountain."

"Way out there. I call that out past nowhere."

The waters shifted and moved beneath the boats. Ben thought of his dream that morning. Could his mother know, somehow, that he'd come back here?

Through the dusky drizzle, they made their way down into the city. Ben looked straight ahead until he saw a sign between two brick posts: Queen Victoria Public School. He turned to look, sending a shot of hot lightning behind his eyes. Past the oaks and down a long path, he caught a glimpse of a turreted building, each window lit, three chimneys exhaling smoke. And then it was gone.

"My friend goes there."

Billy swung his large head and whistled. "Rich kid."

Ben sat back. "I don't think so." Then he thought about it—their food stores, their land, those healthy cows. "Well, maybe."

Billy dropped Ben off in the middle of the road, with directions to Wharf Street. Gulls called and swooped as he watched the cart rattle away down the cobbles, black spots bouncing before his eyes, like flies in summer. He tried to recall Lily's place, but the things he remembered were of little help. The rasp in her voice, her striped stockings. The whisky feeling of falling through his own thoughts. So he kept on toward the harbour, the smell of fish and seaweed heavy in the air.

There was only one butcher on Wharf Street, so it was easy enough to find. At its door stood a wooden pig, three feet tall, hind-footed and saluting in a coat painted bright blue. Through the window behind the smiling pig, real dead pigs hung naked and pink from hooks, and beneath that lay a sheep stretched out on a board. Its eyes were lumpy, like grey poached eggs, and its skin seemed lumpy as well, until Ben looked closer and saw a scrolled pattern carved into the fat of its back. This seemed about the strangest thing you could do to a sheep before eating it, and this shop seemed about the worst place you could be with a stomach turned over.

Ben looked away and opened the door, a bell ringing above him as he entered. The smells of blood and spices made his eyes water.

He was alone in the shop, the air cold on the back of his neck, and the floor inches deep in sawdust. Coils of sausage were draped over the rafters. A barrel full of pigs' feet stood near the door. On the wall hung a picture of a bearded man with his heart in flames, and small carved figures were arranged on the counter. A kneeling woman. A baby with one arm snapped off. A man with a staff, and some farm animals with heads too big and the bodies of dogs. From behind a swinging half door came the sickening sound of a knife sawing bone. Ben felt light-headed and strange in this room.

"Yes?" A Black man poked his head through the doorway, then stepped all the way through, wiping his bloody hands on his apron. He was wide in the chest and silver-haired.

"I'm looking for Lily," said Ben.

"You're not buying anything?"

"No. I don't have money."

The butcher looked up to the ceiling. "Of course you don't. And what do you want with Lily?"

"I have to give her something from her uncle."

"James?"

"You know him?"

"He stopped paying her rent a few months back."

"He was sick."

"Didn't much care for him." The butcher turned away. "She's around the side and up the stairs."

The alley was narrow and the stairs were steep. Lily opened the door as he reached the top step, holding it wide with one straight arm and the other braced against the doorframe. She was much smaller than he remembered, wearing slim trousers held up by suspenders over long underwear. He remembered the braids wrapped around her head but not the black eye-paint smudged around each pale green eye.

"You were looking for me." She smiled, tapping the door open further with her bare foot.

Her apartment was dim, with grey light coming through a gap in a curtain. The floor was layered in rugs, and a small fire burned in the stove. All of it was familiar now that he saw it.

"I saw you down there, so lost," she nodded to the window, where a pair of white binoculars sat on the sill. "I thought to myself, now there's a boy doesn't know his way."

Ben took off his hat.

"Do you remember me?" he said. "My father is James. Your uncle."

She leaned back against the door and it clicked shut.

"The boy that fell in the sea?"

He nodded.

"Little Mouse." She smiled again, showing a gap where a tooth once was. "Come all this way. I wouldn't have known you, but now I see it. Do I look different?" She held out her arms.

"A little."

"Old, I suppose."

"No. Not old."

A cool damp prickled his forehead.

She stepped close and placed her palm against his cheek. "Are you unwell?"

"I think so."

"Sit down and rest."

Ben sat on the sofa, his bag at his feet and his hat in his lap. Lily opened the curtain farther, revealing the brick warehouse across the street. Above the flat roof, gulls called, dropping and rising against a heavy grey sky. She busied herself at the stove, pouring, stirring, humming.

"Last time you visited you were sick as well. How funny. The city doesn't agree with you. Or you don't agree with it."

She handed Ben a cup of pale tea and sat next to him, her elbow on the back of the sofa, her cheek in her hand. The tea was barely warm and he smelled the liquor in it. It tasted bitter.

"What are you now? Sixteen or so?"

"Seventeen, I guess. Or eighteen."

"As old as that? A man." She brushed the hair from his eyes. "But still a boy."

He sipped again and looked into his cup. It looked like any old weak tea, filmy and pale, but the flavour was strange. Metallic. A vinegar taste at the back of his tongue. He looked at Lily, who sipped hers without bother. She didn't seem to wonder why he'd come.

"I have news about your uncle," he said. "James."

"Mm?" She finished the rest of her tea. A slight shake in her hand rattled the cup on the saucer.

"He died. Last week."

Lily touched her hair lightly, and for a moment she was still. Then she took out a pin and pinched it in her lips. One long braid fell down the front of her. "Did he really?"

"He'd been sick a long time."

"Well." She began to pull the braid apart. "Well anyway, I should tell you I don't get too sad about dying. You might as well get sad about eating. Or fucking." She grinned with the pin clamped in her teeth.

Ben's throat was dry. He reached into his bag.

"He left this for you. There's a note in the lid."

Lily took the tin and ran her fingers along it. Her hands were small, with black rims around each nail. She pushed it open and peered inside. "Look at that. It smells like mould."

"My friend says it's a lot. A month's wages."

She handed it back. "I figured he was sick when he stopped sending rent to Gus. Do you know Gus?"

"The butcher?"

"He talks tough, but he's a gentle pup. A buttercup."

"He looked busy."

"He *acts* busy. His shop is always empty, poor man."

Ben's headache was softening. A pleasing warmth spread through his bones. He finished his tea and set the cup on the table, then settled back.

"And Agda's dead as well," Lily said. "How strange."

"That was years ago."

"Was it?"

He leaned his head against the sofa and looked at the ceiling. "She died because we came here." He had trouble holding on to what he said, understanding each word for only a brief moment before it disappeared completely.

"Hmm," said Lily. "She was weak, I suppose, if she died over that."

The ceiling was stained with lamp smoke and something else that had dripped from above, spilling outward in rings and causing the plaster to flake off in brown patches.

"She wasn't weak."

"Well, I remember her." Lily ran her fingernail over her teeth. *Click, click, click.* "Horse's teeth."

Ben put his hand over his eyes and now he was floating. He saw his mother, dead under her quilt, her teeth showing through dry lips.

"Are you lonely out there without my uncle?"

"No."

She took his hand. Her own felt like water, formless and cool, but when he looked, nothing seemed unusual. She spoke in a soft rasp that fell nicely on his ear.

"Sometimes I imagine people don't die at all. They simply go away and leave us behind."

Ben tried to hold on to that. "Do they think of us?"

"Of course." She leaned over so he felt her breath on his face. It smelled of whisky. She kissed his forehead. "I can tell you're good," she said.

He opened his eyes. A spider skittered along the ceiling stain, moving its legs in a quiet dance. *Tap, tap, tap.*

"Do you know how I know?"

Ben shook his head.

"I feel it." She thumped her hand against her heart, and Ben felt it in his own.

"No. I'm—"

His voice sounded low and outside of him, like someone else spoke into his ear. He rested his hat on his head and tilted it over his eyes. The pull into blackest sleep was strong. His body sank into the sofa like he was being dragged into it, absorbed by the old worn velvet.

He opened his eyes. Lily was at the window watching through her binoculars. It was black outside and rain hit the glass in messy splatters. She turned to him and smiled.

"You feel better?"

He did. His blood ran warm, gently pulsing through his veins. His headache had dissolved like sugar in water.

"You'll forget you're sick for a while but it'll soon wear off, and then you'll feel worse than ever. That's the only thing."

She disappeared behind the faded curtain where her bed was and continued to speak. He let his eyes fall shut. The pleasant swirling in his head grew stronger, and he was a boy again, in a little red boat that floated above the water. Higher and higher as Lily talked in rhythm with the rain. *I knew Agda would name you, but I thought it would be something French. Pierre. Or Jacques. Not Ben. Little wren. Come back again. Where's my other stocking?*

He couldn't feel his arms until he lifted one and watched it fall. He couldn't feel Lily's tin but saw that it was still clutched in his hand.

You liked the shells the most. Do you remember going out at night?

Her voice became muffled and, somewhere, something banged shut.

I prefer to wear britches, but you should hear what people say. Oh look, a button fell off. Goddamn.

She came from behind the curtain in a striped dress.

"What do you think?" She pushed up each breast with a half stumble, then adjusted her skirts. "I need a better dress, don't I? Something fine."

"You knew me? Before?"

She smiled wide, leaning one hand flat against the wall, the other on her hip. "I carried you in my belly, didn't I? Have you forgotten?"

Ben leaned forward, elbows on his knees, head in his hands. He had been sick on Lily's floor before and it was all starting to seem like a dream repeating itself. Lily's boots stomped back and forth as she busied about. All the while, she talked and talked but her words were muffled, as if spoken underwater, and the words in his head were loud. *Forgotten … I carried you … in my belly, you knew me …*

"Ben."

He opened his eyes. She stood at the window, again looking through her binoculars. She turned to him, her braids gold in the lamplight, her eyes freshly painted. All the smudges gone.

"Gus is coming."

Heavy footsteps shook the stairs outside.

"I'm happy you visited," she said.

When Ben stood up, Lily took his hand and held it to her cheek. "Come back later. I'll treat you to a meal, poor skinny Mouse."

She opened the door, and the sound of rain erupted into a roar. The butcher stood on the landing in the dark, hat soaked through and dripping. Ben stepped outside to make room for him, then turned to Lily.

"No one ever told me—," he said, but she was already shutting the door and, behind her, Gus was taking off his sopping coat.

As Ben walked along the street, each drop of rain felt pleasing on his bare head, each thought that came to him disappeared like smoke. He still held Lily's tin, so perfectly fitted to his hand as if made for it, but when he looked back, her place was gone.

And then he was standing at a railing and looking out. The black ocean had blended with the night sky. He could hear the waves lapping against boats he couldn't see. Time didn't move forward or back, but hung like a powdery light, filtering down over the water.

An inky shape lay on the dock.

A man?

Merritt.

Or the wet impression of him still soaked into the salted wood.

It lifted. Not as a man stands, but as a shadow—stretching and contorting, then hovering long in the air before the rain swept it away.

Then he was in the middle of the street, looking at a woman. She sat on the edge of the sidewalk, her boots in the mud, her face long and her mouth small over so many teeth.

"I'm looking for—"

But his thoughts were slipping away. She lifted her skirts to the tops of her stockings. Was he staring?

"Lockwood's Lair," he heard himself say.

She lifted her skirts higher still, letting her legs fall open to reveal pale inner thighs, plated like the white belly of a crab.

"You mean the boarding house?" she said, her mouth full of pearls. She pointed.

He was at a bench, wet and slick in the light of the yellow gas lamp. He sat down, his bones melting like candle wax. It seemed he could slip slowly between the slats of the bench, drip like warm honey to the dark grass beneath.

"Are you looking for someone?"

A young man. A group of young men, smiling, laughing.

"For Will Stenhouse."

More laughing.

"He's out with Marjorie."

"Who's Marjorie?"

But the young men were gone.

* * *

"Ben?"

Will stood tall in the dark, a hazy glow behind him. "What are you doing?" It was a whisper, and there was a harshness to it.

Ben sat up, shutting his eyes against the gaslight. The pleasant strangeness of Lily's tea was gone, and he now felt the full force of his sickness. Cold bones and hot skin, a head full of churning nails.

"Are you sick? How'd you get here?"

"I'm fine."

Will slipped his arm under Ben's to help him up.

"You shouldn't have come."

"I'm sorry."

"Be very quiet."

He led Ben down the path and up some stairs, through a door. Their footsteps echoed in a dim hallway. Then Ben was on a bed, sinking into a dark untethered sleep.

"He can't stay here, you know that."

"I know."

"Who is he, anyhow?"

"An old neighbour. He's sick."

"You'll get caught. I won't cover for you."

"I'll make sure he's gone by morning."

"He looks like a vagrant."

"What kind of thing is that to say?"

A cool hand on his forehead.

"You're burning up."

LILY

1864

SHE MOVED QUICKLY IN THE DARK, THE SOLES OF HER BARE feet slapping the rain-soaked planks, her father's oilskin past her knees. She saw a man by the red tip of his cigar and dodged around him and another two under the flickering lamp of the Brown Jug. The black dog followed—sometimes it did and sometimes it didn't, it was old. In the day, its bones showed, joints large, back swayed deeply, but now she only saw the gleam in its eyes and heard its nails on the planks behind her.

If she wasn't back by the time her father went to bed, she'd get a smack or a pinch or worse—as last time—a hot poker to her neck. Only meant to scare her, of course, with the threat of heat near her skin, until a tremor shook his arm—*Tsss*—then her own howl like a screeching raccoon.

She peeked around the wall to see in the window. Her father had his back to the door. He polished things and poured things, his shoulders moving in small, neat jolts. The place was full, and when she stepped inside, the sound of men's voices boomed like rumbling thunder. One of the men at the bar spoke to her father. "You don't want her down here, do you, Connie?" And her father turned to look at her, nodding his head to the stairs.

Lily sat on the top step. She counted the bedsprings and the grunts and the squeals. The men all sounded the same, but she knew which sound belonged to which woman—Penny laughed, Pearl said nice things loudly, Flora *hmm*-ed and *HMM*-ed. Lily hoped Penny's door would open first, but it was Pearl's that did. She pointed her sinewy arm down the hall.

"To your father's room or the kitchen, Miss Lily. Or I'll tell him I found you here."

So she ran, elbows out, down the hall and waited in the kitchen. It was a long time before the noisy men left and the ladies settled quietly in their beds. Penny came down, tired and dishevelled, but she always smiled for Lily. She heated milk. Lily drank it while Penny brushed her hair, gently pulling the bristles through tangles before braiding it. She spoke softly of her mother, who, back in England, had made hats with live canaries attached by tiny chains clamped to their tiny bird legs. Fancy women would buy the hats and wear them all day as a sort of joke, then once the birds became downcast, around dinnertime, they would set them free. Lily imagined the wild chirping, the yellow flutter of wings flashing past the windows of dark buildings and onward toward the setting sun.

They both stopped talking when Lily's father passed the doorway, his fingers deep in his mouth, digging at his molars. He headed up the stairs. They listened to his steps above them, slow and familiar in their uneven rhythm. When it fell quiet, Penny wrapped the braids around Lily's head and pinned them, then kissed Lily on the crown they made.

"Don't wake him, he's surly today."

Lily nodded and slipped up the stairs, down the quieting hall and into the room she shared with her father. He lay fully clothed on top of the bed, the lamp flickering next to him. When asleep, his shaking stopped and he looked dead.

She stepped closer and looked down at the slack of his cheek, the dark smudge in the hollow. The skin would be rough if she touched it, but she didn't. She only let her hand hover above his open mouth, then pulled it back when she felt the hot touch of his breath. She tightened her arms against her ribs in a quick spasm of relief. She wanted to call down to Penny, *Not dead!*

Instead, she unhooked the wiry arms of his glasses from behind his ears, washed them in the water basin and dried them on the rag. Next, she took off his boots. She filled his whisky glass and slipped a tablet from the little blue bottle onto the table. The pills were a sort of magic. A trade with the devil, as she heard her father explain it to Penny. They took away his lesions and in return gave him trembling bones and black teeth.

Lily lay on the strip of mattress next to him under the blanket. Early sunlight peeked through the gaps in the curtains. As this place went to bed, the rest of the town woke up. She imagined the people—bakers setting out fresh loaves, fishermen stepping into wobbly boats, young women walking to the cannery in blue woolen jumpers, arms linked. Sometimes, instead of sleeping, she watched it all from the window.

Later, she'd wake up again. She always knew he was gone by the stillness in the bed, the unbearable quiet of being left alone in a room. She lay awake until the ladies moved about, readying themselves for another day.

LILY

1872

Lily grew fat with child, having not yet lost her own baby fat. She stood in front of the mirror before her bath. Small, round-cheeked, and smooth-chested. Penny said she'd grow a bosom for a while after the baby came, until her milk dried up. And her milk would dry up when the baby left her for Father Michael's Home for the Children of Unwed Mothers.

Lily flattened a palm over each breast. Nothing like Penny's, which hung over the waist of her apron, swaying and soft.

"Then I'm like a cow," she said.

"A pretty little cow. Now get in the tub."

Penny—woolly-haired and sweet-voiced. A woman so good she could have mothered ten children, but instead shared Connie's room and mothered his whores. Her long sharp nose and small black eyes would have looked severe on most women, but not on Penny, who was generous with her affections and therefore beautiful.

Lily hugged her before stepping into the steaming water—face to her pillowy shoulder, a faint whiff of peony. She'd never known a mother, but in moments like this, Penny was hers and hers alone.

After her bath, she went back to her very own room, paid for by her Uncle James. This after much convincing, most of which Lily listened to from the other side of the door—her uncle's voice pitched high, pleading, and her father's cool. She was someone else's problem now, her father said, and James raised his offer, then raised it again. Again, she was like a cow. Bartered over at market, while the cow stood there, chewing grass and swatting flies, thinking nothing in its big cow head. She had felt funny about it, as she listened. Not anxious, but stuck, as if each word they spoke was a pebble sewn into the seams of her dress, weighing her down just that little bit more.

In the end a decision was made and she was informed. James was allowed to pay for a room, as long as Lily stayed out of the way.

And not much later, there she was again, listening at another door as the doctor discussed her ill-health with Penny in the hall.

"She is too young and too small," the doctor said. "She needs bedrest and broth, and God's holy word."

And what did she feel this time? Penny and the doctor spoke in fearful tones, but Lily wasn't afraid at all. Quite the opposite. She wanted to throw open the door and yell, "Look at me, you silly old goats! Do I look like someone about to drop dead?"

After Lily became too big for anything but a nightdress, her uncle's wife, Agda, came to visit. She was a timid, pale woman who lurked around the edges of the room, fussing and fretting. Shall I make tea? Are you warm at night? Does the baby move every hour as it should?

Anyway, this was fine by Lily, as she'd only had the ladies in the house to chat with, and they'd grown weary of her.

"Do you eat plenty of liver?" Agda asked. "It strengthens the blood."

Lily grinned at her from her bed while she went on and on. They'd met the day Agda married her uncle, and she seemed as strange now as she did then.

"Did you see the cattle go by?" Lily asked. "They kick up all the dust in the street. Look." She ran her finger along the side table, leaving a clean streak.

"Shall I close the window?"

"No. I like hearing what goes on. Anyway, they've gone. Where is my uncle? He hasn't come to visit."

"Don't you know that he is at the jail?"

"No one tells me anything," Lily said. Jail was nothing new. His job was a risky one. But usually her father bailed him out. "For how long?"

"Until late next month."

"And then he'll come to see me?"

"I hope so. He is unused to the idea still."

"Why? All women have babies." Lily's eyes dropped to the tie around Agda's narrow waist. "Well, most."

Agda stepped forward and handed her a brown paper package, then sat in the cane chair next to the window and watched her tear it open. Inside, a blue calico dress. Lily stood and held it out, an enormous thing, dragging on the floor and wide as a revival tent. She pressed it close and it pooled at her feet.

"Ha! Made for a circus woman."

Agda held her fingers to her front teeth that forever showed through her lips, her other hand clutching her side.

"We can hem it," she said. "If there is a treadle, I can fix it now."

"I'll be done with all this soon anyway," said Lily, holding her swollen belly. "I don't really need any dresses." She laid it on the bed and moved to the window. "Did you see the paddlewheeler come in? I can't see it from here, but I know it comes midday. I can hear all the fuss."

"I did not see it."

"Last time I was at the docks, it brought Chinamen." She looked at Agda, whose eyes were still on the dress. "I asked one of them how long was his journey, but—" She shrugged. "I guess none of us understand each other. I wonder how you say that in China—*How long was your journey?*"

Talking with Agda was like talking with a broomstick, but still she stayed another hour. When Lily ran out of things to say, Agda did speak—of dry summers and the state of the gardens, her baby goat named Myrtille that ate two potato plants. Lily nodded and yawned and went to look at the busy street out her window. Then she lay herself atop the bed, flat on her back, her belly pressing against the buttons of her nightdress.

When she began to doze, Agda said her name and Lily opened her eyes, looking straight up at the freshly plastered ceiling.

"It would be best if I raised this child, yes?" Agda said. "As my own?"

Lily let her head fall to the side, cheek to mattress, to better see the woman. The sun shone behind Agda's orange hair so that it seemed she glowed.

"You want my baby?"

"I can give it a good home. But this place..." Agda looked at the door, her hand fiddling with the button at her neck.

Lily turned back to the ceiling.

"Father Michael was going to take it, so you can talk to him. I want to go to the islands again and sell whisky. Do you know I've only been twice?" She pressed her hand to her belly. "And I want to go see the new lighthouse on Sandpiper Island. Have you gone there?"

Agda was smiling, one hand to her mouth, the other to her chest. Her eyes filled with tears as she stood. "No. I have not been to any island but this one."

"You should go."

"Perhaps not, as it wouldn't suit me." She went to the door and turned. "I am in charge of the farm with James away, so I will write to him. When he is released, he will come and get the baby. It seems the timing is perfect, no?"

"Yes, I suppose."

Lily watched from the window as Agda walked stiffly to her horse, her dress the colour of dust and her face hidden under the wide brim of an old garden hat. With her forehead pressed against the glass, Lily tapped until Agda looked up. Lily placed her palm flat on the pane and the woman nodded, then covered her smile and left.

Lily's stomach swelled to a full moon, lined in delicate purple marks like tree roots climbing upward. Then the pains came. They rolled forward and back like the waves of a tide. She cried and fussed until the doctor gave her laudanum.

"You best be strong," he said. "You've got a fight ahead of you."

The girls came into her room. Some of them stood along the walls, biting their nails, and others held her hands and smoothed her brow, saying sweet things. Everything moved in swells, like breathing, warping and expanding, then shrinking back. The doctor sweated between her open legs like a man having his way.

"You having fun with me, Doc?" Lily asked him, her voice echoing between her ears.

When she woke, the sun lit up the room. The window was wide open to the warm breeze and city sounds of wagons, voices shouting, seagulls calling. A Songhees woman sat in the chair next to her bed, breast out and nursing a baby. She showed Lily the tiny red-faced thing with a shock of black hair, a milky dribble on its chin.

"*S,hehie,lec,*" she said, her smile gentle.

"It's for Agda." Lily said. Then her eyes fluttered shut. "I'm so tired."

BEN

1890

***HIS MOTHER STOOD BARE, KNEE-DEEP IN WATER, HER ARMS** limp at her sides and her hair in jellied ropes down her shoulders. She wept and her round belly moved and rolled, so the skin stretched parchment thin. Her crying grew louder, her tears harder, and from her wide mouth a slippery stream reached to the murky sea at her feet. She was water. Her wail, low and flat, filled his ears.*

Ben startled awake. His throat was parched and his eyes scratchy. Soft grey light filled the room, and from outside came the continuous noise of the city. Downstairs, pots clanged, crashing and loud like they were being roughly stacked. He was at Will's boarding house. But he could barely remember how he got here.

He swung his legs off the bed and sat up, steadying himself with his hands on the mattress. A little dog barked below him, before being told "Hush, Minna!"

Ben's headache was gone, the searing heat in his bones, and the fever, all replaced by a light-headed hunger. He felt his shirt, sour and limp, and the sheet a little damp. He'd never been that sick, and now that he was better, he wanted nothing more than to get cleaned up and gone.

When he stood, the room swayed, so he waited for it to settle, then looked around. It was a small room, crammed with two narrow beds, two dressers, two low bookshelves, a sweater on the back of a chair, a stack of books on the table, a towel on a bedpost. Under a cup of cold coffee next to the bed, Will had left a note.

The bath is down the hall. I'll be back at lunch. —W

PS Don't leave the room until old Mrs. Lockwood goes to the ladies' guild. She'll have our hides.

Ben stretched his neck one way then the other. Will could have been sent home because of him. He remembered something about that. Then he remembered what Lily had told him.

Little wren, come back again…

He pressed the heels of his hands to his eyes.

Had his mother ever mentioned Lily? His father had. *Nothing but trouble.* He tried to reach through to the old memories, back and further back, to the time before his arrival at the cabin. The old horse. The bread and molasses. Mother, *Mere.* Before that, only darkness. Nothing to grab hold of.

Mrs. Lockwood was still moving about downstairs, quick and vicious little movements. Ben drank the cold coffee while he waited, then, when the front door slammed shut, he went to the window and peered out into the foggy street. Mrs. Lockwood marched stiffly to the gate, a straight-backed woman in grey, with a little dog bouncing along beside her. When she was out of sight, Ben slipped out the door to the bathroom, a cold, tiled room that smelled strongly of vinegar. The tub was huge, long enough to stretch out his legs and deep enough to slip fully under. He considered it for a moment, but instead filled the sink. Clouds of steam rose as he caught sight of himself in the mirror. Glassy-eyed and gaunt. Hair stiff and unwashed. Cheeks pale. He felt better than he looked.

He splashed his face, then took off his shirt and plunged it into the hot water. As he scrubbed with the green bar of soap, he sorted through the long, strange journey that had brought him to Will. *A wide black sea, a woman's lifted skirts, a tin that fit perfectly in his palm...*

He stopped, hands blister-pink in the hot water, then wrung out his shirt, snapped it twice, and hurried back to Will's room.

There, in his bag, he found Lily's rusty tin, the banknotes rolled tight.

He put the lid back on, his mind buzzing. He needed to see Lily again.

With his bag packed, Ben sat on the bed and waited to say goodbye to Will. Outside, the fog was lifting, and the sun was a white glare behind clouds. Midday. To keep himself from falling back asleep, he looked at the books on Will's bedside table, running his finger along the leather spines. *Harvey's Grammar. Elements of Rhetoric and Composition. Ray's Algebra. Our Surroundings, An Elementary General Science.* A whole world of ideas that he didn't know about.

Underneath the books, the edges of a few loose pages poked out. Ben recognized Effie's handwriting. He shimmied the letters out from under the stack and skimmed them.

Father's morose again with you gone...

Do you know Horrid Eli paints? Ha!

It's true that Sarah is uninteresting but what will become of me in this house once you are all gone?

And do you think Father lets me help with the accounts now you're not here to do it? Let me tell you the answer is NO.

Tucked in with the letters was a small photograph. A young woman with soft curls, her direct gaze focused on something beyond the camera. Ben flipped it over. *With love, Marjorie.* He took it to the window and angled it into the light—dark lashes, strong chin, lace at the edge of her collar, the swelling below where small buttons formed a neat, curved row. He clicked his jaw, recognizing the face of someone kind and intelligent, at odds with the hard knot in his chest.

Voices sounded at the door and, as the latch clicked, Ben slipped the photograph into his pocket. It happened quickly, as if his hand had made the decision to do it without the rest of him agreeing. Will walked in, followed by a young man carrying a suitcase.

"Oh good," Will said. "I saw this morning that your fever broke." He looked at the other fellow—the shared look between two people who had discussed something they didn't agree on.

"Thanks for letting me stay." Ben nodded his thanks to Will's friend, who turned his wide back to both of them and tossed his suitcase on his own bed. He began to unpack.

"You need to be gone before Mrs. Lockwood gets back," said Will. "I'll walk with you. I have a bit of time."

Ben could cross the room in three long steps and slip the picture back, but Will was waiting, easy-mannered with his hands in his pockets.

"You'll want new bedding," the roommate said to Will, nodding at the bed where Ben had slept.

Will lowered his chin. "Let's go."

Ben grabbed his bag, feeling the roommate's eyes on him. He couldn't see his hat anywhere, so, bare-headed, he followed Will out.

"That's Anthony," Will whispered, when they were on the stairs. "I had to pay him to stay with one of the other boys. And a little extra to keep quiet about it."

"I'm sorry."

"He's an old crank, anyway. I'm asking to switch rooms for next term."

"I'll pay you back."

"Don't be silly. You have no money."

Will led them through the kitchen to a door at the back. Outside, the air was cool, with only a few ribbons of fog remaining.

"You must be starved."

"I am." Ben's stomach gnawed with emptiness. "I was with you one night?"

"Try three. Don't you remember?"

"I don't remember anything. Three nights?"

"I nearly called a doctor, but that would have put me in a rough spot."

"I'm sorry."

"It's fine. I didn't get caught."

"I slept that whole time?"

"You talked a lot of gibberish. French too. I suppose you get that from Agda."

"Three nights. I need to get back to the farm."

Will shrugged. "You'll explain, my father will get over it. And Ben—keep an eye on Effie for me, will you?"

"An eye for what?"

"She's awful sometimes, isn't she?" Will smiled. "I mean, be a friend to her, you know?"

"We are friends."

"She writes every couple of days and I try to write back, but I'm busier than she is. Poor Effie. Lee was born sweet, if you remember. Effie sour."

They stopped at a cart and Will bought a meat pie for Ben. He tried to eat and walk, but the crust was soft and falling apart, and the gravy spilled out if he didn't catch it quickly. He'd never been so hungry.

"I'm staying here this weekend," said Will."Maybe next weekend too." He shrugged, then smiled. "I met a girl."

The last bite of pie stuck in Ben's throat. He swallowed hard.

"That's good," he said.

"Anyway, I can't really help you here."

"I don't need help."

"I know. But if you ever come back... You understand." Will held out his hand and Ben shook it. "I'm sure glad you're better. Goodbye, Ben."

He started away, then turned around. "I forgot to ask. Did you find that woman?"

"I did. Her name is Lily."

Will continued on. Once he disappeared around the corner, Ben headed back toward Lily's. It felt wrong that he hadn't told Will more about her—and there was so much to tell. And even worse, that he still had the photograph of Marjorie, burning like a hot stone in his pocket.

The muddy mineral smell was thick near the harbour. At the dock, men drove cattle and sheep down a ramp from a paddlewheeler, and others hauled crates to waiting wagons. Children had gathered to watch, as gulls screamed, wild for fish guts in the water.

Ben found Lily at the butcher's, leaning on the counter in her slim trousers. She was talking to Gus, but when the bell rang above the door, she turned to face Ben, elbows on the counter behind her. In her hand was one of the carved figures, the kneeling woman.

"You're back," she said, tilting her head with her hand to the flat top of her hat. A man's hat, stiff and new.

"I came to see you before I left," he said.

"I'm happy you did." She put the carved woman back with the wooden family, then turned to Gus. "This is Agda's boy, if you remember. James and Agda."

"Your boy then."

Lily shrugged. "I suppose he's his own boy," she said. "Since no one belongs to anyone."

Gus glanced at Ben. "We met earlier."

Ben shifted his bag, waiting for more. Some mention of the time before the cabin, how he could be born here and end up there. Instead, Lily came closer. The black around her eyes was greasy and smudged, like she'd used char from under a spit. She took off her hat and placed it on Ben's head—a tight fit and sitting high.

"I got this for you," she said, the gap in her teeth showing. This close, he could smell alcohol on her and the salty sea. "Well, I got it for Gus but he doesn't want it."

"Because it's not yours to give, Lily."

"Whose is it then?" she asked.

Gus groaned and threw his rag into a pail of water.

"Do you mean the beaver who gave up his fur? Or the man who felted the fur? Or the one who made the hat?"

"I'm not playing your games, Lily."

Gus went into his back room. Again, Ben noticed the picture of the bearded man beside the swinging half door, his strawberry red heart in flames. Ben imagined the heat, a chest filled with smoke. He turned to Lily and set his bag on the floor to open it.

"I have your tin," he said, handing it to her. "I didn't mean to take it."

"Mm, funny. I wondered where it went." She scratched a spot of rust on the lid with her ragged nail, staining her thumb orange. "I hope you bought yourself something."

He looked up from his bag as he tied it shut. "I wouldn't do that."

"No? I would want you to. In any case, we can get a meal together. I promised to fatten you up, remember?"

Behind her, the sun hung dull white beneath the low cloud.

"I'd like that," Ben said. "Only I can't stay long."

"According to who?"

"Mr. Stenhouse needs me. At the farm."

"A farm? You worry yourself, little Mouse," she said. "All those chickens will be there whether you return this day or the next."

They walked together to the Brown Jug. Lily dragged her finger along its window, humming flatly to herself. Ben looked through the glass. It was busy inside and a fire burned in the hearth, much like when he was there, dripping cold water onto the floor. He opened the door for Lily, reading a painted sign next to it: *COME IN AND VIEW THE MONSTER CHICKEN EGG! LARGEST EVER SEEN IN THIS CITY!*

Inside, the Brown Jug seemed smaller than Ben remembered. There were pictures on the walls that hadn't been there before—the countryside in summer, a horse and rider, the stern-looking queen. The bar was darkly polished with a row of stools in front and brass spittoons next to them. On a shelf behind the bar was a fairly large egg under a glass cloche.

The place was full of noisy men eating roasted meat while a woman heartily played a piano in the corner. Clouds of cigar smoke hung below the tin ceiling.

Lily walked to the bar, where a man was smiling at her.

"Take some of this, Oland," she said, dumping her banknotes in front of him. "I believe I owe you."

The man, Oland, was tall, heavy-faced, and droopy-lidded. He looked down at the pile of curled bills, took one and flattened it on the bar.

"Aw, Lily, what've you done to get this then?"

"Outlived an uncle."

He nudged the pile of money with his knuckle. "So James died. Who will take care of you now, I wonder?" He looked at Ben.

"I take care of myself fine," Lily said.

Oland laughed, a silent shake of the shoulders. He counted out some of the money and slipped it in his pocket. "Be mindful with the rest of that now," he said.

Lily scooped it up and led Ben to a table near the window. She slumped back in the chair with a sleepy smile, leaving the money scattered in front of her.

"I feel good about today," she said. "Do you know why?"

"Why?" Ben stacked the bills, then rolled them and put them back in the tin.

"The weather will soon turn. I can smell it coming off the water."

He looked outside where the cobbles were wet, the sky heavy and holding rain.

"I have a knack with weather," Lily said. "When I used to help my uncle with whisky runs, I would predict the rains for him."

Two boys set full plates and mugs on the table, forks standing straight up in the mashed potatoes. Ben took off the tight new hat and felt his scalp release in a tingling ring around his head. He took a bite of warm lamb, strongly salted, and watched Lily drink long from her mug. He studied her face for features like his own, but she was round-cheeked where he was cut sharp. Her colours were soft and Ben's stark—black eyes, pale skin. Her ears were small and his stuck out like they attempted to break free of his head. She wasn't old. In fact, he'd be taken for her brother more than her son.

"You must have been very young. When I was born."

She set her mug down. "I suppose I was. I'd only bled once, anyway."

That didn't mean much to him, though Effie had explained some of it. Sarah bled, so she could have children. Effie would never do either, which was fine by her.

"And my father?"

"James?"

"No. My father by birth. Who was he?"

She finished her drink and held two fingers up to Oland.

"You think I track men like days of the week, little Mouse?"

Out the window, an old woman crept by, so bent she faced the ground beneath her. She stopped to reach a slow hand into her basket and Lily traced her hunched form on the glass.

"Seamstress," she said softly, as the woman carried on. "Anyway, all that matters is the father you had, and James was a good man who raised you well."

Ben swallowed gritty potato then took another drink. The beer was dark and curled his tongue. He figured Lily had the habit of calling every man good, as he'd heard it three times from her already.

"You are much like him, you know," she said, regarding him.

Ben shook his head, feeling heat in his face. "We're nothing alike."

"You drink your beer slowly as he did. He had no stamina for drink. His nerves were tender things."

"I wouldn't say tender."

"They broke easily and often." She reached across the table and took hold of his sleeve, where a hole gaped in the cuff. "This was his shirt. I remember it. He worried it right through, poor man."

"He was cruel to my mother," Ben said. "To Agda."

"Yes. Well, I suppose she provoked him."

Ben rested his hand on the table, the fork held loosely in his grip. "She died because of him."

"Hmm." Lily cocked her head, showing the long purple scar along her neck. "I don't like to argue, Mouse, but earlier you said she died because of you."

"I meant us. Him."

"Well. It seems no one's to blame, really, but the snake that bit her. Although even that's unfair as it's only in a snake's nature to bite ankles."

One of the boys set two full mugs in front of Lily. When he was gone, she pulled a little brown bottle from her sleeve and added three drops, then drank it all at once. She hadn't touched her food.

"What I mean is," said Ben, leaning forward, his hands pressed between his knees under the table, "everything turned after we got back—because of what he did."

Lily looked at him, her face blank.

"What he did to Merritt," Ben added.

At this, she blinked, with a slight wobble to her head as if it was briefly unmoored. Then she leaned back and smiled through the glass at a man on a bicycle, bumping along on the cobbles with a dead goose in his basket.

"Poor goose," she said. "He'd enjoy the ride, I wager, if he were alive for it."

Ben said nothing more. He felt nauseous and the food had congealed on his plate, but he made himself take another bite and another sip of beer. As he pushed his plate aside, ready to go, Lily ran a finger along the rough bone handle of her knife.

"Perhaps you don't understand this yet," she said. She pressed the tip of the blade against the tabletop and turned it. A tiny sliver curled away from the wood. "Most men are good. They only turn now and then. Something in their nature that can't be helped. It means little and is best ignored."

"You think I'll turn?"

"Perhaps. On occasion."

Ben looked toward the dark bar.

"Don't worry," said Lily. "You won't be overburdened. Men turn, but they also forget." She took his hand and held it to her face. It was meant as a comfort.

He nodded and put on the new hat, then stood and held out his arm for her. She was already heavy with her medicine and leaned softly into him as they left.

Back at the apartment, Lily walked to her bed behind the curtain, the weaving walk Ben remembered from when he first met her. She lay down and pulled the quilt up to her chin.

"Did you know a person can recall their time in the womb?" she said, her eyes closed. "You must conjure it while sleeping. See if you can remember floating around my belly."

"I don't remember anything," Ben said, but he imagined it—curled tight and submerged, seeing the world through a layer of thrumming, blue-veined skin.

"I suppose the unborn never want for company," Lily said, her voice heavy. "Always attached to someone in that way."

"I suppose," he said, wondering if Lily was, perhaps, lonely in this city full of people.

He looked around her room. It was tidy and spare, save for a shelf in the corner filled with odds and ends—papers, buttons, thimbles, feathers, shells, a Bible, mugs.

"Is my hat here?"

"You have a hat."

"I meant the one I came with."

"I gave it to someone. This one is better."

Lily's eyes were closed, but she didn't sleep yet. Her breath was uneven and her finger picked at a thread on the pillow.

"Why did I live there?" he asked. "Why not here?"

"Hmm." Her eyes fluttered, then she fixed them on Ben. "You don't understand men, little Mouse, and you don't understand women." She rolled over, her voice muffled in the folds of her quilt. "Wouldn't I be a wretched mother?"

"I don't know. I don't know you."

"And I don't know you. As an example, I never imagined you'd be so full of questions and ideas."

"I can come back to visit, if you like."

"I hope you do. I enjoyed our time. Did you?"

"I did."

When she was asleep, he left her, pulling the curtain shut behind him. He stoked her fire, then saw the tin she'd left on the small table. Crouching in the light of the stove, he peeled the note from inside the lid and read enough to catch the angry words he was certain would be there.

tho you be a whoore child and a deceever... yor boy is stranje... evrything ruint... and now wat I lae heer to die?

The coals were hot on his face as he placed the paper on top. It lit, a soft flame that burned a hole in the middle and spread outward, the edges turning quickly to ash. Then he took the picture of Will's Marjorie from his pocket and tossed it in. First her hair caught, then her eyes and mouth. A sleeve. A final corner of lace.

Ben woke in the dark room with the lamp lit low. A rain-soaked girl sat at the end of the sofa, chewing her lip and watching him. He could smell her cold and damp.

He raised up on his elbows, still half dreaming, and tried to anchor himself. He was at Lily's. He'd fallen asleep when he'd only meant to rest. He should be at the farm by now. He didn't know this girl.

"I'm Mae," she said.

Out the window, all was black but the watery reflection of the lamp's flicker on glass. Lily's curtain was open, her bed empty.

"Do you know what time it is?"

The girl shrugged. She was pale and slight, faint on eyebrows and lashes. This gave the impression of someone both old and young at once, though Ben took her to be near his own age.

"Is it still Thursday?" he asked. He got up and crossed the room to look outside. Days seemed to slip away from him in this city.

"Let me think," the girl said, her voice pitched high and soft. "It must be early Friday."

The street below was quiet, save a few men shouting from somewhere, the sound of a dog's nails on planks as it ran by. A cold gust came through gaps in the window frame.

"I shouldn't have slept." Ben sat back down on the sofa and pulled on his boots, tucking the broken laces inside.

"Where are you going?"

"I work on a farm."

He sat forward, resting his elbows on his knees. If he left now, in the dark, he could be there by morning. But he'd need light. He looked around the room and saw only one lamp, but Lily would need it.

"You must have lots of animals there."

"Mr. Stenhouse does. Do you know where Lily is?"

"She's out." Mae placed her hand on his knee. Her eyes on his were solemn and patient. "She says you don't yet know about women."

Ben had a brief thought about Mae's skirts and what was beneath them, but he shook his head and stood, spotting an unlit lamp on Lily's shelf. He grabbed it.

"Would she let me use this? She has two."

"You should ask Lily. Preacher speaks against stealing."

"I wouldn't steal. I'd bring it back."

Mae shrugged, her mouth pinched up on one side. "That sounds like stealing."

Ben went again to the window and Mae joined him. She was taller than he'd thought. Everything about her seemed ill-fitted and limp—her too-small dress, her too-large boots, her wet hair, slipping from its tie.

"I live down there," she said, pointing. "You can't see it now, but you probably passed it. The grey building beside the tobacconist?" She pushed open the window and leaned out into the cold rain. "I think that's Lily there."

Down the street, past the warehouse and near the docks, Ben could see a small woman in a pool of gaslight.

"It is her," said Mae. "She wears a new dress now. Have you seen it?" She touched her fingers to her neck. "Blue. With lace at the collar."

Lily was facing out to where the black sea became inseparable from the black sky, so that it seemed she stood at the edge of the world and could disappear entirely with one step forward. She turned as if she could see them and began walking home.

Mae shut the window and Ben grabbed his bag and set it next to the lamp. Their shadows stretched tall on the walls, like long-limbed creatures.

Lily's footsteps sounded on the stairs and the door opened. She was pale and damp in her new dress, which dragged on the floorboards, six inches muddy along the bottom.

"How are my two lambs?" She shrugged off her shawl and draped it on the back of a chair. "Gratified, satisfied..." She walked to the sofa, unbuttoning the bodice of her dress and letting it fall to the floor with a heavy thwack. "Starry-eyed."

"Do you feel all right, Lily?" said Mae.

Lily sat carefully, holding her hand to her ribs. "Oh, she did get me then," she said, looking down at her side. On her corset was a bloodstain the size of an apple.

Mae gasped.

"It's nothing, really," said Lily. "Her blade was dull, I think."

Ben held the lamp close. "What happened?"

Through the tear in the linen, the gash showed, several inches long and leaking blood, thick and black. Ben's throat tightened like he'd swallowed vinegar.

Lily leaned back. "I don't think Mary cared for my dress. Or the matter of me being able to buy it, I suppose."

"We need a doctor," Ben said.

"Gus will stitch it."

"It could fester." Ben looked toward the table, where Mae was pouring a glass of whisky for Lily. "Where's the tin?"

"Everyone thinks I have money." Lily took the glass from Mae and drank it all at once, then she laid her head against the back of the sofa. She lifted her skirts and let them fall. "Do you not see my new dress?"

Ben looked down at the swath of wet and muddy fabric. "All the money's gone?"

She closed her eyes and smiled, reaching blindly for his hand, which he took. "It never lasts very long, does it?"

Gus groaned when he saw her. Lily was bare-chested now, with one arm behind her head, the other at her side near the wound. Mae sat next to her, holding the corset.

"What's this, Lily?" he said, gravel in his voice. "Cover yourself, will you?"

"How will you stitch me if I'm covered?" She slid a finger along her pale skin, scooping the blood that trickled there, then wiping it on her dress.

"Do we need a constable?" Gus asked.

"For what?"

Sighing, he knelt next to her while Ben held the lamp. Lily's medicine was taking effect, and she had softened into the sofa, her eyes half closed as she watched Gus.

"This wouldn't have happened when I was young," she said. "I used to be admired, if you remember."

"I don't remember." Gus probed the gash with his finger. "It's not too deep. Hold the light closer."

Ben leaned in as Gus opened his pouch, which contained different kinds of needles, all of them large. He dug in his pocket and brought out a small spool of black thread and worked it through the needle's eye.

"Be still." He nodded at the lamp. "Take off the glass."

Ben removed the chimney and Gus held the tip of the needle over the flame.

"Have another drink, Lily."

She held out her glass, a slight tremor to her hand. Mae poured, and Lily shot it back.

"This won't be a pretty scar, though, will it?" Gus said. "This needle's meant for sewing up a hog's bladder." He chuckled and Lily did too, but she winced when he stuck her, the needle pushing and wiggling through her flesh.

"What are you doing to me, Gus?" Lily said. Her forehead was damp but her face still calm as she watched.

"You can't leave it gaping open to the bad air, can you? Rot sets in. That's what kills a person."

As Gus pulled thread through skin, Ben tried to hold the lamp still. He barely breathed, his focus on Lily's flat humming, the patter of rain on the window.

Lily lifted her head. "You don't have a better needle?"

"I do not." Gus stitched quiet and steady, his breath loud through his nose. Then, with the wound nearly closed, he stopped, the needle poised above her skin.

"How'd you steal a dress, Lily? Something as big as that?"

"I paid for it."

He looked at her and when her eyes fluttered shut, he nudged her leg with his elbow. "With what, Lily?" He nudged her again. "You come into money?"

"She did," said Mae. "From her uncle who died."

Gus sat back on his heels. "James left you money?"

"You're upset." Lily's voice was thick with sleep.

He looked toward the door. "I've had no rent from you for months and you go off buying dresses like the Queen of France?"

Lily reached out her hand but he didn't take it. "You'll hurt your heart," she said, her words strung together. "It's not good for you to fret."

No one else spoke as Gus finished his work. The stitches were black and messy, with beads of blood showing between the knots. He poured whisky on a rag and dabbed the blood away while Mae stitched the holes in Lily's corset and dress with the same black thread.

Ben tore a long strip from Lily's old dress. He helped her sit forward while Gus wrapped it around her waist and ribcage. They all looked at him when he straightened up and wiped his hands on the front of his shirt.

"You've done me wrong, Lily," Gus said. She reached her hand out again but still he wouldn't take it. "Do you hear what I'm saying? I have debts because of you."

She dropped her hand but kept her tired eyes on him. "What is it then, do you think? Is my mind broken?"

Gus began to shove things back into his leather pouch. When he left, his steps were like thunder on the stairs. His door creaked open and slammed shut.

This startled Lily awake. Shadows fell on her face so that, in the lamp's dim light, her eyes were like empty sockets.

"How will you pay him?" Ben asked her.

"Don't worry about Gus." She stood, holding his arm to steady herself. "He's like a husband to me. Sometimes we bicker."

Still uncovered, her small breasts showing above the bandage, she walked to the stove and poured hot water in the teapot.

"Tomorrow he will have calmed," she said, then bent her head over the steam, breathing in old tea leaves. "He always does."

Ben left most of Lily's special tea in his cup, so the effects were gentle and pleasant. He felt himself melt, his bones warm, the hard edges of his concern softening. He and Mae both laid their heads back against the sofa. Lily had gone to sleep in her bed behind the curtain.

"All that money gone," he said, his voice low.

"It's a pretty dress," said Mae. "I'm a shirtmaker, but I'd rather make dresses. I sew on the buttons. Look." Taking Ben's hand, she ran his finger along hers. There was a hard callous like a small stone at the tip of her pointer. "It doesn't hurt. Preacher says calloused hands are God's hands. When I close my eyes, I'm still sewing buttons. At night I dream about buttons and thread."

"Those aren't bad dreams."

"My sister dreamed of sitting on the moon. It was small, like a chair, and her legs hung off the edge."

He imagined himself reclining in the moon's creamy glow, with a view of the earth, its black ocean, swirling silver rainclouds. He let his eyes fall shut, but just for a moment. As soon as the sun rose, he would be on his way to Stenhouse farm.

He opened his eyes. "What if she needs a doctor?"

"You don't have to worry about Lily, Ben."

Mae straightened and, without any word about doing so, sat astride his lap, a knee on either side, her pleasing weight on his legs.

"I don't know—"

She began to undo his trousers. "Preacher says God clothes the flowers of the field and each sparrow is fed."

This close, he smelled the damp of her dress and the heat from her skin—milk nearing sour. Honey and pepper. His eyes went heavy as her fingers fluttered and worked each button.

"God cared for the fallen woman and she now sits at his right side." She stopped her fingers and looked at him. "Ben. At his right side in full glory!"

He nodded and her fingers worked again, her eyes cast down, nearly lashless. He felt her warmth and imagined her heart glowed a fiery red.

"This will be quick for you."

She slipped down to the floor between his legs, her head in his lap. He sucked in breath, his hands grabbing the sofa, and like that, every thought was gone. His boot scraped hard on the floor and the stain on the ceiling flickered black as Mae *hmm*-ed in her throat. She sat up and took his tea, lowering her face to spit into it, then wiped her mouth on the back of her hand.

"There."

She looked up at him and Ben had the urge to take her hand, to pull her onto the sofa and fall asleep beside her. But she stood and took the cup to the window. She was talking about birds.

"What I mean to say is, God uses us to feed the sparrow," she said. "As with a birdhouse?"

He nodded as she pushed the window open wide. She swished then tipped the cup into the dark.

"Do you have a dollar?"

"I have no money."

Mae shut the window and looked at the fire.

"It's all right. Lily paid me already, but I was here a long time. But it's all right." She put on her coat. "I should go, I'll soon be at the factory. Will I see you tomorrow?"

Ben shook his head. "I have to leave first thing."

"But it's snowing."

He stood and went to the window. Fat snowflakes hung like goose down under the streetlamp, forming drifts around the base.

"I can walk in that," he said. He thought of Mr. Stenhouse digging a path from house to barn. It would be worse there, up on the mountain, with no man to help. Ben leaned his forehead against the cold glass, fogging a wide arc. "It'll quit by morning. I can walk in it anyway."

He watched it fall for a moment longer, then looked at Mae in the lamp's dim light. She was fine-boned and bendy, her spine slightly rounded between her shoulder blades to the base of her neck, as if a soft swelling pushed it outward. He thought of the bent seamstress from earlier that day, Lily tracing her form on the window.

"You think Lily will be all right?"

"Mm-hmm. She's the sparrow, remember?"

"But you said we have to feed the sparrow."

"That's right."

EFFIE

1890

EFFIE FOLLOWED ELI TO THE SMALL BARN. SHE WAS NO fool—his look invited her. She felt the ache and the wonder, and though she was uneasy as he walked in front of her—squat stride, untroubled hitch to his shoulders—she didn't turn back.

In the barn, he lifted her onto the railing and she waited while he shut the door. She had expected they would go to the bed in Ben's room, but knew little about any of it.

He stood at a distance and undid his pants. Effie looked away, at the muddy straw on the floor, then up to the loft where she had screamed for her father. Then back to Eli, who was laughing at her.

"What?"

"You don't know what to do." He smiled, arrogant. "Lift your skirts," he said.

She lifted them to her knees.

"Now Effie." He came forward, pushed her skirts to her waist. "Hold them."

He cocked his head as he looked at her, nudged her knee wider, then the other. He flicked his fingers at the buttons on his shirt and nodded to hers. "Unbutton."

So she did. Her cheeks burned as she opened the top of her dress, breasts exposed to the cold bite of winter. She held her breath and made every effort to not look away.

Of course he would be an animal. The words flew to her mouth but she bit down on them. *You look a panting pig with your thing in your hands.* But she sat there, silent. None of it was what she'd imagined.

He held out one hand to keep her still while the other worked like he was scratching a violent itch. When he spilled over his own stubby fingers, she lowered herself to the floor and limped past him and into the dark. She felt the cool touches of snow on her cheeks, and when she opened the door into the kitchen, she watched the flakes melt on the arm of her wool coat.

So now she knew. Nothing of much importance. Nothing much at all.

Before shutting the door, she took one more look outside.

It would blizzard tonight.

BEN

1890

HIS MOTHER STOOD IN THE SHADE OF A LARGE OAK, DEEP IN the forest where the mushrooms grew. It was dawn, cool and green. The birds twittered and darted like black sparks through the branches. With her back to him, she crouched to pick the mushrooms. She sang.

À la claire fontaine
M'en allant promener

His legs wouldn't move, but still he drew closer. The earth beneath his feet seemed to close up, shrinking the space between them. Her voice grew louder.

J'ai trouvé l'eau si belle
Que je m'y suis baigné

She picked and picked, but when he was close, he saw her basket was empty, and it wasn't mushrooms she picked at but her ankle. She smiled.

Look.

She lifted the hem of her skirt and revealed two punctures, each the size of a peppercorn. She laid a finger on one of the marks, bruised and spongy under her touch, and dug into the wound, knuckle deep. Clear juices eased out the sides. With a twist of her finger, she scooped out flesh.

In her palm, a glistening piece of orange.

She let it fall to the ground then pulled at her collar, where another gash stretched along her neck. She dug into it with two fingers and a thumb, pulling out a longer slithery piece of orange and letting it fall.

Do you not see, she said, moving her wet fingers to a tear in the side of her bodice, where her side had split open and wept a murky syrup down her dress. She pushed both hands into her ribs, dug out fistfuls of pulpy fruit and held them out to Ben. The juices ran down her arms and peppered the ground like soft rain.

Look.

Ben opened his eyes to the stain on the ceiling, the spider in its web in the corner. He sat up, thrumming inside. Lily was gone.

Wrapped in his blanket, he opened the door to a blinding white world. Lily's footprints, already filled with snow, led down the stairs and into the alley. With the icy slap of air, he knew he couldn't leave her with a wound that could fester. Maybe he'd decided it while he dreamed, or before that, when Mae talked of sparrows.

He thought of Mr. Stenhouse, stuck without a farmhand when extra hands were needed most. Ben would have to be quick.

There were two whisky jugs on the table. He put on his boots and coat, pulled on the tight hat, then grabbed the heaviest jug and followed Lily's footprints.

After his mother died, he'd shown his father all the things they could have traded for a doctor's visit—eggs, chickens, the painted bowl, jars of preserved blackberries, braids of garlic, a chair. He yelled at his father's retreating back, "We don't even need chickens!" And his father only waved him away while keeping the worst to himself: that he had all that money sitting hidden and useless.

Voices came from beyond Lily's alley, and when he turned onto Wharf Street, it seemed the whole city was gathered there. In both directions, men were shovelling and shouting. Steaming horses carted off snow in wagons, their iron wheels crunching. Children with frost-burned cheeks climbed the white hills piled along the sidewalks.

Ben passed it all.

"Hey, kid!" someone yelled. He pointed at the wall of the ironworks, where shovels were lined up. "Grab a digger!"

"Sorry," Ben called back. "I have to find someone first."

He was right to think Lily had gone to The Jug. When he opened the door, he saw her sitting at the bar with Oland, a stack of playing cards between them.

"Little Mouse," she said. "Come."

The place was filled with winter light and empty of customers. Chairs were still turned over on the tables. A low fire burned in the grate. Lily pushed a half-eaten plate of stew toward him.

"I thought you might have left by now," she said, rubbing his arm. She was pale, the bloodstain on her side a wet and muddy bloom.

"I'm going to go find a doctor," he said, taking a bite of stew. "Will you be here a while?"

Lily looked at the whisky jug and leaned back in her bar stool. "That may be a fair enough trade, if I needed a doctor in the first place."

Oland leaned in, his droopy brown eyes on Ben's. "You get that doc, friend. Look at her. All pasty."

Ben nodded, downed another bite, and left.

He remembered the brick house from his walk with Will. Green shutters, black steps, a brass plate by the door. *Dr. C. M. Silman*. He used the knocker, then waited, hunched under his coat and blowing on his hands.

A woman answered, very small and round and almost entirely lacking a chin. She wore a black dress and a lacy black cap on her grey head.

"I'm looking for the doctor," Ben said.

"Yes." She looked up at him. Her pale eyes bulged slightly, as if she blew a trumpet. "What is the problem?"

Ben began to explain. As he did, the woman wrapped a black shawl around her shoulders, grabbed a leather bag from a table next to the door, then held out her hand for the jug. Ben gave it over and she popped the cork and sniffed.

"The doctor is tending to someone," she said. "I'm Mrs. Silman."

She led the way past the shovelling men and the shouting children, her steps swift for a woman so short, her black lace cap fluttering. When they arrived at The Jug, she walked in, set down her bag, and said to Lily, "Let's see your trouble, my girl."

"Oh hello, Mrs. Silman." Lily was smoking a dark cigarette. She held it between her lips while she undid her bodice and her corset. She pulled them aside to show the flame-pink gash, held together with chicken-scratch stitches.

"Sloppy job, this," Mrs. Silman said. "It's all dirty and inflamed." She opened a small jar of clear liquid and doused a clean flannel rag. "And how'd it happen?"

"My friend Mary." Lily watched the woman's small hands dab her side. "I owed her money."

"I see." Mrs. Silman opened another jar, the contents dark, but orange when she painted it on the wound.

"She only meant to tear the dress," said Lily.

"Yes."

Mrs. Silman worked quickly and gently as she unwound a spool of gauze and wrapped it around Lily's ribcage. When she was done, she buttoned her back up like one would a child.

"Now," she said, holding Lily's gaze. "You don't want this to turn foul, my girl. No baths, no fumes, no men in your bed."

"I don't generally take baths."

"And you should go home and rest."

"Hmm." Lily sucked long on her cigarette. "Like a prisoner."

"No." Mrs. Silman brushed aside a strand of Lily's hair. "Like someone with a badly stitched stab wound. You can come and go as you please, I only ask you rest in between the wanderings."

Mrs. Silman snapped her black bag shut and wrapped her shawl around her shoulders. She looked at Ben. "We'll know in a few days how it fares."

"A few days?" Ben looked outside, where the sun had already lowered to the roofs of the buildings.

"Get her some Pink's Ointment from the chemist and come fetch me if the wound weeps or reddens." She stopped at the door. "I don't much care for whisky."

They watched her through the window, a bustling form against the white street, skirts and cap and shawl flapping like black feathers. After she turned the corner, Ben's gaze remained stuck there. *A few days.*

"You're proud of yourself, little Mouse," Lily said. "I believe I see a puffed-up chest beneath that old coat." She took a thoughtful drag on her cigarette. "Or is it something else?"

"Of course he's proud, Lily," said Oland. "Stay and have a pint with us, Ben."

Ben turned from the window. Lily's dress was still open and her bandage showing. She absently picked at it with a dirty fingernail. He needed to think.

"Thanks," he said to Oland. "But I was asked to help clear the streets." He ate the last bite of stew and put on his hat. "I'll see you tonight, Lily."

"I'll see you, Mouse."

Ben stepped outside and began walking. Each step brought a thought of Mr. Stenhouse, or one of Lily. If he could, he'd talk to Will, who would be quick to form an opinion and just as quick to share it. Ben was slower at figuring things, a plodder. Still, he knew what Will would say. She'll be fine, Ben. This place isn't for you.

Ben stopped. He turned back and poked his head in the door of The Jug.

"Do you have a penny I could borrow, Lily? I want to send a letter to Mr. Stenhouse."

She smiled at him through the curling strands of smoke. "I'll bring you one tonight, Mouse."

Ben found himself a shovel and was soon in the thick of it, snow inching into his boots and under his pant legs. Many of the men knew each other by name, but they seemed happy for a new set of ears in Ben. One of them put out fires for pay. Another was a stove merchant, married four times. Another made gloves for small children from the skin of small pigs.

Ben talked to a Black man who had purchased his freedom and moved north to open a hardware store. Another man who years ago had harpooned a whale, then bought drinks for everyone, and later cried himself to sleep. "A glorious beast," he said to Ben, shaking his head. "A grand and noble fish."

One man had just opened a soap factory called Wonderful Soap. "Made with cloves." He raised a finger. "Each square stamped with a fine curling *W,* then wrapped in pink waxed paper."

They continued working in the dark, their torches lit and stuck in icy, flickering hills along the edges. When they were done, the streets were clear enough for two wagons to pass. Everyone said goodbye, lanterns swinging and disappearing through doorways and around corners. Ben thought of Mae.

Her building was easy to find, grey and four stories tall. He leaned against the wall, thawing his hands under his arms, until he saw her. She carried a tin lunch pail, her head down against the cold. When she neared, she didn't smile, but there was a warm familiarity in her eyes.

She led him inside and down the dark stairwell to the stone basement, where it smelled like river rock. She spoke all the while of her day sewing on buttons. Tomorrow she would clean the church.

"You have a lot of jobs," Ben said.

"Preacher says God smiles upon the ready worker."

Mae undid his pants. Something different this time, held up by the damp wall with her forehead to his and her hand in his trousers. Sounds echoed in the cold room—a scuff, a sharp breath, and Mae's voice a light bell against the stones. He agreed with everything she said—he would send her a dollar, pray for her mother, warn her before soiling her dress—

"Sorry," he whispered.

She slipped aside. He heard the rattle of her tin pail, felt her place a flannel rag in his hand. They cleaned up, buttoned up, then felt their way back up the stairs, emerging like squinting moles in the gaslight.

From the entryway, he watched her climb the three flights to her flat before disappearing in the darkness, her large boots flopping so each step sounded like two. All the while he thought how this city was nothing like he'd expected and certainly not what his mother thought it was. He didn't mind this place at all.

"Goodbye, Ben," Mae said, her voice falling from the top floor.

"Mae? The church you work at. Could they use another worker tomorrow?"

"You mean you?"

"I need the work."

"Then come. The preacher always wants for helpers." A door creaked open and there was a shuffle as she spoke softly to someone. Then she called down to him again. "I'll get you in the morning."

On the walk to Lily's, Ben thought of what he would do with a day's wages. Pink's Ointment from the chemist. More money for Mrs. Silman, if Lily took a turn. Money for Mae for her kindness. If any was left, money to Gus for Lily's rent.

Ben found Lily on the sofa, arm draped over the side, fingers grazing the floor. Her dress was twisted around her, the sheen of it catching light from the fire. The same old feeling stuck Ben in the doorway, his feet rooted to the ground.

Then Lily opened her eyes and smiled, slow and sleepy. Ben closed the door and relaxed against it.

"You were off to see Mae," she said, leaning on her elbow. "I can tell a man recently relieved."

Ben pulled off his snowy boots and hat, then sat next to Lily. She shivered.

"You brought the cold in, Mouse."

"I thought you said the weather was turning."

"Did I?"

"You smelled it off the water."

"Well, I don't know what I meant. Maybe I smelled the snow. You can stay as long as you like, you know."

She placed a penny in his hand, her unpainted eyes clear and dark in the low light.

"Mae would be happy to have you here. You like her, I think?"

"She's nice."

Lily lay back against the arm of the sofa, closing her eyes. "She would appreciate a young man like you. The older ones require too much."

Ben imagined a man like his father, his ticky eyes on her, broad hands like paddles. He pressed a thumb and finger to his eyes to clear the image. "Why does she do it then?"

"She only does a little—" Lily ran her hand languidly over her buttons. "Sewing doesn't pay well, so like any good woman, she's learned to make do." With her eyes still closed, she smiled. "I suppose that means I'm not so good."

"I think you're good."

"Do you really?" She looked at him for a moment, no smile, only thoughtfulness. "And so are you, little Mouse."

He turned his hat in his hands as Lily's eyes fluttered shut and her breathing deepened.

"I can tell you're still recovering," she said, her voice low and heavy. "I hear the rattle. Let me make tea."

"It's all right. I don't need it."

As she fell asleep, he found a slip of paper on the table and wrote:

dear mr stenhous I will be a littel late and I hope you dont mind it. when I get back I will work extra for the trubel —Ben

AGDA

1872

IT WAS A WARM SPRING DAY AND SHE'D JUST PLANTED HER garden when James came home in a dark mood. He threw his bag on the floor, his face purple and his eyes bulging. Agda hadn't seen him in weeks.

"That girl," he said. "My brother's girl set to help me with the whisky runs?"

Agda nodded. "Yes?"

"With child!" The words came from his mouth in a hissing whisper.

It took no time for an idea to form. It surprised her how quick she was to think of it.

"How far along?" She placed a hand on her stomach and took a breath. "Is she showing?"

But he was all muddled and batted at the air, then stormed outside. From the window, Agda watched his broad back disappear into the cowshed. She sat at the table lost in thought, then, slowly, she began to smile.

God knew she couldn't tempt him in the bodily way as her age was against her and her angles all wrong. So she made him his favourite dinner, a rabbit pie from the traps she put out and set herself. The crust was tender and the gravy rich and dark. She added wild mushrooms and young nettles.

As he ate, she picked at her food and waited until he was full-bellied and satisfied. Then she spoke.

"James?"

"What?"

"How does your brother handle the matter? This business with Lily?"

He spoke around his last bite of pie. "You think I'd tell him?"

She was glad of this secrecy. Connie had no heart for his own daughter. He handled people like farm animals, from his tiny cabin in the woods.

She took a small bite. "That girl is too young for a child, yes?"

"Of course she is. That's what I'm telling you."

"And not fit for it, would you agree?"

His hand clutched his fork so tight the knuckles looked like sun-bleached bone, and she saw what she often saw in James: a man afraid.

"I set her up to have a good life," he said. "And she casts it aside! Spreads her skinny legs for any fool that comes along."

Agda had no stamina for such talk, but she forced herself to meet his eye. The man was pained, sad and sallow, his watery eyes shifting back and forth.

"What will become of her?" she said gently. She thought to touch his hand, then changed her mind. "There is a way though. Do you understand?"

"Mrs. Silman says it's too late to get rid of it."

"No. Not that. Tell her I will raise the child. It will be nothing to you. I will care for it, and you will do as you do, with no trouble or burden."

His jaw hung slack, his eyes stilled in their sockets. "We're too old for that—"

"Your own mother suffered," she continued. "Young and with children. You would ask this of your niece, who is like a daughter to you?"

She shouldn't have said that. Shouldn't have mentioned his mother.

He thrust back his chair and stood over her, the muscles in his neck in flickering spasms. She raised her chin and kept her eyes on his, but her hands were sweaty on her skirts under the table.

For the rest of the night, James railed. He threatened fists. He stormed and sulked and kicked the goat that stood on the porch. He called Agda old and unfit. The child, still a bean in a girl's belly, he called "the devil's bastard."

Then, without touching her, he held his finger just near Agda's chin so that she was forced to face him. "Who are you to talk of mothers?"

Agda was used to his outbursts, the drawn-out length of them. His insults fell around her but not in her. A man who had never outgrown his boyhood tempers. A man whose fury lit quicker than his brains.

She cleared the dishes and set bread to rise, mended a hole in the cuff of his sleeve. Then she slipped into her nightgown.

When he'd worn himself out, James sat by the fire. From the bed, hidden in darkness, she watched his face move in the orange flicker, chin to chest, sniffing wetly and wiping his eyes.

For so long she'd waited, wondering why she was denied a child, the only thing she wanted. How many times had she searched her memory for some forgotten misdeed, some moral failing. But after it all, she'd only needed to be patient.

Here, then, was her gift at last.

Next morning, Agda rode the old mare to Petrenko's Dry Goods & Post and bought nine yards of blue calico.

During the summer months, Agda prepared for the baby. She knitted six tunics, two caps, three blankets, and a jacket for fall. All made from the creamy Stenhouse wool spun each night by firelight on her drop spindle. She purchased glass bottles with rubber nipples, and a tiny brush with soft goat-hair bristles. She sewed nappies out of flour sacks and a tiny woolen tick for the bottom of the cradle that James would make when he returned from another stint in jail. She'd written to him, instructing him to collect the baby upon his release. To wrap it tight and hold it close. To walk slow. To sing if it fussed.

By summer's end, the garden she'd planted burst with all the good things she would preserve for the baby. The apples were red, the chickens were plump, and the goats were giving rich milk. Any day James would return, carrying a tiny bundle. She smiled from her chair on the porch, and continued knitting a sock so small only two fingers could fit inside, her eyes flitting to the trail at the edge of the yard.

A boy or a girl, she wondered, and either one gave her a thrill. Healthy, she hoped. Though her heart ached all the more if a child wasn't well, as when her nephew, Maurice, broke his leg falling down the cellar steps. She had nursed him, sung to him, stayed awake through the night. The truth was, she loved him more because he needed her to. That was the truth of it.

When the sun sank and she could no longer see, she lit a lamp, as sometimes James arrived past dark. The flame glowed yellow, and the moon a milky green, drawing out the crickets and lulling Agda to sleep. When she woke, it was dawn, cool and dewy. The lamp had burned out beside her and the stitches had dropped from her needles.

She went about her chores, finding comfort in the distraction but still running to the window or the barn door when she heard a creak or a rustle. After tending the animals, she waited once more on the porch and knitted the other sock.

Agda had also knitted Lily a pair of long striped stockings to wear under the calico dress. She'd sent them to the butcher's, along with a note.

I hope you rest and are Well. Be kind to your self. Your frend alwaes, Agda.

* * *

When James broke through the trail, Agda stood from her chair on the porch. The sun was high, her neck damp, a trickle of sweat running down her sides and along her spine. All gone cold at the sight of him. Empty-handed. She waited as he neared, stopping before her, two steps down so that he had to look up. That was when she noticed his ear—half missing and scabbed over, dried blood in the whorl.

"It died," he said.

He took off his hat and looked at the cabin door, then put his broad hand on the chicken-flesh of his neck. "Strangled as it came out."

She reeled back and struck the wall. The log scraped the nubs of her spine, and her hair caught in the bark as she shook her head. No.

"Died peaceful," he said. "No fussing or any of that."

He kicked the porch to knock the dirt off his boots, his eyes catching hers sidelong. He went inside. She heard his bag drop to the floor, his chair legs scrape back, a hard sigh.

"I'm ready to eat," he said.

She heated yesterday's beans and mashed a potato. Then she went back to the porch and sat as the sun dipped behind the rustling black trees.

For months afterwards, her feet and hands worked while the rest of her slowly drowned, a soft and weary sinking.

She walked the muddy path to the Petrenko's. She needed kerosene and salt, and James would soon be home.

A fire crackled in the stove in the corner of their store. Only as she warmed herself in front of it did Agda realize how cold and numb her hands were. Mrs. Petrenko was away.

"Mr. Talbot came and fetched her," said Mr. Petrenko, pausing his pencil over his ledger. "His poor wife was going on three days of birthing pains." He shook his head, his face in full cool sun from the window.

Agda's eyes filled and spilled over. She wiped them with her fingers.

"Mrs. Maclean! Sit, sit. You are unwell."

Mr. Petrenko came out from behind the counter and guided her to a chair. Then he made tea on the stove and they sipped it in quiet. Agda felt his eyes on her, the weight of his concern, and she wanted to lean into him, absorb that kindness the way old moss absorbs rain.

"We have felt loss as well," he said finally, though she hadn't yet told him she'd lost anything. "My dear Mrs. Petrenko and I. It's why she is so strong, and why I—" He placed his hand to his chest, then swatted the air and leaned back. His eyes were wet like Agda's.

Customers came and went throughout the day, and Agda remained in her chair by the stove. Mr. Petrenko chatted and weighed coffee beans and poured molasses, or cut wide bolts of cloth with heavy scissors. Every time she looked out the window, the shadows were deeper, the trees darker.

She was still there that evening when James stopped in on his way home from the city. She didn't look at him when he said her name, but she did when he spoke to Mr. Petrenko.

"She's been strange," he said, nodding at her, as though the sight of her was evidence enough.

Mr. Petrenko paid for the three jugs of whisky James brought him. "Not strange at all."

"Well, she won't do it again. Agda, do you hear me? Don't go barging in on these people again."

"She's no bother at all, James. I enjoy the company."

When they were outside and starting to walk, Mr. Petrenko came out of the store and called after them,

"She is our friend, James. You needn't keep her from visiting."

Agda followed James down the road, the last of the evening light showing through the branches above them. She placed her hand on her stomach and wondered how poor Mrs. Talbot had fared with her labour.

When they arrived back at the cabin, she slipped into her nightgown and brushed her thin hair. She set beans to soak and crawled into bed where James snored.

It was days later, as she was filling the last jar of stewed tomatoes from the pot, when she realized she was thinking about kindly Ed Petrenko again. She poured hot wax into the rim and nearly smiled. She was almost out of wax, and she still needed to buy kerosene and salt. It seemed she would again have to make the long walk to Petrenko's Dry Goods & Post.

BEN

1890

IT WAS EARLY MORNING AND BEN WAS WAITING FOR MAE ON Lily's sofa, hat in hand, foot drumming on the dusty carpet. Lily had gone in the night, something he'd grown used to, but he saw her wound before she left—flame-red and puffy.

When he heard the double thump of Mae's large boots on the stairs, he met her at the door. She stood on the landing biting her lip, hair brushed out smooth and tucked behind her small ears. In the alley, snow melted, a continuous rapping as it dripped from the roof.

"You ready?" she said.

Though Ben and Mae were of similar height, she had a way of looking at him with her chin tilted down and her lashless eyes on his. The effect was one of shyness, but he already knew there was boldness to Mae beneath her soft voice.

He grabbed the letter for Mr. Stenhouse and put on his coat and hat. At some point in the night, Lily had brought home a bowl of apples, waking him to see if he was hungry. He wasn't then, but now he gave one to Mae and ate one himself as they hurried down the rickety stairs and walked along the newly cleared street. Mae led him to a post office, where posting a letter was as easy as blinking, if you had a penny to do it. The postmaster gave Ben an envelope and pencil, on which he wrote *stenhouse farm, west cane lake, ash mounten*, then watched with great relief as it was tossed into a canvas bag behind the counter.

Ben and Mae were soon leaving the busy part of town for the quieter part, where the trees were more plentiful and the houses less so. A colourless morning, everything some shade of white or black, shadowed or muddy or untouched—even the sky had been washed of colour. Snow fell sloppy from branches, hitting the ground in splatters.

They passed the mudflats where the Songhees used to dig for clams, where fishing shacks and storefronts now edged the shores. Then they came to a cleared field with snow-topped cairns where children were playing.

"All the fancy houses will go here over those Indian graves," Mae said. Ben's eyes wandered over the field of bones and the children. "Preacher says it's fine because our bodies are as dust and our souls everlasting."

The road became winding and rugged, and they used wagon ruts in the snow as their path.

All the while, Mae talked. First about her mother who, when Mae was small, sewed dresses at the window of their tenement flat. Then one day, whoosh, the whole building caught fire. Flames shattered windows as they ran down the outside stairway, clutching half-stitched linen sleeves. She spoke of the woman who, running all the way from the cannery in fish-greasy skirts, screamed and swore and stormed along the edges of the smoking rubble, taunting the men who searched it. Three days later, her two charred boys were found and she collapsed cold.

She spoke of the man who moved his chair to the front door of the tenement, since rebuilt of brick. He wanted to watch the birds and the people passing, and that's how he went to be with God, just sitting and watching with a seagull on his hat.

Then she talked of her sister, who like herself sewed buttons until sickness rattled her chest and turned her fingers blue. She died soon after they moved into their new flat, her eyes rolled back and her tongue swelled up, dreaming of sitting on the moon, or so Mae hoped.

Ben found himself looking over at Mae as she talked—a quick study of her face to see if she was broken up by her dismal stories. But it seemed Mae wasn't so easily brought down. She floated on sadness like a gull on a breeze.

The narrow road turned and the first thing Ben saw of the church was its wooden steeple above the snow-laden branches. The rest revealed itself as they came closer, a small, sturdily built church of stone. The path to the front step curved around tree stumps, and a patchy white wagon, filled with clutter, was parked in the yard.

The preacher, Mae said, had built the church himself, and paid for it with butter donated by congregants. The butter became known as Church's Butter, sold on the mainland, and the church became the Butter Church, with its own profitable creamery, run by women hard done by. The preacher had a reputation for hot-tongued sermons and cold-river baptisms, and Mae spoke of it all with awe.

A small, bespectacled man hurried down the church steps.

"Mae! I always know you'll show, whatever the weather." He crossed the yard, his manner quick, his hair wild about the ears. "And you've brought a helper."

"This is Ben," said Mae. "Lily's son. You remember Lily?"

"Of course I remember Lily. She took my inkwell." He laughed and shook Ben's hand with a hard grip. Behind his glasses, his eyes were lively but red-rimmed and stubby-lashed, as if prone to infection. "Welcome to our humble church, Ben. I didn't know Lily had any children."

"I was raised at Ash Mountain."

"Ah yes, I see. So then you are blessed with not one family but two."

As Ben considered this, and the way it didn't quite lie flat, the preacher hopped up in the back of the full wagon. He picked his way through bins and baskets, glass jugs, weathered fence posts, an old carpet, a cupboard door cracked down the middle.

"How about we do the windows today, Mae?"

When she agreed, he pulled a bucket out of the jumble and found a few balled-up rags, passing it all down to her. As she headed to the pump, the preacher studied Ben.

"Do you know your letters?"

"Yes, sir."

"Very good!" He rummaged deeper in the clutter. "I've been intending to get this done for some time, but I can't tolerate the fumes. And Mae can't read." He poked his head up and waved a finger at his eyes. "Muddled sight."

Ben looked back at Mae. She had filled the bucket at the pump and was struggling to get it up the church steps.

"I've tried to teach her," the preacher continued, his voice muffled as he pulled something from under an old treadle. "But where we see letters, she sees some other code."

He hopped down, holding a tin pail and a paintbrush.

"Does she see everything that way?"

"Ha! I hadn't thought of it, but maybe we do look strange to Mae. Noses on our chins or some such. Here you are. Now, you open this once I've stepped away or my eyes will swell shut."

Holding the full pail, Ben faced the whitewashed sides of the wagon. "I've never painted letters," he said.

"I have it all written out here." The preacher dug in one pocket, then another, finally producing a crumpled piece of paper. On it, he'd written:

CHURCH'S BUTTER

For the people were hungry so GOD fed them Church's Sweet Butter!

Sweet! Nutritious! Yellow!

A Songhees man was picking his way through the snow toward them, carrying a three-legged chair over his back. The preacher waved to him, then nodded to the paint can.

"Stir it well. Until there are no lumps."

With a slap on Ben's shoulder, he went to meet the man, and together they headed to the back of the church.

Ben pried off the lid. The can was full of thick, vaporous red paint that burned his nostrils, and when he stirred it with the brush, it dripped in clots like half-churned butter. He looked back. The men were gone and Mae was blurry in the church window, circling a wet rag over the glass.

He applied the brush to the top board, and a heavy, red drip ran down the white wall of the wagon. He quickly scooped it with his thumb, then painted the red crescent moon of a *C*. He continued on, scooping drips and checking the preacher's note now and then when he felt stuck on the spelling. After a while, he found a steady rhythm, and time slipped by unnoticed. The sun arced above him. The shadows stretched longer across the snow.

As he finished a *W*, footsteps crunched behind him. He turned to see the Songhees man, now holding a shovel and a coffee grinder instead of a chair. He was tall and large-built, older than Ben by several years.

"You ever painted before?" the man asked.

"No. Not like this, anyway."

"Uh-huh." The man nodded, then shook the hair from his eyes. "I'm Charlie."

Ben held out his hand and Charlie gave it a loose shake.

"Ben."

"I know. Mae told me who you are. I knew your father."

Ben pushed back his hat and squinted. He didn't want to ask, but he knew he was meant to. "How'd you know him?"

"He used to sit at our fire. Eat our food. We called him *stete,álkem*." His mouth twitched, as did the faint moustache above his lip. "Beetle."

Ben nodded slowly. "He wasn't actually my father."

"Always scurrying," he said. "Hiding. If he heard a noise, he'd run for the bushes."

"He did that?"

"Scared of police, scared of his brother. He charged too much money. My uncle told him to stop coming around. He did us no good."

The paint fumes stung Ben's nose and made his eyes water. "He wasn't really my father."

"*Stete,álkem.* Little scurrying beetle. Eats our food, then—" Charlie whistled through his teeth, cutting his hand flat through the air.

He nodded at Ben's boots. "Your paint's dripping."

Ben looked down at a red splotch on the old leather. When he looked back up, Charlie was already started toward the path.

Ben stirred the paint again, feeling the scorch on his cheeks. It hadn't been himself who scurried into the bushes but it might as well have been for how he felt. James seemed to leave no good impression behind, wherever he went. Not one good word spoken, except by Lily. But Lily held no grudges. She even spoke well of the woman who'd stabbed her.

Somewhere behind him, the preacher was singing cheerfully. The snow continued to drip, the birds to sing, and Ben went on painting, lost in thought. By the time he had done both sides, he realized the preacher was quiet and Mae had vanished from her window.

He put the pail back in the wagon and went inside. The church was empty and smelled of long-sitting water and cool earth. Along each wall was a row of three windows, all beaded with damp so the trees on the other side looked like blotted paintings.

Behind the pulpit, a second door was open as wide as the front, and the cold winter air walked right through, filling all four corners. The church felt not like a room where people gathered, but like part of the outdoors, where moss would sprout on the floor, branches would unfurl from the tops of the pews, and cold rain would fall from the rafters.

He went to the window and looked out the wet glass. He saw the preacher and Mae, cloudy figures against dark trees and white ground. The preacher was talking, his hand sweeping through the air, and Mae's face was tilted toward his. They were friends, loose and easy with each other. Mae saw Ben and waved, so Ben went outside to meet them.

"There you are," the preacher said. "I was admiring your handiwork. It looks like the work of an old hand, Ben, not someone new to painting."

Ben shifted his hat back on his head to get a better view. From this distance, he saw the wagon whole—his painted letters curving upward as if they steadily climbed a hill, shrinking in size as they went. Blurry stains spotted the whitewashed background like sloppy pink clouds.

"A few errors," said the preacher, "but nothing that can't be touched up if we feel the need."

Heat rose under Ben's collar. He read again. "Errors?"

"Well. Church has no *t* and people has an *o*, though don't ask me why." He smiled. "Most won't notice."

Ben shook his head. "I should fix it."

"No need. It'll be dark soon, and tomorrow I load up at the creamery right after service." He nudged Ben with an elbow. "Two hundred and forty pounds of butter to the docks. Can you imagine so much butter?"

The preacher turned to leave and Ben looked at the mucky ground at his feet, then back at the work he'd done. His face burned hot when he asked the preacher if he'd still get paid.

"Oh dear." The preacher stopped and turned to him. "None of us are paid here, my friend. This is God's work."

Ben's heart dropped to his belly.

"God doesn't deal much in coin, you see." The preacher grinned, then turned around and kept walking, but he held his hand in the air and beckoned with two flits of his wrist. "Come with me!"

The preacher's cottage was out back, a one-room, one-window cabin next to the small cemetery. There were about a dozen wooden markers, each carved with a last name and the cause of death—OLD AGE, FEVER, HEAVY-LADEN.

Inside, the cottage was stuffed full, nearly to the ceiling in places—crates and papers, crocks, baskets, chairs stacked every which way, clothes folded and hanging. A path led through to a stuffed chair by a stove, but there was nowhere else a person could properly fit and nowhere to sleep.

The preacher bent over and sorted through an open cedar box. "I ask for donations from those more fortunate, see. It allows for this exact sort of joyous encounter." He stood up, holding a pair of shining black boots. "A poor man like myself can offer a fine pair of boots to a young man who needs them."

Ben took the boots, ankle-high and buttoned down the side, the soles barely scuffed. They were indeed fine, but he had boots.

"It's only that Lily needs Pink's Ointment," he said. "And maybe a doctor."

"And you need boots. Try them on!"

Ben looked at this own, his toe poking out the seam. "I don't—"

"Or take them with you and try them later. If they don't fit, bring them back and we'll round up something else. And now, about your letters. Have you been to school?"

"My mother taught me."

The preacher lifted a brow. "Lily?"

"No. My mother who raised me. Agda."

"Ah. And I'm sure she did a fine job." He turned his back to Ben and moved farther to a stack of books taller than himself.

"Knowledge is freedom," he said, his finger running along the titles as he bent down. "One will only know truth and goodness when he knows himself and the world he lives in. I address this in my sermon tomorrow."

He shimmied a book from the bottom of the pile and handed it to Ben, a slim green volume, its fabric cover faded and its pages speckled with black dots.

"I didn't go to school either," the preacher said, "but taught myself. This is *The Book of Psalms and Proverbs.* Bring this back and I'll give you another. In this way you will become as learned as any man."

With bird-like energy, the preacher flitted from crate to pile to basket. For Lily, he found a jar of homemade ointment, half used and, so he claimed, better than any store-bought salve. He found clean flannel for bandaging, and lastly grabbed a tin of honey cake.

"Baked last week by one of the congregants." Then he added, in a low voice, "Walnuts make my tongue itch and my lips swell, and I haven't the heart to tell her."

All of it together was better than any amount of money, as far as Ben weighed the matter. He thanked the preacher again, his arms full, and they left the cramped cabin. They walked back through the graves, the low sun cutting through tree branches and warming the headstones.

Mae waited on the church step, a willow branch of a girl. She stayed behind for a lesson with the preacher, and Ben headed back to Lily's to give her the ointment.

Down the road, he stopped to change his boots. The new ones fit well and looked fine, with room to move his toes. The tiny buttons shone in the setting sun, black and glossy as a bird's eye. He tossed his father's old boots into the woods and continued on, his new boots squeaking with each step back to Lily's.

Lily was not at the apartment. Ben set her ointment and bandages on the table, then lit a fire and opened the cake tin. He recognized the warm cinnamon smell—two fragrant sticks, an orange, his mother bent to his ear, warning him not to go with his father. *Écoute-moi.*

He took the cake to the sofa along with the preacher's little book, and as he sat back, it came to him. His mother had likely never been to this city, and that's why she was afraid of it. She didn't know all the good things.

Eating sweet cake, he flipped through the pages of the book until something stirred, lovely or violent or sad. And so much of it was—the earth trembling at God's steps, a soul's longing as the deer pants for water, the rising up of vile men who make haste to shed blood, a good man's peaceful dwelling on a holy hill. All of it thrilling and fleeting. Every man a shadow, every man a vapour, so it said in this little book.

He read aloud in a whisper, several times over until he sounded the words out right:

He made darkness his secret place

His canopy around them was dark waters

Ben was filled with the creeping wonderment of it as he fell asleep, his new boots shining until the lamp's flame sputtered and died.

He woke to a scattering of things in the corner, where the small table stood. Lily's voice came to him in the dark.

"I don't mean to wake you," she said. Her skirts swished wetly along the floor, the fabric rustling then quieting near his face.

"Is everything all right?" His tongue was heavy with sleep.

He heard a clink and a catch, then light, and there she stood in front of him, swaying with the lamp held high, her breath an icy vapour.

"Do you know, little Mouse, why I don't worry too much about Gus?"

Ben shifted onto his back on the narrow sofa and laid his arm over his eyes. "Why?"

"There is no truth to money."

He peeked at her from under his arm, her face showing then hidden in the sway of the lamp.

"What is it, anyway? Paper. Metal. And such." She shrugged and the lamp swung wildly. Ben leaned up on his elbows, ready to grab for it.

"Paper—," she continued. "If it's paper he wants, he can have one of those old songbooks on my windowsill. I'll gather up all the old songbooks from every church, if that's what he wants."

"You bought your dress with money."

"Hmm. Well, you are right there," she said. "And wasn't I lucky? That the clerk was willing to trade such a fine dress for a mouldering pile of old paper? Remind me to explain this to Gus in the morning."

"I'll bet she has a hearty appetite. Look."

Ben opened his eyes to the morning light. Lily sat bare-chested on the window's ledge with her binoculars. The black stitches showed along the ridges of her ribs, where the skin flamed red through a sheen of ointment. He could smell it—like juniper boiled down to a pungent syrup.

"She's very pretty," said Lily. "Fat people have smooth cheeks, like dolls. Well anyway, I can already tell she's unfriendly by the way she tilts her chin. Look."

Ben sat up, blinking and groggy. The fire was lit, but still he saw his breath.

"She won't fit in my bed, especially if she wants that man with her. He's small. Maybe he'll take the sofa."

He stood and moved to the window, his blanket around his shoulders and bunched up near his ears. Outside, a Black woman and a White man stood next to a buggy in matching red scarves. They were speaking to each other with their eyes on Gus's shop window.

"I should eat more bread, I think," said Lily. "I'd have a fine large bosom for it." She covered her breast with her hand, her thin arms prickled in gooseflesh.

"Who are they?"

"Renters."

Ben looked at her, his chin buried in the scratchy wool of the blanket. "You said Gus didn't mean it."

"Usually he doesn't."

The woman moved out of sight and soon footsteps sounded on the stairs. Ben grabbed his coat and tossed it to Lily just as the door opened, letting in a gust of cold air. The woman greeted them with a nod, then marched inside. Swift and strong, like a man set to work. She swung back the curtain, revealing Lily's bed.

"Small rooms," she said, looking at Lily with pretty brown eyes. She didn't look at Ben at all. "Gus is my cousin," she said.

She opened the door to the stove and poked at the fire. Next, she looked in the teapot. They moved out of her way as she went to the window and felt along the edges for drafts. Her eyes fell on Lily's cluttered table—a red ribbon, a pamphlet for liver tonic, a tin pie plate. She picked up a jar of brass buttons and rattled it.

"Will all this come with the place?"

"If you like," said Lily, leaning against the wall, her hands in the pockets of Ben's coat, leaving it open enough to show a strip of flesh from breastbone to naval.

The woman set the jar down with a thunk, then rubbed the tips of her fingers with her thumbs.

"I'll talk to Lester, but I think this will do just fine."

While Lily changed behind the curtain, Ben watched the woman and her husband from the window. They climbed onto their buggy, took one last look up at the apartment, then left, their heads whipping back when the horses jumped ahead.

"What will you do?" he asked.

"With what?"

He turned from the window. Lily, in only her skirt, was holding up her arm to better see her wound. She touched the red edges with a finger.

"I mean, where will you live?"

Lily stepped behind the curtain, then opened it a moment later, fastening blue buttons. Her new dress already looked worn—mud-stained and dragging on the floor. Mae's black stitches puckered up on the side of the bodice.

"I'll talk to Gus," she said, facing the mirror and undoing her braids. Her hair fell down her back in waves. "His moods overtake him and then he recovers. It's his way."

"That woman seems set on moving in."

Ben leaned back, his fingers tapping the wall behind him, his insides twisted and bothered. He watched Lily plait her hair, swift and easy, before winding the braids around her head. She kept her right arm low so as not to stretch the stitches.

"I can help you move," he said. "While I'm here."

She looked at him in the mirror.

"To where, Mouse?"

Downstairs, Gus's door slammed, then his footsteps sounded slow and steady on the stairs.

"You best go see Mae so I can hearten him. He'll be feeling poorly."

The door swung open and Gus came in. He looked at Lily, his eyes puffy and his jaw set.

"You drove me to it, Lily," he said. "You asked if something's wrong with your mind." He struck his temple with a finger. "And I say yes. Your reasoning's all mixed up, and I'm done dealing with it."

Lily nodded. "I know." She swayed, then opened her arms and Gus went to her. "I know I vex my closest friends."

Ben took his coat from the floor and his hat from the table and left. He considered seeing Mae as Lily had suggested, but when he stopped at the end of the alley, he went in the opposite direction. He wanted to see the preacher, who'd already proved helpful in unexpected ways.

* * *

It was a long walk in the snapping air, the sun rising, vast and glaring, and the road patchy with cold puddles. The hard leather of his new boots rubbed fiercely, and it wasn't long before he felt the skin roll off his heels like peeling bark. He picked moss from a fencepost and stuffed it in the backs of his boots, then continued on to the little stone church.

The preacher's voice called out as Ben walked up the steps. The church was full, all heads turned to the front.

"Does God not know your deepest stirrings?" the preacher shouted, red-faced and joyous. "Does He not say in His holy word, 'I form the light and create the darkness'?"

Something moved at the edge of Ben's sight—Mae in the back row, waving him over. Ben took off his hat and sat next to her.

"I thought you'd gone," she whispered.

"Soon. I have to talk to the preacher."

He looked around the small church. The stove in the centre provided some heat, but the edges were cold and the windows damp. Congregants filled pews—Songhees, Kanaka, Whites, families and old folks, some listening, some not. It seemed this city had people without end. You could walk its streets, enter its shops, and every day see new faces. Along the wall sat a row of women in faded dresses, hair in identical knots low on their necks.

"The butter girls," whispered Mae. Despite the name, they were of all ages—a collection of women that seemed gathered at random and given similar frocks in pinks and yellows.

"For what is wickedness," the preacher called, "but the absence of understanding? And from whence comes suffering, but through one's own ignorance?"

He moved eagerly around the front of the church, pressing his arms to his sides as though containing himself.

Ben half listened. He let his eyes wander back to the butter girls, who murmured and fidgeted. Suddenly and without intention, he imagined

Lily among them, dressed in yellow, hair twisted and tied at the nape of her neck. But the image quickly changed. The dress took on muddy stains and Lily sat splay-legged, smiling sleepily and smoking a dark cigarette.

The preacher raised his voice higher.

"And do we not each of us have that bruise on our hearts? That tender prick of unknowing? This is the hurt that leads to all manner of sin. This is the dark seed within each of us."

He listed these sins: lying, cheating, sloth, foul tempers and rages, jealousy and impure thoughts, self-righteousness, drunkenness, violence, mistrust, and hysteria.

Mae leaned forward, biting her lip to rawness. Ben thought she might cry. Then some excitement stirred in her and brightened her face.

The preacher was singing now, and everyone joined him. All but Mae, who stood, and did so alone. She squeezed past Ben and walked up the aisle to the front. The preacher greeted her with an outstretched arm, his other holding his Bible to his chest. They whispered between them as the hymn came to an end. Then he faced the congregation.

"Brothers and sisters, I hope you will join us at the river as our dear Mae dedicates herself to God's work once more." He smiled and held his palms up. "In case God has forgotten."

Everyone laughed and Mae stood radiant before them.

As people began to leave, Ben turned around. There were two old women behind him, sisters perhaps, with similar long chins. "Do you know what she's doing?"

They didn't understand the question, so he asked again.

"Mae makes a habit of getting saved," one said.

"We don't go," said the other. "Spurs on our hips."

"It's a little tiresome, truth be told."

Ben looked to the front. Mae was walking through the door behind the pulpit, speaking in the preacher's ear as he guided her.

Ben turned back to the women. "But what is it?"

But they were already sidestepping out of the pew, buttoning up their matching black jackets.

Some people left in wagons, others on foot. The rest lingered in the churchyard, waiting for the preacher and Mae.

The butter girls draped about the front steps. One of the youngest, sitting on the bottom stair, smiled at Ben, and he adjusted his tight hat. She smiled wider, leaning with a sway into the handrail, which she held at the top while peering at him through the slats.

"I don't know you," she said, her look unsettling for its long and intimate hold.

"I don't live here."

Her eyes lowered to his fine-looking boots. "That's a true shine."

"They're from the preacher."

"He does that. Gives people things."

"How do you like it at the creamery?"

She shrugged, slumping back and letting her head loll. But she kept her eyes on him. "Fine."

Another girl, sitting on the step above and holding her large pregnant belly between her knees, leaned toward them and said, "Better than what we'd be doing otherwise. Better than what I was doing."

He was about to ask how long they'd been at the creamery but the preacher came out the door and down the steps. All the girls looked at him. He shook hands with congregants and asked after sickly grandmothers, wagon repairs, and the recent acquisition of milking goats. When there was a lull, Ben stepped up and the preacher clapped him on the arm.

"Pleasure to have you join us, Ben!" He pulled off his spectacles and wiped the glass on his shirt.

"I came to talk to you about Lily."

"Yes. Has she been thrown out?"

Ben straightened and looked at the little preacher. "How'd you know?"

"Seems a Lily sort of event that would drive her son to church on a fine day." The preacher smiled. "And you're wondering if I know of a place for her."

"Yes, sir."

"There's the creamery of course. We welcome any woman, if she's willing to get on well and work hard, as pleases God."

Ben looked at the girls on the steps, trying again to imagine Lily among them—milking a cow or turning a butter churn. But, as before, she veered off in his mind, wandering away from the cows with a piece of straw between her teeth.

"If you don't think she's suited for us, Ben, I know a spinster on Fort Street who would rent her a room. I assume you'd share the place with her, help cover the rent. For that, you could get work at the docks."

Ben shook his head. "I have a job to get back to. I can't stay."

"I see." The preacher smiled wide with a shake of the head. "Lily's always made her own way, hasn't she? She'll do so now, and God will watch over it all."

Ben moved to say that her uncle had always paid her rent, but Mae stepped out of the church and both men turned to look at her. She wore a white robe that reached to the tops of her large boots. She was proud to be in something so pristine—Ben saw it in the way she bit down on her smile.

The preacher called for everyone to follow. They walked down the side of the church, past the cemetery, then into the woods along a narrow path. The snow was unmelted in the deep shade of old firs and hemlock. The pale sun reached through the branches, spots of light on hanging moss and glossy salal leaves.

They stepped into the preacher's footprints, ducking low branches that sprinkled snow on their heads. In the distance, the thunder of water tumbled over rocks, becoming louder as they went deeper into the woods.

Finally, they came to an edge and the preacher began to traverse a steep slope down, where Ben could see glimpses of the black river through the trees. The preacher moved quickly, sure-footed, and the others followed more carefully, feet seeking out roots or boulders under the snow, hands pressed against tree trunks, cold moss beneath their palms.

They gathered at the bottom, where there was a deep pool at the river's edge. Light fell in shifting, murky shapes on the pool's surface, and the sound of the water was deafening now that they were near it.

Mae kicked off her boots. She followed the preacher barefoot through the snow and into the pool, puffs of breath in front of them. Shaking, she held her arms above the water, and her skirts floated smooth all around her.

Ben felt every gasp and spasm, knowing well how cold water locked your bones and ripped the breath from your lungs. But Mae smiled, unafraid and shivering as the preacher put one arm around her thin shoulders. With the other, he took both her hands and pinned them to her chest. Then suddenly and without a word, she arched her spine and her hair fell back like a curtain touching the water, her throat long and her chin to the sky. Ben stepped forward and, as he did, the preacher plunged her under.

Something gave way—a boulder in Ben's chest plummeting hard as Mae's white dress shot to the surface of the dark pool. Her face was pale and tinted green, held firmly under by the preacher's straight arm. Ben heard nothing but the blood pounding in his ears, a current down his spine. As he took another step, Mae burst upward.

Water spilled from her eyes, her lips dark blue, her face as white as her dress. She smiled at the preacher and at the two women who rushed forward with blankets, helping her out of the water.

As the butter girls clustered around Mae, Ben moved his sore jaw, loosened its tight hold. The women held Mae's hands and pressed their cheeks to hers, then guided her to a red blanket on the ground where her boots waited. Some people stayed and sang, others followed the sloppy footprints back up to the trail.

The preacher, wrapped in a wool blanket, his spectacles halfway down his nose and splattered with river water, came and stood next to Ben.

"What a glorious day, do you not think so?"

Ben studied the preacher as he took off his glasses and wiped his face on the blanket.

"But why does she do it?" Ben asked.

"It gives her hope. In life eternal." He leaned in and said softly, "Mae doesn't have much in her earthly life."

The butter girls' voices rose and fell like cooing birds as they helped Mae get her boots back on. One of them embraced her and another rubbed her back, all of them petting and warming and calming Mae's shivers.

It didn't quite come together for Ben—how an icy river plunge was hopeful. But he knew that, somehow, it was for Mae. He turned to the preacher. "Do you have the name of that woman? With the room to rent?"

On their way out of the woods, Mae walked with the preacher, both hooded under their wool blankets. Ben followed with the others, relieved to have sent Mr. Stenhouse the letter, and pleased that he'd arranged a new home for Lily. It occurred to him that Will must often feel this way—making up his mind about something and acting on it without trouble. There was a sturdiness to it. Feet well planted.

Back at the church, Mae went inside to change, nodding at Ben so he'd wait for her. The preacher, still wet and bundled, climbed onto the front seat of the painted wagon, and the butter girls sat on crates in the bed. As the wagon turned and pulled away, the preacher waved.

"Goodbye, young Benjamin! Tell Lily to be fair to Mrs. Cartier!" And before they rounded the bend, he turned in his seat again. "She is welcome to join us at the creamery any time, should it strike her to do so!"

Ben watched the wagon leave.

Churtch's Butter! Sweet! Nutritius! Yelloe!

Soon Mae joined him, sunny and breathless. She was in her dry clothes but her hair was dripping wet and stringy. They headed back along the darkening road. She spoke brightly of her coming week, which in its details didn't sound especially bright. Ben was still thinking of Mae at the creek, going under, so he asked her about it.

"It pleases God," she said. "I see him when I look up through the water."

Ben lifted his hat and pressed it back down. He had watched the whole thing—Mae still as stone under ripples, face tinted green. It was the preacher her eyes were fixed on from underneath.

She took Ben's arm and leaned into him, bendy and slender under her coat. He slowed and she leaned in farther. They stopped, and she pressed her icy forehead against his. She smelled clean, like snow. Her lips were blue and tasted like the cold river. He slipped a hand into her coat—she was cold there, too, through the thin fabric of her dress.

She pulled him into the trees. Her hands were fast and strong, and all over. Yanking his shirt from his trousers, unbuttoning his trousers, in his trousers.

"Don't worry," she said, pulling him closer, her back against an old fir. "I won't get knocked up."

On the road again, Mae spoke cheerily. By the time they reached her building, the sun had set. Ben offered to walk her up to her apartment on account of her muddled sight, but she said her eyes fared well in the dark, so they said their goodbye outside.

Ben thought about Mae all the way to Lily's. It was curious and something to ponder, how she saw things differently than most. Shapes instead of letters, hope instead of drowning, God instead of a regular little man in spectacles. Of course he had to wonder, what did she see when she looked at him?

Lily was standing in the dark at the top of the outside stairs, smoking a slender cigar.

Ben looked up and asked after her wound.

"It's funny," she said, looking briefly at her side. "I sometimes forget it's there."

For a moment, Ben took comfort in the small, dark shape of Lily, the warm rasp of her voice.

"I'm quite pleased to see you," she said. "I thought you'd left."

"I would have said goodbye." He climbed the stairs. "What did Gus say about the place?"

She lifted herself to the landing rail, a long drop behind her. "He used to love me, you know."

"He still does, I think."

"You're probably right. He did cry in my bed today." Lily sighed. "I'm tired. Usually I don't care for sleep, but tonight I'm weary."

Ben shook his head, confused. "So you can't stay here then?"

"No, I can't. All these years he's hated butchering." She said it softly, and Ben wondered if she was perhaps a little sorry. "Now he'll move back with his brother's family."

Lily leaned far back, clutching the railing to keep herself from tipping completely.

Ben pulled his hands from his pockets, ready to grab her if he needed to. "It's all right anyway, Lily. I talked to the preacher and he knows a woman who'd rent us a room."

"Us?"

"Until I've paid some rent, anyway."

"Hmm. Then what?"

"I'd go back to the farm. I'll send money from there."

"As my uncle did." She drew on her cigar and smiled. "This is funny, Mouse. It's as though you're the parent and I'm the child."

"That's not it."

"Or doctor and patient."

"You have nowhere to live."

"People have always said that about me. Anyway, I know the woman he speaks of. Mrs. Cartier. She'll have us stay in at night for prayers."

"It's only for a short while. The preacher says there's room at the creamery too, but I don't think you'd like it much."

"Not much, no. You must see I'm not suited to churches. Or creameries. Or old ladies' quiet rooms."

Ben kicked some snow off the step, listened to it land. It stung him, this quibbling over prayers and old ladies when the idea was better than all that.

"Would it please you?" Lily asked, and he waited as the red tip of her cigar glowed, then faded. "Would it please you, Mouse, to stay here a while longer?"

A flash of Mae. A flash of the farm. His gaze fell to his boots. He thought of Mr. Stenhouse, a fair man but unbending.

Lily reached out to him. When he stepped nearer, she took off his hat and placed it on her own head, then ran her fingers through his hair. "You're a fretful boy. Perhaps it's Agda's influence."

Ben stepped back, a flare in his chest. "I'm trying to help."

"Yes, you've a good heart," she said. "I'm pleased to see it. But I hope you know there's a time to use your other side. Perhaps a time like this." She dropped her cigar behind her, then slid down from the railing and took his hand. "What I mean to say, Mouse, is that you may want to get back to those chickens."

"It's not just chickens."

"Chickens and pigs then." She went inside the flat and kicked off her boots. "And girls named Effie."

"You know Effie?"

Lily unbuttoned the bodice of her dress and let it fall to the floor, then disappeared behind the curtain.

"Maybe you've spoken of her. I knew of her somehow."

Sometime in the night, Lily woke him, breathless.

"I had a dream," she said. "I was a cow at that creamery. Chewing grass while the sun warmed my back... Are you listening?"

It was dark and he couldn't see her. "Yes."

"Then someone tried to milk me."

Ben pulled his blanket up against the cold.

"I had no milk, little Mouse. None. I was dried right up and no good to anyone."

"It's only a dream." His voice was hoarse from the cold. "You're not a cow."

"And what of the real cows?"

"At the creamery? They have milk or they wouldn't be there."

She fell silent for a moment. "Where would they be then?"

They'd be supper, he thought, but he knew better than to say it. "I guess they'd be on a different farm."

For several moments there was no sound at all.

"Are you thinking of going to the creamery?" he asked.

"It wouldn't suit me."

"No."

She started walking round the room, her skirts swishing and her boots loud. Ben turned and faced the back of the sofa, pulling the blanket over his ears. Lily added wood to the fire and rattled the teapot, paced about, then sat at the window. She opened it and spoke to people walking home from the taverns. *How's the night, Nigel? How's your boy? I have a story for you next chat, Pete—I think you'll laugh.*

Then the front door opened and closed and it was quiet.

Ben woke again in the early hours. In the moonlight, he saw Lily's curtain was still pulled open and her bed was empty. He went to the window and looked down at the silent street, then farther to the docks. How would it be to work where Merritt once lay dead? To work so near the same waters that tried to kill Ben as well? He shivered and went back to the sofa, where he slept fitfully and dreamed of his mother, her hand reaching out as he sank beneath the waves.

Then he fell. Not through water but through air—

He woke with a start to Lily's soft and tuneless humming. The curtain was drawn back. The dawn sky was clear and green. A few stars were still visible over the warehouse roof. Lily sat on the floor with her back to him, digging in her cedar chest.

And her braids were gone. Chopped off. Her hair was cut at the nape, jagged and stringy.

Ben leaned up on his elbow. "What happened?"

She turned to him with a fistful of old handkerchiefs, her wide smile faltering.

"My hair? I sold it."

"Why?"

"Not to worry. I have no attachment to hair." She continued searching through old clothes and rags. "I gave the money to Gus for his move. Are you very happy to hear that?"

"I guess I'm surprised."

"Hmm. Well, sometimes I'm surprising."

Ben sat up and pulled on his boots, careful of his blisters. He stuffed squares of the preacher's flannel into the backs.

"I considered it last night, Mouse, and thought I might stay at that place and make butter."

He stopped hooking the buttons and looked at Lily. "The creamery?"

"We can go together, if you like, since it's on your way."

Her face was more painted than usual—black around her eyes, lips red, cheeks dark pink. She'd readied herself.

Ben leaned back into the sofa. He felt as if he were lifting. Even his heartbeat rose in his chest. "Really?"

"I decided I might like cows. I've only seen them herded down the street in a storm of dust, poor things." She nodded to the table in the corner. "See if you want anything."

"It's good, Lily. It won't be for long."

"Yes, I know."

"And then I'll send rent. I'll help you move back here."

"I know. I know all that."

He watched her for a moment as she continued to dig, opening crumpled rags and tossing them.

He said, "It's only— Do you know about the creamery?"

She stopped and looked back at him. "You think me incapable of hard work?"

"No."

"Then you needn't worry."

Ben went to the table. It was loaded with bottles and jugs, pamphlets, songbooks and Bibles, a stack of letters, a pair of men's gloves, and the fine drinking glass Ben remembered from when he'd visited as a boy. He flicked the carved glass and the sound filled the room, then faded. His eyes shifted to the letters, yellowed and addressed in slanted writing. The ink had aged to brown. He picked one up and turned it, his mouth suddenly dry.

"Are these from my mother?"

Lily looked over her shoulder and squinted.

"Yes, from Agda. She used to write to me."

He shuffled through them, his breath catching in his throat. There were more than a dozen.

"They're unopened."

"Are they?"

He checked each one. "You opened two."

Lily tossed an old shirt on the ground. "You can have them if you like," she said, without looking up. "Her English was poor, but I suppose you know that."

He took the letter from one of the open envelopes.

Ben is a fin Boy with strong Bones and his teeth are with out rott. Each day he gathers eggs and lerns his numbers and lettres. You see, I teach him myself. What a carefull Boy is he and so gentle with the animals. You must never worry. He is safe and eats well—Mon garçon affamé!

It is strange, yes, that he will sleep in the day as he does? And he is awake at night? I've never seen such in a child. I cared for the sons of my Brothers and I tell you it is not usual. I show him the proper time for sleep, but still I find him about when the moon is high. He wanders or pokes at the coals and at times he cryes with much kicking and fussing, but I settel him. I sing to him and hold him and he sleeps finne.

Ben refolded the page and slipped it back in the envelope. Lily still had her back to him. He sat on the sofa and opened another.

Ben is near my sholders now, as well as he is good with his manners. He will Be strong when he grows—alredy he holds pace with

James when chopping the wood. He wishes for scool and James tells me he should go. But you see no good can Be found there. Perhaps you knowe this. He is fin here and has frends on the farm so his life is full and well. At times his temper is shown and I wonder where he learned it. Perhaps some influence in the city or even your uncle.

Ben lifted his hat and pressed it back down. It felt good and tight like that, holding in his thoughts. He didn't remember any nighttime wanderings or any kicking or tears. And she hadn't lived to see him outgrow it. Perhaps she thought he'd grow to be like his father.

Always you are welcom here. If you would like to visit you only need come with James. I am sure you have no wish to stay in such as that place where you live.

Lily had dug down to the bottom of the chest, flapping moth-eaten linens open and tossing them aside. The smell of old clothes and cedar reached Ben across the small room.

"She invited you to the cabin," he said.

"Did she? That was friendly of her."

"Did you come?"

"Well, how would I, Mouse? Ah!" She held up a piece of lace, then sat back on the floor with her legs folded beneath her dress. "This was made in France by children with tiny fingers. Do you know how I know?"

Ben shook his head.

"Penny told me back when my own fingers were still small. She had such pretty things, Penny did. And she always smelled good—peony powder."

Lily ran her fingertips along the small scrap of lace, then held it to her face and breathed in. It looked frail, like an old leaf decayed down to its fine web of veins. Something that could disintegrate at the lightest touch.

"Penny was like a mother to me," Lily said. "Do you remember her?"

"I don't remember anything from then."

"Not even when she died?"

He shook his head.

"You watched it happen from the window—no, not this one. My window above the Brown Jug."

"How did she die?"

"Mmm." Lily stood and steadied her hand on the back of the sofa. She leaned into it gently, like an old woman would.

"A spooked horse," she said. There was a hollow sound to her words, as if she meant to soften the violence of what she was saying.

Ben watched her pick at the stitches on her dress. "Did you ever write my mother back?"

"Agda? I had no writing paper."

Ben nodded, because the answer didn't surprise him. He slipped his mother's old letters into his bag and, in doing so, saw another opened envelope on the table. This one was not from his mother, but he knew the handwriting well. Effie. He held it up to Lily.

"This one's for me," he said.

"That's right. I left it there for you."

"But it's opened."

She swayed, slightly. "Yes. I read it, Mouse. I didn't think you'd mind."

He pulled the slip of paper from the envelope.

Dear Ben,

It snowed heavily last night, as I'm sure you know, and who do you suppose showed up first thing this morning, with snow up to his knees and whiskers frozen to sticks? Our neighbour's ridiculous son, Rudy Lamb, that's offered to help with repairs. Ben, he's already put his things in your room. I moved them into the barn over lunch and when I came back, there it all was again piled on your cot. I told him not to get too comfortable, and do you know what he said? Don't trouble yourself, Effie, you worry too much. I held my temper, which might impress you, and then spoke to Father. You won't believe what he said. Effie, it's not your trouble. So what am I doing here if nothing is my trouble? Should I just sit by the stove like a simpleton? Instead of trying to hold your spot while you're away doing God Knows What? I'll tell you this, I had great plans to grow old here alongside my friend. That's you. I had no plans whatsoever to spend a moment of time with turtle-faced Rudy scurrying about, bow-legged and grinning like a fool.

You said that you would return in two days. I went to your place to see if you were back at your cabin, sick or insane or otherwise afflicted. But NO. It is empty and by the way, a Great Rotting Cow lays in the mud. One of our cows, and if Father knew you mistreated a carcass, he would likely not trust you to work again. So of course I didn't tell him. Mother and Father were in a frenzy that I disappeared for half a day but I won't bother you with all that.

When are you returning? I haven't told you yet that I found myself a hobby a while back and it's painting. Well. I am quite good and eager to show you my work and hope you will enjoy it more than Sarah or the others, who all wonder what I am on about. And if you think it terrible, you should tell me and I will listen. We understand each other don't we? Of course you haven't always felt that way. I used to be a pest at your ankles and ugly to boot. I suppose I'm still ugly. Unlike Sarah who we all know is beautiful and could find a much better husband than that obnoxious oaf Eli. Would you believe that he paints as well? Ha! I'll tell you this—with his painting and Sarah's poems the two may be well matched after all! Their children will be just as dull, and together they can grow a vast empire of witless men and terrible cheese.

I'll say one more thing about it and that's all you'll hear from me on the subject. I never worried, because I knew you never saw much in Sarah's beauty. Perhaps you have no appreciation for comely women, having met so few, and in this way can see me as better than I am. Don't we bare all in letters? Although I expect a full twelve words in your response. If you respond at all.

Father is taking the sleigh to Petrenko's for provisions and he's agreed to post this letter, so I say goodbye now. Old Ralph Blitterswick has never missed a pickup in his whole life and I count on him to get this to you this evening. You will come back quickly to claim your room, won't you? Tomorrow? Enough with this foolishness.

Waiting your return,
Effie

Ben looked at Lily, who sat at the window with her binoculars.

"She sent this on Friday morning," he said.

"Did she?"

"When did you get it?"

"I suppose I got it Friday afternoon." She leaned close to the glass, her face to the morning sun. In the full light, her eye paint showed uneven and her red lips grotesque. "I forgot about it, really."

"I was meant to leave days ago."

She looked at him, quite still.

"I should have been there. They needed me," he said.

"I never asked you to stay."

He put the letter in his bag with the others, feeling hot on the back of his neck.

"Well." Lily stood and grabbed her bag. "Let's leave directly. I walk fast, when pressed. And anyway, those farm people will prefer you over that other one—that Rudy. He sounds a poor catch."

Lily didn't pack much—the lace from Penny, the jug of whisky, her binoculars.

Before they left, Lily wanted to see Gus. The front of the shop was empty, but the sound of a blade sawing through bone came from behind the swinging door. A crate sat open on the floor, filled up with straw. All the little carved figures nested on top with their faces to the ceiling—the misshapen family and their large-headed animals. The pictures from the walls were gone, including the bearded man with his heart on fire.

Gus came from the back, wiping his hands on his apron. He stopped when he saw them.

"So you're off then," he said. "You have a few days yet before my cousin moves in. I insisted on it."

"There's no need. We'll steal away now, like bandits." Lily looked at her friend. "I'm going to work at a creamery, Gus. Perhaps the next time you eat your bread, you'll be using butter I churned myself."

"My brother's wife will make my butter."

"Perhaps I'll become devout under the preacher's instruction," Lily continued. "In which case I'll have to close my legs to you when you visit."

Ben went to the window. Everything glistened in the morning sun—even the bricks of the warehouse were clean and bright. By now, Rudy would have woken in the room at the back of the barn. Cracked the ice on the water jug to splash his face before crossing the frozen yard for breakfast.

"Lily," Gus said quietly, "there won't be any more visits between us."

"Well. It's like you to say that, isn't it?" She dropped her bag on the floor and dug through it. "I have a gift for you to remember me."

She pulled out her binoculars, and Gus took them in his large hands. He rubbed his thumb along the pearly white.

"I wouldn't likely forget you anyhow," he said. "Don't you want them?"

"For what? Looking at cows?"

"Why not?"

"It's people I like."

He kept his eyes on the binoculars. "Well, you take proper care and don't go fighting with those butter girls. I hear they're tough."

"You know I wouldn't fight with anyone."

"I just stitched you up for some kind of fighting."

Gus walked with them to the door, then stood next to his saluting pig to watch them leave. They hadn't gone far when he called behind them, "Lily! Once that thing scabs, pull the threads out!"

They picked their way down the snow-lined street, through slush that had frozen overnight, making for perilous walking. Shop windows and doors showed Ben his limping reflection, new hat sitting high, new boots pointed and gleaming. He carried a bag over each shoulder and Lily's whisky jug sloshed behind his ear. Ben stopped.

"I should have said goodbye to Mae," he said.

"She'll be at the factory. It's too late for that."

He looked down the street. "She'll wonder what happened to us."

"Mae's fine, Mouse." Lily stepped near and rubbed his arm. "She's the type to attach herself to one thing only, and it's not you or me."

He looked at Lily, shivering under her shawl, and knew she was right. Maybe that was why Mae was so untroubled—she wasn't all caught up in wanting. It left him colder than he already was to think that.

They continued on past the harbour, where the air was salty with the smells of cold fish and seaweed. Few people were around this early, only gulls coasting over the empty docks, the tops of the piles crusted in barnacles.

"I don't much like the docks in the morning," Lily said.

They walked past the old banks and the long inns, the pigs penned between buildings, their steaming noses pressed between the wooden slats. Soon, the cobbled streets gave way to muddy roads. The shops thinned out to houses in large lots as they climbed out of the city. Here, the snow was still deep and each step more work.

At the top of the hill, before the road cut into the thick forest, they stopped for a rest. While Ben adjusted the pads in his boots, Lily caught her breath.

"Isn't it funny?" she said, looking down on the city. "We're all just little ants on a hill, aren't we?"

The road twisted through the trees as they followed sleigh tracks and wagon ruts pressed into snow. Lily struggled and Ben's blisters burned, so when a sleigh overtook them, Ben waved to the young man and his wife. They were ruddy and unsmiling, but they stopped and gestured for Ben and Lily to get in the back with three red-cheeked children and a curly-haired dog.

"We're going to the Butter Church creamery," Ben said. "Do you know it?"

When they shook their heads, one of the children said, "No English!" her voice ringing out in the cold, quiet forest.

"Don't worry, Mouse," said Lily. "It can't be missed."

The children crowded to one side with their dog, and Ben and Lily sat opposite, facing them.

The ride was quiet, with only the heavy hiss of the sleigh runners and the horse's hoofbeats and puffing breath. Lily kept her eyes on the road behind, while the children stared openly at the two of them, their pale eyes peeking from under fur hats. They played a game that involved string and a small rubber ball. Each time it landed at Ben's feet, he tossed it back and they laughed behind their mittens.

After a while, Ben turned and looked up the road, tucking his cold hands under his arms.

"Lily?" he said. "Do you think we passed it?"

She glanced ahead, the road a white tunnel through the trees. "Are we near West Cane Lake?"

"It wouldn't be as far as that."

Ben watched as Lily's head bobbed gently with each dip and bump of the sleigh. He suddenly wondered if she was trying to land herself at the Stenhouse farm with him. He imagined her pacing their house at night, pocketing items and baring her breasts.

Leaning forward, he tapped the man on the shoulder and the sleigh slowed, then stopped. Ben hopped down and helped Lily, who protested quietly.

"What'll we do here, in the middle of nowhere?"

Ben thanked the man and his wife for the ride. Before they drove off, the woman held up a hand. She reached into a basket at her feet and retrieved a piece of black sausage and a wrinkled apple, handing these to Ben with a stern nod. The sleigh pulled away, then slipped quietly through the trees and disappeared at the first bend.

Slinging the bags over his shoulders, Ben turned to Lily. Her eye paint was smudged now, the red on her lips all faded but the edges.

"Do you know where it is, Lily?"

"It's not far," she said. "But I had the idea we could go to the lake on the way." She smiled, weak and uncertain. "I want to show you my father's cabin."

Ben stared at her, then pressed a thumb and finger to his eyes. "I've seen that cabin. I don't need to see it again."

He scanned the fields of sparkling snow behind them—no hint of human life except the road they stood on.

"We passed the creamery, then," he said. "Is that what you're saying?"

"It's only a few miles behind us, Mouse."

"So back near the city." He shifted his jaw, heard the grinding pop.

"Well, it's rather near the Butter Church, as it should be," said Lily. "But we're close to the cabin now, aren't we?"

With a long exhale, Ben studied the ground for a moment. Then, without looking back at Lily, he turned and began following the tracks of the family's sleigh toward West Cane Lake.

They eventually came to the split in the road where one way led to the Petrenko's and Stenhouse's and the other to the school. Ben kept on toward the school and cut into the trees at the path to Connie's cabin. It was overgrown now and buried deep in snow. He slogged onward, his back sweaty and his boots full of slush. Lily's laboured breathing came from somewhere behind him, growing quieter as the gap between them lengthened. He finally stopped to see her struggling through a patch of snowy ferns to her waist. He continued on.

The cabin was well hidden, but Ben caught a glimpse of its tin chimney. The whole thing would be missed by someone not watching for it—mistaken for a large tree stump or a mass of vine, covered in untouched snow.

He checked once more on Lily, then reached his leg over a snow-buried log and caught his boot. With a wild step to save himself, his foot plunged into a tangle of branches. The grip was tight and the fall swift—face down and elbow-deep in the snow, with a searing twist to his ankle. He heard himself groan.

Planting his good foot, he cautiously righted himself, then eased his leg from the trap of branches. He cupped both hands around the injured ankle and pressed—a hot, liquid pain pooled in the muscle. Holding a young tree, he took a step, then another. He kept on, bracing himself against trunks and branches, until he stood in front of Connie's cabin.

No smoke issued from its bent chimney, no footprints led to the low door. A snowdrift hid much of the woodpile, and the chopping block was unused, with a hatchet's handle reaching from the snow like a bone.

Ben limped to the door and pushed it open, stepping inside. It had the feel of a place long unused—still filled up but colder than outside and hollow to the ear. Old leaves and pine needles had come in through gaps along the crooked door. Ragged cobwebs were thick in the corners, some still holding dry spiders.

He was stiffened up with cold and his burning ankle needed rest, so he eased himself onto one knee beside the little stove to light a fire. Kindling had been left behind, blanketed in cobwebs and dust. Ben stacked it in the stove with frozen hands, then took the flint from his bag. He was clumsy, his fingers too numb to get a good grip, and he struggled to get a spark.

Lily watched from the doorway as Ben gently blew life into a tiny flame. She pulled her shawl tight around herself, her breathing shaky.

"I almost expected him to be here," she said, stepping inside. She turned slowly, taking everything in. "I thought maybe he'd leave something. A note or..." She sat on the narrow cot, its ropes groaning beneath the thin mattress. "I suppose he wandered off like an animal would."

With the small fire lit, Ben stood and checked the hanging lamp. It had some oil that he'd save for the walk home. He forced the crooked door shut, blocking out all light, and sat in Connie's chair.

"Penny called this place the shiver house," said Lily. "It's where he came when his tremors took a turn. It's very small, isn't it? And dark. Is this how you remember it?"

"Mostly." He thought back to Connie looking at him through his thick and murky glasses. The choking woodsmoke that clogged Ben's throat. "Mostly the same, I guess."

He lifted his pant leg. His ankle was so swollen it had pulled his boot laces taut. He dragged the kindling box closer and rested his foot on top, then unstrapped the blanket roll from his bag and handed it to Lily.

Lily was speaking of her father as if he were still alive and needed tending.

"I'd run errands to the chemist... little white pills in little blue bottles... a slow poisoning, Mouse, it's terrible to witness... rotting teeth... feet so swollen, the skin peels off in sheets..."

"Sometimes he'd become a wild animal," she said. "Like a dog or a bear. When he started snapping his teeth at me, I knew he'd be gone in the morning."

"Sounds like he shouldn't have taken those pills."

"The pills saved his life."

Ben handed Lily the apple and sausage, along with her whisky. She drank and handed it back.

"It'll warm you."

As he sipped, the heat spread from his throat until the hollow in his chest was filled with warmth. They passed the jug back and forth, his arm loose over the edge of the chair, fingers grazing his mother's letters at the top of his bag. He imagined her writing them all those years ago. Sitting at their table next to the small window, then walking all that way to Petrenko's to post them. Just so they could be stuffed away, hidden and unread in Lily's cedar chest.

"It's good I lived there with her," he said, realizing that the words were unkind. He turned to see if he'd hurt Lily, but the fire cast strange shadows and her face was hidden. "I'm sorry," he said.

"Don't be sorry—it's likely true. But you shouldn't think her without flaws, Mouse. That's a dangerous way to see people." She leaned forward and handed him the jug. "We're all saints and devils both. If you know that, you'll walk easier through life."

Ben watched the small fire snap and flicker from under the brim of his hat.

"We're more alike than you think, anyway," Lily said. "Agda and I. Both given to our own way."

Ben took another drink. The whisky was warming him, easing the pain in his foot. He had no interest in arguing with Lily.

"I have a present for you." Leaning forward on the cot, she reached into her bag and pulled out a packet. "Here."

He held out his hand and she placed something small and light on the palm. It felt like he held a dead bird, stiff and wrapped in lace. He knew, even in the dark, that it was Penny's lace. As he carefully unwrapped it, he felt with his thumb a wooden head the size of an acorn, a roughly carved body. The firelight reflected off two glass eyes.

He looked at Lily. "You took this?"

"It's a gift."

"No." Ben shook his head, the wooden baby staring back at him with too-large eyes. "It's not. This belongs to Gus."

"I saw you admiring it."

"I didn't admire it. I don't even know what it's for."

"It's for looking at," she said. "Well anyway, you can give it back if you like."

"How can I? I'm already late getting to the farm. And you know Gus leaves soon." He turned to the fire, the baby held loose in his hand. The old ache burned along his clamped jaw. "You say you're like her," he said. "But she would never do this."

Lily shifted on the cot, a rustle of fabric.

He continued. "This is something James would do. Steal. Lie."

"Everyone does both those things, Mouse."

"No. Not everyone."

"You're still young so you don't yet know the depths of people. My uncle was a good man beneath the bluster."

"Not so good, Lily." The fire mellowed, then smoked. Ben shut the iron door with his good foot. "You just don't want me to say it, I think. You don't want anyone to say what he really did."

He stood and handed the baby back, then rolled his blanket and tied it to the bottom of his pack.

"Merritt drowned," she said.

"No." Ben shook his head. "He was strong in the water. He saved me."

With the fire out, he couldn't see her face at all—as though he spoke to a dark, empty corner.

He swung both bags over his shoulders and opened the door, blinking against the low sun that cut through the trees. It felt good to have said what he hadn't said before—like a burning coal in his stomach had finally been extinguished. Perhaps his mother felt that way when she spoke the truth to his father that night—*You have let misery into our house.* Maybe she slept well after that, one restful night before she began to die.

Ahead lay the sloppy path they'd made coming here through the trees. It would be a rough hike on his burning foot. Ben yanked the hatchet out of the chopping block and limped through the snow to a leafless maple. He hacked off a forked branch and trimmed it to fit—a crudely-made crutch, but good enough.

He turned to get Lily, but something caught his eye, a flash of movement—real then gone. His mind leapt to the impossible. The Howland dog? Connie himself? Or maybe his father's broad back, leading the way once more. The forest was full of shadows, moving as the sun moved. Old shadows lingering like ghosts.

"I suppose we shouldn't have come here," said Lily. She was standing in the doorway with one hand on either side, the hem of her blue dress brushing the threshold. Like this, she seemed to be holding herself up by her arms alone, while the rest of her floated. "The feeling of this place... It's all wrong, isn't it, Mouse?"

Ben put his weight on the crutch and it held firm. "This place never had a good feeling."

"I didn't know." She leaned her head against the doorframe and smiled. "I'm filled right up with bad ideas, aren't I?"

"It wasn't so bad, Lily." But of course it was. Some places had a certain darkness to them, and little good could happen within their walls. He knew that well enough.

They were slow and cumbersome moving through the trees, even with their old footprints to follow. In silence, they reached the road, where the sky opened up to a vast pink veil. The moon barely showed itself—a clean slip of glass.

Ben started in the direction of the creamery, but Lily stopped him.

"Your foot won't last, Mouse. You go on to the farm and claim your room."

"It's too far for you to go alone."

"Not for me. I'm a strong walker. I'll be fine." She took his hand, kissing the top, then rested her ear against his chest as if checking for a heartbeat. "What a good Mouse, coming all that way to give me an old tin of money."

He put his arm around her shoulder and laid his cheek on the top of her head. When she stepped back, he lit the lamp and handed it to her and they said goodbye. He watched her walk for a while, then he turned and headed for the farm.

LILY

1872

SHE WAS TORN RIGHT UP. SPLIT RIGHT OPEN. THE CHILD HAD spilled from her like she held the sea itself in her belly. She didn't know any of this—that babies came from water or that they grew from a long root that also attached to her.

The doctor gave her laudanum and she warmed to it, softening like putty in a hand. Her dreams were strange and wonderful. Penny brought her the baby, fed and washed, for Lily to hold now and then—a funny wrinkled thing that moved its mouth like a tiny bird and stared at her with slow-blinking eyes.

"I promised it to Agda," she said, handing it back. "How long till my uncle comes?"

"A few weeks yet," said Penny, the baby a sweet bean in her arms. Penny cooed and calmed and stroked its red cheek. "What a fat little thing. What a funny little mouse," she said.

Lily watched them for a moment. She touched her finger to the downy earlobe, then drifted into sleep.

Merritt showed up three nights later. Lily knew he was there before opening her eyes. She felt him like she felt the weather stirring. He sat next to the bed, holding the baby in his strong, lean arms.

She smiled. "How long are you back?"

"I leave tonight. If you'll come with me."

She hadn't seen him in months, back when he had placed his long hand on her small, round belly and felt the baby flutter like a bird's wing. The next morning he was gone, but he always did that—roamed free, as only men could do, and did.

"To where?" Lily asked him now.

"I have work at a camp."

"What if I say no?"

"Will you? Say no?" He looked pained.

"Probably not."

"We can leave tonight."

Lily whispered, "But the baby—"

"He doesn't belong to her. James's woman."

"Her name's Agda."

He was fine to look at, Merritt was. Strong boned in a way that gave Lily a shiver down and all the way down. She reached across the bed and took his hand. She kissed it and kissed it and turned onto her side to face him, kissing it some more. His eyes remained on the baby in his arms.

Weeks later, Lily snagged a piece of paper and a pencil stub from McEvity's dirty store at logging camp 57.

Dear Penny—this camp is a wild place & the men are wilder than those at the jug. There are only a few women & non of them espeshally frendly. I wish Id asked you about caring for babys before I left but sure I snuck out in the dark while you slept & I am sorry about it. You see he cries and wont eat. My milk wont come so he naws away at my finger. I give him potato water & bread soffened in cow milk if I have it. Guess what we named him Penny? Maerrit chose Jabez because I was all torn up. He read in the bible it means sorrow and born in pane. Well I call him Jabe as somehow its frendlier. Harriet next door glares at me for naming my baby stranje but she is the sort to glare anyway & I'm not too bothered. All she does is clean & wash & scrub & so she must have her own problems & when she came to check up on the baby crying she looked around my place & glared some more all the wile holding her fingers under her nose. I told her to stay for tea anyway but she didn't & so I have yet to make frends here with thees women. Tho she did one thing only once & I'll tell it to you. Without a word she came in the eerly hours still in her nite dress & holding a lamp. Jabe was screeming to wake the world all that nite. She took him from his cradle & out popped her full titty with milk dribble running down—mothers milk is not like a cows or goats see its a little blue & a little perly coming out of her like a leeky fausset. My baby suckllled while Harriet glared at me meanly the whole wile then she handed him back sound asleep & she left. She only did it the once & I wish she would again but she tells me she has four of her own to mind & a lazy husband on top of it wich she said is gods curse on her for being hasty & not insted marrying Martin the baker down island when she had the chance. I told her go to Martin the baker now & she slammed her door at me but I only ment well by it. Anyway the men are a whole other story here Penny. They get vishus & drunk its true & you'd be surprised by it. I haven't seen the like before not on the wildest nights at the jug. Old Pat from too doors down bangs on my door all hours to have his way whenever Maerit is gone wich is often. I dont let him in. Ive seen his wife black and blue so I know better then to put myself in his path wich is what you taut me. Well I think men use hands like women use tungs—for good or bad wich you also taut me & I find that rather funny about people. Maybe you'll come visit me and bring your plum bread with nuts and synnamon. I also need more lodanum as it costs too much here tho I can snag some now & then when Mr. McEvity goes in the back room. Maybe I'll just go back home with you Penny if you come to visit. Would my father take me in again? If my uncle pays for the room? I should guess not but you could ask him after hes well fucked & sleepy & contented. Thats when you can say to him—what about we let Lily back. I wont live with my uncle tho he'd have me. Its because Agda would take the baby so I wont go there. Did you know shes after babys? I didnt mind it then but I do now as Mearit says a child suffers when away from its tru mother. And so. Well. Mearit is often away and I think hes the type to leed an aventursome life no matter what else. As men are wont to do or able anyway. When he is home he is dutyful & quiet as is his nature. Sometimes I think him part animal staring into the fire as he does & long in the face with no word at all. I wonder if hes blind to me sitting only feet away or if his mind is so full up there's no room for much else or I often wonder if he is somhow all broken up in his mind. Sometimes he cries see and I dont know what to say when he does that so we sit quiet—his face wet & me watching him. Is that not stranje? But maybe everyone is stranje in there houses. Well. So long Penny I count you as a mother all those years at the jug. I pray I will see you again soon. Dont we have a time when we are together? You feel warmly toward me dont you—even now after I left in this way? And so long then. Your Lily.

The camp women did slowly warm to Lily, in their own time and their own way. Not with friendliness, but gifts of food left at her door—a couple eggs, a jar of milk, a pork chop in paper. Lily tried to catch them for a visit, such was her loneliness, but these women weren't the visiting type. They were the doing type—strong, tough, quiet. There were only six of them in this sea of men. Strong men, tough, and roaring loud.

But Lily was no cooker of pork chops or any other thing. Hungry as a bear after winter, and with Jabe crying on her hip, she tossed the piece of meat into a pot, filled it with water from the bucket, and set it on the small stove. Once steam curled up, she pulled out the pork chop with a knife and took a bite right there. It was grey and rubbery to chew, the taste entirely unpleasant.

With Jabe howling on her hip, she sat to feed him the milk while forcing down the pork chop herself. And lucky for him he had no teeth to share it—that night she endured a fiery stomach, cramped so tight she lay sweating and shaking, knees to chest, while Jabe cried in the corner.

She was hungry, and some of these men relentless, and Penny still hadn't responded to her letter. As well, Merritt had been gone nearly a month—the longest of all his absences.

"Lily," Mr. Brockenheimer pleaded whenever Merritt disappeared, "these cabins are for workers. Workers who pay rent."

And each time, Lily assured him it was only a short while.

But now, here Mr. B. stood once more in her little shack, with two giant Swedes behind him—twins with yellow moustaches. They unpacked their bags while Lily packed hers.

"Would you tell Merritt I went back to The Jug? Mr. Brockenheimer?" she said.

"Little girl, you go on and forget that boy."

"Forget him?" She hefted her bag over one shoulder. "How do I do that?"

With Jabe in her arms, she hitched a ride to town. First with a farmer and then with a priest. Then she walked for a while until a soft-faced boy offered her a ride on the bouncing seat of his wagon. As he drove, he squirmed away from her baby's cries.

Lily no longer heard it—the crying. Her arms did what they should, they rocked him and held him to her empty breast where he chewed and sucked and wailed tearlessly. His face was so red she thought he didn't look like a human baby at all, but a sort of undersea thing or a bird newly hatched. They both were odd animals, mother and son. Her from lack of sleep or feeling, a bony girl emptied right out. He from lack of all she was supposed to give him but couldn't.

"There's milk," the boy said. "In the back. Just scoop it with that ladle."

Turning in the seat to look at the bed full of cans, she cried out, "I thought it was whisky!"

She climbed into the back and sat with Jabe on her crossed legs. Her hand trembled as she unscrewed the lid and fed him straight from the long-handled scoop. She fed him so fast he nearly choked, his face wet with rich, white milk, frothy bubbles at his mouth.

"I've never seen so much milk," she called to the boy.

He looked over his shoulder, still nervous. "It's all going to be made into cheese."

"Is that so?"

"You know those Chadsey men? At Ash Mountain?"

"Never heard of them." Lily pushed the hair from her eyes and settled back. The bumping and clanging shook her and Jabe too much to sleep, and he spit up plenty of milk. But she just fed him all over again, and a little for herself.

The boy dropped Lily off outside of the city, holding the baby for her while she climbed from the wagon. "You'll be all right, miss?"

"You're very serious for a boy," she said. But as he left, she had a funny thought. *That smooth-cheeked, glossy-haired boy is older than me.*

A seagull swooped by and splattered white on the road, tiny dots on her boots.

"Well, fuck."

She walked a couple miles with her bag and her baby. He was heavy when sleeping, like a bag of stones. She adjusted her hold on him to ease her shoulder and looked around at the town. All these months and it was just as she'd left it. Everyone she knew called out hello, and she felt herself lighten just being back on these streets.

"I'll see you tomorrow," she called back. "I'll come by for a chat and show you my baby. Named Jabe!"

Penny saw her from the third-floor window of The Jug and called down. She met Lily at the door, kissed the top of her head, held her close, then scooped up the baby and kissed his face all over. He slept through it all, milk dried to a shiny crust on his cheeks.

"He's skinny," she said, placing a hand on his ribs. "Oh heavens, he's a scrawny one." She held him and smelled his black hair. "Poor baby. He needs a bath."

"I sent you a letter," Lily said, with her head on Penny's soft shoulder.

"My girl, there are dozens of camps on this island. I had no way of knowing where you were. My little lost mice." Then, whispering, "James has arranged to pay for a room. We knew you'd return to us."

Upstairs, freshly washed, with her hair in braids like when she was small, Lily sank into a clean bed. Penny had powdered her so she smelled like peony, slipped a clean nightdress over her head, then snuck in a bottle of laudanum. Her father hadn't yet come to see her, but still Lily was happy. She fell into a dreamless sleep for the first time in months.

LILY
1875

THERE WERE ONLY A FEW PEOPLE ON THE STREET PAST MIDnight. Back at the camp, people referred to this place as a quiet town, though she had nothing to compare it to, other than the camp itself, which certainly wasn't quiet. Were there cities that stayed busy through the night? Bustle and noise and lit up shops? The idea thrilled Lily—a buzz in her fingertips, a shiver in her knees. Down the hall a man shouted and a woman laughed.

She'd seen Merritt only once since leaving the camp, when he came back to make deliveries for her father. When he took her into the alley and did his work as he used to. She asked where he always went off to, and he spoke of small fishing villages where bears lumbered down the one dirt street, and logging camps that floated on crystal lakes. But mostly he kept alone, he said, doing odd jobs, sleeping in barns, eating berries and stealing food from people's cellars.

"And we're not invited like before?" Lily asked. "Me and Jabe?"

Merritt pressed the heels of his hands into his eyes, then looked at her. "I'm not very good at that."

They stood in the dark alley, two faceless shadows near each other. Lily leaned on the stone wall behind her.

"Well, neither am I," she said.

Now, Lily turned from the window and looked at her bed, where Jabe lay in the moonlight. She slipped under the blankets next to him and placed her hand on his cheek—warm and a little sticky from eating stewed apples before bed. He'd asked for more, with the manners Penny taught him. *Mo peas.*

"Jabe," she whispered, but he didn't flinch. "Wake up."

She smoothed her thumb over a delicate eyelid, then took a silky strand of hair and gently tugged just enough that his lashes fluttered against the edge of her hand.

"Do you know what time it is?"

He blinked then squeezed his eyes tight, pretending to sleep. Clever boy, and only three years old.

"It's night. Let's go outside."

She held his hand as they went down the back stairs, three flights with loud moans and squealing laughter heard on each landing. Outside, an icy nip bit at her eyes. Penny didn't like Lily taking Jabe out at night, but she was too busy to have a say. Besides, Penny had Jabe in the day—bathed and powdered and fed to roundness. In the evening and through the night, he belonged to Lily, warm and milky, soft to hold, fun to play with.

They walked to quiet beaches, where he crouched, shivering and damp, while salty waves licked his feet. It was the seashells he liked, touching a finger to their spines and ridges in the moonlight. He called them *seabows*, so she did too, and it came to be that she would wake him at night and say, *Should we go look for seabows, Jabe?* And he would nod yes.

From her window, Lily watched Penny die—a robust woman taken down by a runaway wagon. Thundering hooves and rattling wheels. The driver shouting in panic. But not a sound from Penny, just a sudden crumpling, a swath of red skirts in the dust.

Lily had been sleeping while Jabe played at the window. Usually Penny watched him in the day, but today she had errands and wanted to visit her sister. It was Penny's scream that startled the horse. Penny's scream that woke Lily. Two sharp notes—*No, Jabe!*—barely out of her mouth before she was trampled.

Lily jumped up to grab him. One step forward and he would have plummeted three stories. As the horse and wagon disappeared down the street, she pressed her face to the back of his neck and stayed that way for some time. Everything slowed. The world below. Her own thoughts, her breath.

They watched in quiet as Penny's limp body was carried inside by her father and one of the cooks. Jabe reached his pudgy hand out the window and said, "Mama." But Lily barely heard him and only fully realized what he'd said much later.

When next Lily turned from the window, her boy was off with the girls, and her arms were empty. She looked back outside. The street was filled with onlookers, men with hats removed and women with hands over their mouths. The police chief and two constables stood in the spot where it had happened, now just marks in the dirt, a little patch of drying blood, black as tar.

Then it was dusk.

One of the girls, Mary, stood at her door, holding Jabe's hand. Her face was streaked with tears and patchy red.

"Poor Penny!" she sobbed, and Lily turned once more to the window. It was all a dream and she would soon wake.

Then Mary was gone and Jabe was asleep in the bed. Lily lay next to him, stared at the ceiling, and imagined it opening to the starry night. Where was Penny now? Nowhere? Vanished. Water boiled out of a kettle. A shadow snuffed once the lamp goes dark.

Gone.

"Everything is all wrong," she said to her father, days later. She pressed her hands into her ribcage, which felt constricted, squeezing her lungs to dust. "Nothing's the same."

Her father had closed the place down. Chairs were on tables, the light through the window dusty and drab. He sat behind the bar with his mercury pills beside him, his body in spasms. The girls wept on the stairs until he shouted at them to go to their rooms.

Because everyone loved Penny. Every single one. People in town loved her, and people who only just met her, they loved her too. And her father. He loved her the most, if only because love was nearly impossible for him.

"You best not talk to me," he said to Lily. He knew why Penny had died and who was to blame. He leaned forward with both hands on the counter. "I open again tomorrow and you need to stay out of my way. Understand? Tell James to rent you a different room, you hear me?"

She nodded, but lingered, one hand on the bar.

"How will it be, though?" she said. "Without our Penny?"

Her father didn't ignore her. He simply didn't listen. So she went upstairs to get Jabe and took him outside, through the back door.

Later that summer, Jabe was gone and their nights at the sea were gone too.

LILY

1882

LIFE HAD SETTLED, AS LIFE DOES, AND EACH YEAR SETTLED further. Until her boy showed again, looking at her with eyes as black and shiny as molasses. A clever boy at eight, but a quiet one—he was like Merritt in this way.

And then a canoe flipped.

One small nothing, and Merritt died and her boy was gone once more. On top of that, James wouldn't return to the city, such was his fear and trembling when it came to her father's wrath.

And Lily continued to drink her tea, letting in all the colour and light.

It was during the winter rains, a month or so after the canoe turned over, when she came back to her flat to find her father had returned. She slumped against the door's frame, her hair wet and sticking to her face. He was on her sofa, his left hand rocking and his other digging around in his mouth. He looked at her, so she smiled.

"You're back." She shut the door, and with the click of the latch, the downpour went from a roar to a whisper. She held onto the cool doorknob behind her back. "Did he tell you?" she asked.

He extracted his hand, and a string of saliva with it. "James? Of course not. He's a coward. I came back because I'm healthy once more."

She kept her eyes on his so they wouldn't drop to his rocking left hand or his foot skewed outward, or his teeth stained black in his mouth.

"It was only an accident," she said. "These things happen all the time."

"Come here." He patted the sofa.

She stepped toward him and sat. He smelled like meat gone rancid. Later, if he let her, she'd run him a bath back at The Jug, but it wouldn't fix the smell inside him.

He looked out the window at the silver sheets of rain. "I won't have you lying to me."

"I don't lie."

He sighed. Closed his eyes for a moment, then looked at her. He had the face of someone sleepy and calm, and it often deceived her. This close and able to see better through his murky glasses, she noticed one of his eyes was as skewed as his foot. And so. The poison was finishing its slow crawl, having now reached his head. The end of a long uphill climb.

She reminded herself to take a breath, her fingers digging deep into the old sofa cushion. She blinked her stinging eyes to dry them.

Bit by bit, everyone left and she was alone.

Lily put her hand on his rocking one and he pulled it away, snatched her by her wet braids at the top of her head and forced her to face the ceiling. The scar on her neck stretched, like fabric pulled taut.

For a while he looked at her. She felt his breath but held her own so she wasn't made to breathe it.

"You're all talk, Lily." He kissed her on the forehead then and let go of her braids. "A little character and so easy to spook. You know you used to be such a frightened thing, even in your sleep?"

She did know.

"Used to wake me with your nightmares," he said.

She remembered that too—his hand pressing her face into the pillow until her crying ceased, as well as her breathing. His hand on her neck, thrusting her to the floor till she scurried far enough under the bed to avoid his grasp. That was what woke her—his hands on her. Not the nightmares.

"Those dreams are your bad side, Lily. Your cunning and deceit come back to wake you."

"Only it was you who woke me."

"See?" He shook his head, sadly. "Filled right up with lies."

"I don't lie."

"Then tell me what happened."

"Uncle James tipped the canoe and lost the whisky." She stood and went to the table. Poured a drink for herself but none for her father, who didn't take liquor. "Merritt drowned in the accident."

"James and Merritt together in the canoe? No one with the wagon?"

"It was only to Sandspit. The risk was small."

She leaned against the table and drank.

"See how you lie? You didn't mention the boy."

She drank again, though her throat was half closed. "He was here with me."

Her father stood and stretched, but weakly. His bones had shrunk but nothing else, so he seemed loose, like a sack of skin over sticks.

"Well now, Lily. You know the boy left James and lost the whisky. You know James blamed Merritt. But I see you prefer to think otherwise. Meanwhile, I'm glad to be rid of the lot. See?" He held out his hands, his smile black. "This frees me from all my burdens—James, a fool I could never rely on; Merritt, a wanderer and a thief."

Her father's mind, once sharp, had softened, become formless and spongy. Still, she knew not to argue.

"Oh, Lily. Did you think these were men of strong character? Did you think Merritt didn't intend to take all our whisky and leave you too? That James didn't kill him for it?"

"He wouldn't."

"So tell me how Merritt came to die in shallow waters? Unless there was a man to hold him under?"

"I wasn't there."

"No. You weren't." He went to the door, one foot dragging. "I'll be staying in the city, now I'm healthy. You can help me at The Jug."

She watched him go, then went to the window and watched through her binoculars. Always she'd asked to work alongside him. Even when she was little, she wanted him near. But it felt all wrong, and her body was vibrating like she was going to be ill.

For two weeks, her father ran the Brown Jug, badly, while she served drinks and cleaned dishes. Creditors came and customers stayed away.

Then one night, he showed up at her door without trousers or boots, baring his dark teeth like a wild dog. She watched him from the other side of the room, her back pressed to the wall, wondering if this time he meant to attack. But he only stared, toothy and wild-eyed, then turned and went silently down the stairs.

She ran to the door and called after him, "Will you come back?" And before he rounded the bend, she called again, "What'll I do if you don't come back?"

BEN

1890

The moon glinted off Ben's new boots as he stood on the Stenhouse porch. He leaned on the doorframe and rested his crutch against the wall. From inside, he heard pots clang and women's voices. All went quiet when he knocked.

One of the twins opened the door, eyeing him with a ladle in her hand. She turned to the women behind her.

"It's Ben!"

"Ah," said Effie firmly, like her suspicions on a matter had just been confirmed.

"Oh dear. You're hurt." Mrs. Stenhouse waved for him to sit at the small table, then tested the heat of the kettle with a finger. "Sarah, slice the bread."

Ben eased himself down, comforted by the warmth of the kitchen, the smell of bacon and onion, the relief of sitting after so many hours. His red hands burned as they thawed, and his bad ankle felt ready to burst his boot. It had taken him twice as long to reach the farm as it should have.

One of the twins took his hat and hung it on a peg as Mrs. Stenhouse placed a bowl of split pea soup in front of him.

"Let me see," she said, nodding to his foot. She was gentle, pressing into his ankle, holding the heel of his boot while tilting the toe.

Ben winced.

"What'd you do?" She unhooked the buttons, but the boot was fixed onto him like rind on a melon.

"I got caught up in some branches. I'm all right."

Mrs. Stenhouse straightened as Sarah set two fat slices of brown bread in front of him. Effie hadn't moved from her spot by the stove.

"We may have to cut that boot right off," said Mrs. Stenhouse.

"I think I can pull it—" Ben reached down and tried to tug until Effie dragged a chair over.

"Here." She sat across from him and patted the top of her good leg. "I can do it." She wrenched it off in one painful jerk as Ben sucked in through his teeth. "You'll be glad I saved it," she said, tossing the boot by the door. "It's a good boot."

Ben's ankle was round and dark as a purple cabbage. It throbbed fiercely now that nothing held it.

Mrs. Stenhouse nodded to the twins. "Make a comfrey bath in the copper tub." She brought him tea, and when she turned back to the stove, Effie added a splash of cooking brandy from a jug on the table.

"I only got your letter this morning," he told her.

"I sent it Friday."

"Sorry. I didn't know."

"You didn't know my letter came for you? Odd."

"I'll talk to your father and explain," he said. "I wrote to him too, you know."

She nodded. "Too late, is all."

"You went all the way to my place?"

"To find it empty," she said, then stood and went back to the stove, where eggs were boiling.

The twins had brought the tub and filled it with water from the kettle. They were talking over one another, telling Ben about the blizzard's damage. The small barn had a busted roof from the weight of the snow. Eight chickens had died, frozen solid with their beaks open wide. Two apple trees had lost limbs. A fir had cracked like thunder down its middle. The cows got buggy and distressed, and two of them were so disoriented from snow blindness they wandered off.

Ben ate spoonful after spoonful of the soup as the twins continued.

"One of the cows is still missing. Father's out looking for her with Eli and Rudy."

"And tell him what Rudy did today," Effie said, her back to them all.

"Effie," sighed Mrs. Stenhouse.

"Tell him, girls."

"He knocked over a lamp in the barn, but Father was there to throw a saddle blanket on it. There's a black spot on the floor."

Effie nodded. "He knocked over a lamp is the point."

While Ben listened, he kept his ear trained on the door. But it wasn't until he was on his third bowl of soup that steps sounded on the porch. He turned to look, setting down his spoon.

Mr. Stenhouse came in first. He looked at his wife and shook his head. "Found her half buried in a snowdrift. Died upright, leaning against a tree." He nodded to Ben. "Good to see you, son."

"I'm sorry I'm late."

Eli stepped in, but Ben's eyes settled on the man behind him. Rudy, who took off his hat and showed himself—damp hair plastered to a perfectly round head, small sticking-out ears, and wide set eyes. He gave the impression of being large and well-built, when in fact he was somewhat compressed, as if all his bones had been shortened and put back together while retaining their girth. He had a friendly look—nothing at all like Effie's description.

"Well now, this must be neighbour Ben," he said.

Ben stood on his good foot to shake Rudy's hand, disappointed to find a regular sort of fellow had taken his place when he'd expected a foolish one.

They ate in the kitchen, making plans for the next day. When finished, they carried their plates to the washbasin.

"You can have the trundle tonight, Ben," said Mrs. Stenhouse.

Ben nodded, knowing her meaning. Rudy had his spot now.

It took Ben time to make his way up the cold stairs, a thick blanket in his arm and his bag over his shoulder. When Mr. Stenhouse cleared his throat from the bottom, Ben stopped and turned.

"When you agree to a job, you'd best be available," he said, his face in shadow under heavy brows and his arm braced against the wall. "You understand?"

"Yes, sir."

"These farmhands never stay long. They get married or they get bored. We'll see how it turns out. In the meantime, we can use your help with the damage from the blizzard."

"Thank you."

"Do you think you can you work on that foot?"

"I'll work."

In Will's room, Eli was crawling into bed, his long underwear so tight he looked like a pale plucked chicken. Ben lay down on the trundle and pulled up the blanket. He blew out the lamp. Eli fell quickly to snoring, and Ben watched the moon out the small window over his head. The same moon hung over the city, reflecting in the harbour. It would be shining over Mae's dark flat while she sweetly slept—and over the preacher's cottage.

Beyond all that, it would be shining on the wide open sea, where men plunged harpoons into the sides of giant whales, then later grieved it. Or farther still, lighting the warm places, where heads were turbaned and forests of orange trees scented the air. It hung over Lily, spending her first night at the creamery. He pictured a row of beds, each filled with a snoring butter girl in a pink or yellow nightdress.

But then he thought, *Lily doesn't sleep at night.*

* * *

Ben woke to a bumping sort of knock on the downstairs door. It was dark and Eli was snoring like an aged hog. Somewhere a bed creaked, and outside two cows lowed.

Ben sat up and slipped his trousers on over his long underwear. He limped down the creaking stairs with his hands braced against either wall, then felt his way to the kitchen door and opened it partway. The night was moonless—so black anything could be standing in front of him and he'd only know by its breath on his face.

He quickly shut the door but listened with his forehead to the wood. Only the usual sounds—an owl, the distant chime of sheep bells. None of the animals were distressed. He latched the door and turned as Mrs. Stenhouse stepped into the kitchen. Ben startled and landed on his bad foot—a tearing burn across his ankle. She lifted her lamp.

"Ben," she whispered, hand to her chest. "You gave me a fright."

"I'm sorry. I heard something—"

"Not that damned cougar, I hope." She spoke with ferocity.

He'd never known a cougar to come up to a house. Or Mrs. Stenhouse to curse.

"No," he said. "I think I dreamed it."

He would have left for his bed, but she stood there still, much softer than he was used to, with her hair down.

"I'm glad to see you again, Ben," she said. "Your mother was a good neighbour, and I feel a certain obligation to look out for you."

"Thank you, Mrs. Stenhouse."

She lowered the lamp to elbow height, throwing shadows on the walls.

"Maybe you don't know this, but I supported Will's going to school in the city." She was whispering so he took a step forward to hear. "I arranged for him to borrow the money. Mr. Stenhouse doesn't know all this. All of my involvement. He'd disapprove."

She held his look, her face tight with some deeper meaning that Ben couldn't make out.

"Will seems to like it there," he said, then tucked his hands under his arms. "Do you think he'll come back?"

"I knew when I helped him that he wouldn't."

It was a strange confession, and Ben felt uncomfortable hearing it.

"Deep down, mothers want this for their sons," said Mrs. Stenhouse. "More than for their daughters, who will always be cared for and less inclined toward independence. Whether or not we admit it, mothers want nothing more than for their sons to walk strongly away." At this she motioned with her arm, as if pushing the air from her side.

"My mother didn't want that."

"She didn't know it yet," she said, more gently. "She didn't live long enough to know it."

Back upstairs, Ben slept fitfully and then woke again to see Effie in the doorway. Eli was gone, and the room was full of grey light. Downstairs, the fire cracked and popped, but the air upstairs had an icy bite.

"You're awake," Effie said. She looked comfortable leaning against the door, and he knew she'd been waiting a while.

He sat up and swung his legs over the edge of the trundle, sending a throbbing rush of blood to his ankle. "I didn't mean to sleep late."

"You're not much good to work yet anyway."

"I can work." He examined his foot. Still purple, but the swelling had gone down some. "Where is everybody?"

"The men have started repairs on the small barn. Was the city terrible?"

"I didn't mind it."

"I wondered. Returning late in a new hat and fancy boots."

"The hat's not really mine."

"That's good. It doesn't suit you. Or fit. Did you see Will?"

Ben nodded, hoping she wouldn't ask more.

"He says he has a girl now." She watched him, biting the edge of her thumbnail.

"I saw a picture of her. She's pretty."

"Well, I could have told you that."

When he said nothing more, Effie relaxed against the doorframe. "And James's niece? Did you see her?"

Ben leaned forward and put his head in his hands. "I'll tell you all that later."

"Fine."

Effie reached outside the door and brought in a wooden board—or rather, three boards wired together, flat. She turned it around to show Ben the front.

He got up and limped nearer in his long underwear. Paper had been pasted on the boards, where she'd painted a woodsy scene. But nothing was quite as it should be, everything a little untrue—smooth brown bark and flat blue sky, trees that curved, fine and orderly and all in the same direction. Near the edge, a cabin.

Effie lowered the picture. "You don't like it."

"I like it. Is it my cabin?"

"Yes it's your cabin."

She swung the painting around and carried it back to the room she shared with her sisters, her brace clanging with each step. Ben leaned, one-footed, against Will's doorway and waited as something slid along her floorboards and a cupboard shut firmly.

When she came out of the room, he said, "I just wasn't used to it."

"You don't have to like it, Ben." She started down the stairs. "You're all bones now. Come and eat."

After getting dressed, Ben went down to the kitchen. Out the window, he saw Effie with the other women hanging wet laundry in the snowy yard. Near them, a steaming cauldron cooled over dying embers.

He grabbed an apple and his crutch and headed out to the small log barn. It was one of the first buildings Mr. Stenhouse had built on this land and had since become a shed for storage. A ragged hole gaped wide in the roof, where Mr. Stenhouse and Rudy were perched, looking at the damage.

As Ben took it all in, Eli walked past with a jar of nails. He flicked his finger against Ben's new hat.

"What's this thing all about, anyway?" he said, continuing on into the barn.

Ben clamped his front teeth down on an apple seed, tasted its bitter tang, then spit it out and went inside, where Eli was scrambling up a ladder into the rafters.

It felt strange being in the little barn with dusty light falling through an open roof. Ben's old cow was penned in the corner, staring dumbly at the wall. She'd been set aside for slaughter, first surviving the roof's collapse and then the slaughter itself as the men's attention turned to repairs around the farm after the blizzard.

Ben petted her large head. "Lucky girl," he said, but then he thought perhaps not. A swift death without the waiting may have been a mercy for the old cow, as it was coming for her either way.

With only one foot to bear his weight, Ben was given the job of splitting new shingles. The twins helped by sorting through the fallen shakes to salvage any that could be reused. They were rambunctious workers, chattering gleefully.

The men above talked as well. Eli and Rudy seemed to have developed a friendliness between them, but Ben figured Rudy was the type who'd be friendly with anyone. A few times he poked his head through the hole in the roof and called down, "How you holding up, fella? How's the weather down there in the hollows?"

Ben's hatchet was dull and he had no whetstone, so he grabbed his crutch and made his way across the yard to the large barn. It was empty of animals, but birds were conversing in the rafters, and at the sight of him, a cat tore for the shadows. The only other sound was the distant and irregular hammering from the small barn. After the city, he wasn't used to quiet and felt strangely exposed.

Mr. Stenhouse used one corner of shelves and hooks to keep his tools, and Ben found the whetstone exactly where he knew it would be. But before leaving, he looked at the closed door of the back room. He limped over and nudged it open.

Nothing had changed at all. A cold and simple room, with little sign that Rudy lived in it over any other man—a stove, a cot, a blanket, and a wooden box under a washstand. Ben sat on the bed and pulled out the box, his ears pricked for approaching steps as he lifted the lid.

Everything inside was neatly arranged. A family photograph of ageing parents with Rudy and half a dozen other round-faced sons. A new-looking Bible. A pair of thick socks, patched at the heel. A blue ribbon from a fair. A stack of letters. A painted rock—*RASCAL RUDY WHISTLES LEWDLY.* Half a chocolate bar, wrapped in foil, and a perfectly fine tooth, folded in paper.

Ben replaced the lid and pushed the box back under the washstand. Mr. Stenhouse was probably right. Rudy seemed to have no intention of settling long at the farm.

He stood carefully, looking out the barn doors and across the lumpy white yard, where the path ran the long way to the house. A house he knew almost as well as his own. The chimney was smoking, and Mrs. Stenhouse was shaking out a rug on the porch. From here, she looked small and faceless. He left, shutting the door quietly behind him.

By day's end, Ben's foot was throbbing badly. He carried his plate and fork to the table and sat next to Effie. Her features seemed sharper by firelight—narrow eyes, thin brows, lips pressed together.

She hadn't spoken much to him that day, aside from the usual things when she and Sarah brought lunch out. *Take another slice of bread. You have shavings in your hair.* And when the old cow pressed her head against Ben's shoulder while he was eating, Effie had said, "She hasn't paid at bit of mind to anyone else the whole time she's been here."

Mrs. Stenhouse set a cold pie on the table.

"You'll need to go to town for black beans and molasses," she said to Mr. Stenhouse. "Three times now Mrs. Petrenko has promised to order more, but her bins are still empty."

Mr. Stenhouse dipped his bread in the gravy. "She's slipping."

Ben looked up. "Slipping?"

"Losing her mind," said Effie, then she looked at her mother. "I'll go see her after the baking tomorrow. I've helped her with her accounts before, I'm sure I can figure out how to do up an order."

"I just saw her..." Ben thought back to his visit—the dusty shelves, the wide-open door, Mrs. Petrenko's nightdress hanging off thin shoulders.

"My uncle had a similar affliction," said Rudy. "Each morning, he mistook me for his son who'd died years previous. I played along and he was quite contented."

"Oh Rudy, how sad—," Sarah began, but then Eli arrived, late to the table and loud in his boots.

"Excuse me," he said, pushing behind Ben's chair and bringing the cold air with him.

When Ben inched forward to make room, he caught sight of Eli's hand on Effie—thumb and fingers curled around the back of her neck—then gone before anyone noticed. He continued on to his place beside Sarah and plunked down.

"I do love your kidney pie, Mrs. Stenhouse," he said, dishing out a large piece. "My mother never cooked so well."

Mrs. Stenhouse looked up, her face tight. "You shouldn't say such things."

"I only meant a compliment."

"Mrs. Stenhouse makes an excellent crust," Mr. Stenhouse said, head bent over his plate.

While the twins were describing a school project, Effie leaned over to Ben and whispered, "Father's been sentimental since Will left. No one's quite used to it."

Ben tucked his hurt foot under his chair to protect it from all the other feet crammed under the table. "That's nice, though, isn't it?" he whispered back. Effie shrugged.

"Eli, you should share your idea with everyone." Sarah looked at her father. "He's looking to go into business for himself."

Everyone waited as Eli wiped his mouth.

"Soap," he said, setting down his napkin. "There's no manufacturer yet in the region. Shops order it from Seattle or people make it themselves."

Sarah beamed. "Scented soap. For ladies."

"Lemon, lavender..." Eli circled his hand. "Cedarwood."

"That's fine for those who can afford it," said Mrs. Stenhouse. "Most women prefer to make their own, of course."

Ben leaned forward. "Actually, there is a soap factory in the city."

"I'm sure you're mistaken, Ben," said Sarah. "Eli looked into it."

Eli smiled. "Let's just say, in all my research, I found no such business."

"I met the owner," said Ben. "It's called Wonderful Soap. Made with cloves." He looked around the table and faces stared back like he was some strange animal. He rarely shared an opinion at the Stenhouse table. Effie smiled.

"You really are full of surprises, Ben. You weren't gone two weeks and you return to us newly outfitted with a swollen foot and tales of spiced soap."

"Well," said Eli, eating another bite of pie. "I don't care to argue, so I'll let him have it."

"That's generous," said Effie. "And I wish your venture every success. I've always wanted to smell like a woodpile."

Ben was washing his dish when Mr. Stenhouse called him out to the porch. He stacked his plate on the others and went outside. Mr. Stenhouse looked comfortable in his chair in a cloud of pipe smoke, the smell like leather and cherries. Ben sat next to him.

"Have you figured what you want to do with James's land?" Mr. Stenhouse asked.

Ben leaned forward with his elbows on his knees and looked over at him, all sharp bones and heavy moustache.

"I hadn't thought anything," he said. "It's not mine."

"Well, I considered all that and talked to an acquaintance who knows. As James's ward, you can petition quite easily for the property. Unless there's a will? Some written statement?"

Ben shook his head. "I didn't see anything like that. Only the deed."

Mr. Stenhouse nodded, then straightened his back and looked at the first stars over the black lake. "You see, I'd like to buy that land if you have no need for it. It'll be auctioned off if no one lays claim to it, but I'd rather see the money go to you. That is, if you don't want the property yourself."

Ben felt a quick curling inward, belly to spine. More money was a problem he didn't want, and he had no interest in going back to that cabin.

"You may not need money now," said Mr. Stenhouse, watching him, "but you can sock it away. Use it when the time is right, and one day it will be."

"Yes, sir. Thank you." Ben cricked his neck, then said, "I think you should know that land's no good."

"There'd be work to do," Mr. Stenhouse said. "I'm aware of that."

"I mean to say, it's bad somehow. Everything there dies."

He imagined Mr. Stenhouse walking the yard where the cow lay dead, where the two graves were sunk into the weedy ground, where the goats had died with legs swollen like clubs, and the apple trees were twisted and marred with disease.

"Sounds like regular land," Mr. Stenhouse said. "Things living and dying."

They looked out at the fields and the lake. The snow glittered in the moonlight, having partly thawed before freezing again. Rudy's lamp flickered faintly from his small window at the back of the large barn.

"How much, do you think?"

"Since there's no road and it's not cleared, I can only offer you five hundred dollars."

"Five hundred." Ben let his head thump gently against the log wall behind him. "Well," he said, "that's a lot."

That night, Ben hardly slept, turning over thoughts of his father's tainted land and Mr. Stenhouse's offer. What seemed a burden, on first hearing it, grew warm in his mind as he lay in the dark next to Eli's snoring. Of course he'd first get Lily a place. Then he'd pay Mae what was owed, and more. He'd get a new hat, one that didn't try to press his brains out his ears. Paints for Effie, if she'd accept them. A book for Will's schooling. And books for himself. Cinnamon cake. Socks. A haircut. It meant another trip to the city, if he could be spared for it. And he didn't mind that much at all.

In the morning, after filling their bellies with a full breakfast—biscuits and jam, beans, bacon, and strong coffee—the men went back to the barn repairs. Ben left his crutch behind in his hurry to catch Mr. Stenhouse. Without looking back, Mr. Stenhouse slowed his stride.

"I thought about it last night," Ben said. "I'll sell you that land if you still want it."

"I'm glad to hear it." Mr. Stenhouse stopped and faced Ben. He reached out his hand and they shook. "Once things settle, we'll go into town and get you squared away."

"Yes, sir."

Eli was already on the roof and Mr. Stenhouse climbed up to join him. Rudy, coming from the large barn, caught up to Ben with a friendly good morning.

"And how's the old cabbage treating you this day?"

"Getting better. Thanks."

Ben worked alone alongside the old cow, as the twins were in the house for a day of bread baking. The job was nearly done, and Ben hoped Mr. Stenhouse would have more work for him. Or better yet, that Rudy would be ready to move on and there would be plenty of work for Ben. The men above were discussing Eli's new venture. Or rather, Eli spoke while Rudy tossed in the odd thought. Mr. Stenhouse worked silently.

Halfway through the day, the men went quiet, and Mr. Stenhouse came down the ladder. He walked by Ben and out into the yard. Ben shaded his eyes against the glare of sun off snow as Mr. Stenhouse met with a man on a horse.

"Someone from the city, looks like," Rudy said to Eli.

A short while later, Eli came down the ladder and went out into the yard. Rudy peeked at Ben from the rafters.

"Some kind of news, I reckon."

Ben finished stacking shingles. When neither man returned, he looked outside again and saw Mr. and Mrs. Stenhouse leaving in their sleigh. No sign of Eli.

Ben called up to Rudy, "Should we go see if we're needed?"

Crossing the yard, Rudy slowed his walk and offered the use of his shoulder, which Ben declined. Rudy was cheerful and untroubled, but Ben knew when things were unsettled—the stillness in the air, the quiet.

They found all four daughters in the kitchen, with Eli near the door, his face flushed pink. He stepped farther in, allowing room for Ben and Rudy.

Sarah stood at the window, staring into the empty yard. "Mother would never recover," she was saying.

Ben looked at Effie.

"Will's poorly," she said. "He's in hospital."

There wasn't much to discuss, since not much was known. Will had been sick for a few days, then his fever worsened and he became delirious. Mrs. Lockwood called Dr. Silman, and he ordered Will to be taken to St. Joseph's Hospital. A messenger was dispatched to the farm.

Ben stood against the wall, wishing he could disappear into it. He should have burned Will's sheets. Or taken them with him and tossed them somewhere. He shouldn't have gone there in the first place.

"Aw, well now," said Rudy. "I sure will say a prayer for Will tonight."

"Has that worked for you in the past, Rudy?" said Effie. Then she turned to the three bowls of puffy bread dough and plunged her fist into each. The dough deflated around her thin wrist.

"I say it's worth a try anyhow."

"Mr. Stenhouse has left me in charge," said Eli, recovering his usual manner. "We'll work as if he was here. Let's finish that roof."

When Rudy and Eli left, Ben stayed back. He looked at Effie. She was furiously kneading dough on a floured board while the twins greased pans. Sarah remained at the window. But he found he had nothing to say, so he left.

In the barn, the cow swung her great head to look at him, but Ben didn't pet her. As he stacked the shingles, he tried to think of what Mr. Stenhouse would have him do next, but he couldn't focus. His thoughts kept shifting to Will, sweating in a hospital bed.

Eli whistled through the battens, and Ben looked up to see him peering down through a gap.

"I see you, Dandy Ben in the fine hat. No speed but slow, eh?"

Ben had little room in his mind for the likes of Eli, so he carried on without altering his pace. Then he swept the place out. He sharpened and put away the hatchet, and to keep himself busy, began chopping wood to add to the already large woodpile.

When the sun lowered behind the trees, they crossed the yard to the pump. Their boots crunched old snow and their breath came in clouds. They washed in turns, each man gasping as the icy water hit his face.

In the warm and yeasty kitchen, they all stood around the edges eating fresh bread and cold beans. Sarah reassured everyone that Will was young and strong, that he'd be fine. With some effort, Ben took comfort in that.

"Of course he'll be fine," said Eli. "It's insulting to think otherwise of a strapping young man."

"You didn't look so sure earlier, Eli," said Effie. "You looked like a roasted goose, all dark in the face."

"Effie, not tonight," said Sarah. "Let's all sit in the back room. I'll read, so we can keep our worries at bay before we sleep."

Rudy built a fire while they took down chairs, brought them into the sitting room, and crowded them around the hearth. Sarah stood by the fireplace and read a poem about a great eagle who was close to the sun on its mountain perch. The azure sky was frigid as it watched the wrinkled sea below.

After a bit, Eli stood and put his arm around Sarah, reading over her shoulder and mouthing each word with a nod of his head, as though reciting a school lesson. He was the sort to enjoy the discomfort of others, the sort who made a joke of it. Sarah shifted, uncertain, then looked up at him and smiled before continuing on. For the final line, she strengthened her voice, lifting her arm and dropping it.

"And like a thunderbolt, he falls."

Eli slipped a finger onto the page and closed the book.

"I say we take turns tonight, Sarah. Poems get a little dreary, don't they?"

He placed the book back on the small shelf and picked up Mr. Stenhouse's old Bible, long unused.

"I think it's time we behave as good Christians."

Sarah sat, her cheeks flushed. When Eli assumed her pose—one arm raised, the other holding the Bible, open on his palm—she attempted to smile. Behind her, the twins giggled.

"She revealed her harlotry," Eli read solemnly, "and uncovered her nakedness."

Sarah looked up sharply and was about to speak, but Eli lifted a finger to quiet her. "Then I turned in disgust from her, as I had turned in disgust from her sister. Yet she multiplied her harlotry—"

"Eli, for goodness sake," said Sarah. "Why not read from the Psalms?"

"Because the Psalms would garner no reaction from anyone," said Effie. "If you want him to stop, Sarah, say nothing."

Eli continued, unchanged in tone or manner. "For she lusted for her paramours, whose genitals are like the genitals of donkeys, and whose issue is like the issue of horses."

Rudy guffawed, and Eli looked up, pretending confusion. "Is something funny?"

"Not in the least," said Effie.

From above the open Bible, Eli shifted his look to her. "It's all in good fun, Effie. Everyone's so glum."

"Do you mean we're concerned for our brother?"

"Concern is well and good, but so is a little chuckle now and then. I didn't take you for a prude."

Ben put his elbows on his knees and stared at the floor. Eli and Effie continued to bicker as Sarah tried to dissuade them both. Finally,

Ben stood and dragged his chair into the dining room, where he hung it back on the wall.

From the kitchen, he heard one of the twins say, "You riled Ben."

He added some wood to the stove and filled the kettle, then he took down the copper tub from the high shelf. He could hear Eli attempting to read further, but Sarah sent the twins to bed and soon everyone dispersed.

When Ben turned, he saw Effie in the doorway.

"Do you agree now?" she said, her voice a loud whisper. "She could marry any man, and she chooses a buffoon."

"I never disagreed with that."

Rudy walked through the kitchen with a nod and a smile. "Good night to you both," he said and headed outside for the barn, leaving a cold swell of night air behind him.

Ben pulled the blankets from under the stove and handed them to Effie. They both sat, treating their pains—he with his foot in the tub and she with her leg bundled on the chair.

"Aren't we a pair," Effie said, sighing. "Slow workers. And not much good to anyone when things go awry. You're too quiet and I'm too mean."

Ben picked at the chair underneath the seat, working the wood with his fingernail.

"It's my fault, you know," he said.

"What is?"

"Will."

He looked at the stairs, just visible through the kitchen doorway. Above them, the floor creaked as everyone readied for bed.

"I was sick when I saw him. I stayed in his room."

Effie raised a brow, then looked into the fire, biting her thumb. She nodded firmly.

"All right. You may not want to tell anyone else that."

"I was well in a few days."

He waited, as if she could promise the same for Will, but she didn't. She folded her arms tightly over her chest and watched the flames leap in the stove.

"Don't tell anyone," she said again. "It wouldn't help anything, would it?"

He looked up at the heavy ceiling beams. Secrecy didn't feel right either, but it was the simplest. Maybe the kindest. The sliver he was picking at dislodged and he flinched. A crescent of blood quickly pooled under his nail.

Effie watched Ben suck his finger then wipe it on his pants.

"I suppose they'll bring him back?" he said.

"When he's well enough."

They sat in silence for a while, then Ben stood and went outside to empty his tub off the porch. Effie left her blanket in a heap on the chair, and they both went upstairs, a limping pair. They said good night on the landing.

Eli was already in Will's bed, hands behind his head. As Ben stripped down to his long underwear, he heard the rattle of Effie's brace as she unhinged it, hook by hook, pin by pin. He crawled under his blanket on the trundle, then blew out the lamp.

"I wonder," Eli said, invisible in the dark, "why you continue to stay in this house. Given you're not family and not even the hired man."

A bedspring creaked twice in the girl's room.

"I don't consider what you think at all," Ben said.

A silent dawn, dusty and purple. His mother held his hands. He looked at her face. It was changed—eyes rimmed with black, lips smeared red. Her long orange braid moved snake-like on her shoulder as she rubbed her thumbs along his knuckles.

See what these can do?

Ben pulled away, but his hands remained in her grip, cleanly severed. They dripped dark blood, like molasses, into the grass at her feet.

Benjamin, garde ta rage.

Ben sat up sharply, slick with sweat and breathless. Downstairs, something thumped at the door.

The moon was high, shining through the window and showing the vague shape of Eli's blankets. It took a moment for Ben to see they were pushed back and Eli wasn't there. He listened. Footsteps crunched the snow outside.

He lit the lamp and turned it low, stepped into his trousers, and limped across the landing. With the lamp held high, he looked into the room Effie shared with her sisters. One bed held the twins, and the other had only Sarah, with an empty spot beside her. He went down the stairs, slow on each creaking step.

Leaving his lamp on the kitchen table, he pulled on his boots and went outside. The moon cast blue light on the lumpy snow in the yard. All the outbuildings were dark but the small barn, where a yellow light flickered in the window. As Ben neared, he heard the low tone of Eli's voice, thick like mud.

He didn't slow, but walked right up, ears pricked to hear Eli take a sharp breath, and then a quiet laugh. Ben pushed open the door.

Eli had his back to Ben, and Effie was sitting on the top rail of the cow's pen. She was lit by the quivering light of the lamp at her feet, with steam from the old cow's breath rising behind her.

Though Effie's eyes were in shadow, Ben knew she was looking at him. She dropped the hem of her nightdress, and, with her other hand, held the top closed.

At that same moment, Eli jumped, a skittery two-step as he buttoned his trousers. When he turned, his eyes were panicked, but only for a moment. Seeing Ben, his face fell back into calm and he smiled.

"Seems we have a Peeping Tom, Effie."

Ben looked at Effie again. She was pulling a blanket around her shoulders, the old cow behind her groaning and stomping, steam rising off her back.

"You hate Eli," he said to her.

Effie lowered herself to the ground and walked toward the barn door, leaving her boots and brace beside the flickering lamp on the floor.

"You show up at the worst times, don't you?" she said. "Too late to help my father, and now too early to this barn." She spoke weakly, her eyes on the ground, but as she came closer to Ben, she looked at him straight. Her voice hardened. "Too sick to be visiting Will's dorm, and now look."

Effie passed both men, cheeks dark and eyes wet, and limped barefoot toward the house.

Eli shook his finger at Ben. "I see what you are. A deviant, as they say."

Ben turned to go, but Eli stepped in front of him. He was short, and Ben felt strong looking down on a soft little man that pretended at coolness.

"I'll remind you, since you may not have puzzled it out, that it's Effie who will pay the price if you say anything."

"And Sarah."

"Yes, I dare say both women would suffer."

"Effie can't stand to be around you."

"And yet she's shown herself to me three times. I guess you don't know her so well."

Eli turned to leave, but stopped and tipped his hat. "I put on a small performance for Effie and she found it amusing. The Boy in the Ridiculous Hat."

Ben noticed now what sat tall and new on Eli's well-greased head. He snatched for it but missed as Eli stepped aside.

"Whoa now," Eli said, both hands raised. "Do you not think I'm handsome? A regular dandy in my high-class attire?" He took off the hat and pressed it to his belly, bowing deeply.

"It was a gift," Ben said.

"A gift?"

Eli held the hat out as if admiring it, his smile showing small, perfect teeth. Then, with a quick flick of his wrist, he flung it out the door.

Ben lunged, hitting the ground hard with Eli beneath him. A crack against the railing, a shatter of glass. Ben's fists were directionless, wild, hitting muscle, bone, packed earth. He felt hot and strong, Eli a wriggling pig under his weight, hair splayed like slick fronds against the straw. Ben's ears hummed like a nest of hornets, drowning out Eli, whose mouth moved in gaping, soundless words, blood in his teeth.

Ben's spine cracked as he flipped and hit the ground. Eli was on top now. He felt a blow to his cheekbone, a realignment of his face. The hornets grew louder, and his eyes flickered closed. Behind his lids, he saw his mother, in flashes of lightning—a snap of her flame-orange hair, sparking static, then gone.

Eli pushed off Ben's chest with both hands, his full weight forcing the last bit of air out of Ben's lungs.

And Ben was alone.

Flattened to the ground, he turned his head and watched Eli flail away across the moonlit yard, slipping in the snow. Ben felt no pain. His breath returned, the hornets in his head quieted, and sound came back to him—the cow, bucking and moaning, a windy crackle, Eli shouting in the distance, the pop of burning wood.

"*Fire!*"

Ben scrambled to his feet. Flames were climbing the posts from Effie's shattered lamp, grasping upward like wicked hands. Behind them, the cow bellowed and thrashed in her stall. Ben sought an opening through the fire, or some way around. His face was scorched and his lungs full of smoke. There was no way through.

So he ran, feet on air.

Across the yard, Eli scrambled from the large barn toward the pump with four buckets. Rudy was fast behind him. Eli pumped and Rudy took off with a full bucket in each hand, then Ben. The fire had engulfed half the little barn, the cow silent somewhere inside it. Ben threw the water, as good as spitting, and ran back. Now the girls were at the pump, forming a line.

They worked fast, black figures against the flames, the twins running empty buckets back.

They worked without stopping, but it made no difference. The flames devoured the barn.

By dawn, they were still dousing the smoking wreckage, shivering in their sweat-drenched clothes. Melted snow hissed along the edges as they surveyed the damage. Rough looking figures, all of them—faces smudged and hair singed, their knuckles skinned and pink.

The old cow's black and peeling carcass lay in a tangle of charred timbers, her legs sticking straight out like branches from a swollen stump. Ben felt worse about the cow than the fire or what came before it. She'd been led to death many times over, only to meet it in the cruelest way.

For a while, no one spoke, but they were all no doubt thinking about Mr. and Mrs. Stenhouse, and their return with Will.

"Why are you bleeding?" one of the twins asked Eli. Her eyes shifted to Ben and studied his face, then landed back on Eli. "Did you fight with Ben?"

"You two go wash up," said Sarah. "Effie and I will get breakfast on."

But Sarah didn't go inside. Instead, she spoke to Eli. "You boys'll have to explain this to my father. You best get your stories straight."

She turned back to the house and Effie went with her.

Eli stared blankly at the smouldering rubble. He didn't seem aware of Ben's presence until he happened to look at him, stunned and exhausted.

Ben almost felt bad, but stopped himself. Instead, he scanned the snow for his hat. When he found it, he felt with his finger the two singed holes on the rim, the scuff along the top.

"I'm only sorry for the cow," he said to Eli, placing the hat on his head. "And for Mr. Stenhouse's barn."

"As you should be," Eli said, taking it for an apology. He turned and followed the girls to the house, leaving Ben alone with the ruins.

From the porch, Sarah spoke in a strained voice. "Effie! Where in heaven are your boots?"

Ben looked into the fallen beams until he saw them, both charred, one taller than the other. How would they explain any of it?

He washed at the pump, splashing his face and scrubbing his hands. The icy water soothed his parched skin, so he pumped more and drank until he thought he'd be sick.

After drying his face with his shirt, he looked down the long drive. The sun was low and the sky pale orange along the black tree line. Above that, stars still shone in the deep blue. He found his crutch along the side of the house and began the long walk down the Stenhouse drive.

JAMES

1872

HE LOOKED LIKE A FOOL IN THIS GARB. BAGGY MOLESKIN pants, red shirt, and blue cloth cap. Like some sort of elfin creature in a children's book. He'd waited three days before realizing that Connie wasn't bailing him out.

His job was to carry large rocks from here to there. That was the whole of it, all day long, and it would last for three months. Each big rock pressing him into the ground, the shackles and chains holding his feet inches apart. Drop it on the pile of rocks, then back to do it again, pigeon-footed and panting.

A whole gang of men—shuffle-shuffle, grunt, shuffle-shuffle, drop. Chains rattling. Under-the-breath curses. Grunting, spitting, hacking, a whole gang of them, and James no better or worse. Just another man carrying rocks.

James felt the sharp edges scraping through the fabric of his shirt, the grit and heft in his arms. His ear smarted, what was left of it. He would show it to his brother. *See where you left me? See how I am now?*

On the third day, when he realized Connie wasn't coming for him, he'd lost his temper with wild Baron, a cross-eyed youth accused of burning down his mother's house and taking a girl cousin, too young, for himself. Baron had stood along the wall, managing his private business right there in the open, and James yelled at him to quit it now. *You feckin' deviant.*

The boy flew at him, ungodly strong for his age, and tore into his ear with his teeth. Ferocious as a wild dog, growling and slobbering. After pulling the boy off and locking him away, the prison guard had sealed James's ear shut with a hot poker. When James screamed, Baron's laughter came loud and hooting from the cellar.

The whistle blew and all the men, James one of them, began their long shuffle back to the jail. They went along the harbour and right past the Brown Jug, where he paid for Lily's room out of his own pocket. And now look at him. His eyes turned wet, stinging in the cool ocean air. Who looked out for James Maclean? Not one person. Not ever.

Instead, James looked out for everyone. Did Connie care for his own daughter while she convalesced? Or before that? No! Did he risk his own self for the profit of another? Of course not.

And would James confront Connie, like a man of strength and bearing? Would he boldly speak up for himself? Or would he continue on, knees trembling, bowing to his brother's every demand?

It hadn't always been this way. When they were small, his younger brother had reached for his hand. James had fed him and held him till he slept, while their mother grieved lost children by the window. In some ways, James was the mother, though he'd never say it aloud. When had Con turned? And when did James?

Eyes to the sky, he sniffed and cried as they moved slow and steady. All together, they were like one big snake on its belly, moving past the courthouse, then down the brick passage into the dark jail.

When he was finally released, James walked straight to the Brown Jug, where Connie shrugged and said Lily had left.

"It's Merritt who took her, along with the baby," Penny said, blinking away tears. She reached out as though to touch his arm, but stopped herself. "She'll be back, James."

So he had left as hastily as he came, his thoughts a painful scatter, like pebbles firing off the walls of his skull. He couldn't grab hold of just one. His hate for Merritt. His worry for Lily. The unfairness from his brother. And Agda. He stopped at an alley. Stepped down its cool dark passage and waited for his mind to settle.

What was he going to tell Agda?

He talked it out as his boots crushed twigs and cones on the long path home. He knew one thing: Agda would go batty if he told her the truth. She was a wilder woman than she looked. A ferocious mother, but a childless one. Look out for that.

He thought of his own mother when she delivered a blue baby girl. Blood spread wide and bright on the quilt beneath her, the neighbour woman shrieking out the window for help. The panic and the people and his mother covered in a sheet while he and Con watched from the corner. The baby so blue—a storm cloud in the shape of a tiny limp person.

James found Agda waiting on the porch.

He hadn't seen her since before he was locked up, but she had sent him letters that he kept under his shirt, where they became soft and worn from reading. He slowed as he approached her, sorting the lies in his head as she waited. Her eyes were filled with dread.

"It died," he said. There. Over and done with. "Strangled as it came out."

She stood.

"A blue baby," he continued, and when he described the blood and stillness, he felt the crushing of his own insides as if it were the truth. He went inside and sat in his chair.

"I'm hungry," he said. Anything to fill the silence.

That night, Agda didn't come to bed. When he woke to use the chamber pot, she still sat by the stove, now gone cold. On her lap were the tiny clothes she'd made. In the morning, these were put away. James sawed the rockers off the cradle and used the pieces to patch a leaking pig trough. Later, he watched Agda pluck a chicken on the porch, her skirts in the mud, her bare feet slick in it.

"You'll track dirt in like that," he said, astonished at her carelessness.

And she did. Muddy prints when he came inside hours later with three squirrels over his shoulder. Dried-up mud leading from door to bed to stove many times over. Later, when he found her in the bed in broad daylight, he flipped back the sheets. More mud, everywhere.

"You've lost your mind, woman." And then, softly, "What's wrong with you, anyway?"

BEN

1890

IT WAS MIDDAY WHEN BEN REACHED THE CREAMERY, WHICH was, as Lily had told him, just outside the city. Four squat stone buildings, a farmhouse, and a small log springhouse over the creek—all of it sitting on partly cleared land that sloped down to a dark pond. The rancid smells of manure and sour milk masked any smell of the nearby ocean, but seagulls called wildly in the sun as a reminder that it was near.

Three butter girls walked with weighted buckets across the trodden and muddy yard, the hems of their pale dresses wet and their hair slipping from the knots at their necks. They chattered like birds, but stopped and squinted into the sun when they saw Ben approach.

"I'm here to see Lily," he said. "Do you know where she is?"

The oldest scrunched her brow and the other two looked at each other.

"She came a few days ago." He angled a hand near his ear. "Hair cut short? Blue dress?"

"There's no Lily here," one of them said. She pointed her chin at him. "What happened to you?"

Ben shook his head, then looked back down the road where he'd come from. Everything shimmered wet and white, making his dry eyes burn.

"A barn fire," he said. "Where's the preacher?"

* * *

Ben waited at a scarred oak table in the kitchen. He turned his hat in his hands, the tips of his fingers drawn to the scorch marks and holes. A woman in a dirty apron worked at the stove, plodding and slow. She cast miserable looks at Ben when his bouncing knees squeaked the floorboards, which he couldn't seem to stop doing.

"Sorry," he said, but before he knew it, she was glaring again and he realized his knees had started bouncing without him knowing.

Finally, quick steps sounded on the porch, and the door flew open. The preacher hurried in.

"Ben!" He stopped at the sight of him. "You appear to have been battling a fire."

"A barn fire." Ben looked at his hands, seeing only now that the skin along the knuckles had peeled off, and the small singed holes along his sleeves and more on his pants. He hadn't yet seen his face, but he felt it—tight and dry, lips parched, with a tender swelling along his cheekbone. He would be a sight.

The preacher poured a cup of water and handed it to him. "The girls said a young man was looking for a woman named Lily and I said to myself, now that sounds like Ben."

He clapped Ben on the shoulder, hitting on some bruised bone, then went to the stove and dished out porridge.

"I've come to get her," said Ben. "If she wants."

The preacher plopped the steaming bowl in front of Ben, then did the same for himself. He sat on the other side of the table with a smile.

"She's not here, friend. She must have changed her mind about coming."

Ben shook his head. "I was with her. I brought her. Well, partway."

The preacher leaned back in his chair and blinked. "I don't know what to tell you. Sounds like she went back home."

"She has no home."

"Maybe she found a different job," said the plodding girl, her ladle dripping porridge clumps on the floor. "Maybe she met a friend."

None of which sounded likely to Ben.

"Martha, why don't you round up the girls and see if anyone has seen her."

Martha took her time taking off her apron. She ate a couple of spoonfuls of porridge from the pot, then walked heavily out the front door with her boots untied. Meanwhile, the preacher gathered items from around the kitchen—strips of flannel, a jar of salve, a bowl of warm water from the kettle. He sat across from Ben and dabbed at the cuts and burns on his hands, then smeared green ointment across them.

"What do you think about cheese?" the preacher said, as he wrapped soft flannel around Ben's knuckles. "I'm considering getting into cheesemaking, since our butter is such a hot seller, but the girls all said no." He looked at Ben and smiled. "They think they won't like the smell."

"I don't know much about cheese," Ben said, watching out the window. Martha was crossing the yard with a dozen girls alongside her. He recognized some—the pocked and pregnant one, the young one who stared. They came inside, rosy faces and heavy boots.

"No one's seen a new girl," said Martha. "But here. Ask them yourself."

They shook their heads solemnly, and Ben looked back at the preacher.

"Well now, young Benjamin, it's entirely within Lily's choosing to go where she pleases." He shrugged, his smile easy and bright. "Did you really think her suited to a place like this?"

AGDA

1875

EACH TIME SHE READ THE LETTER, AGDA'S HAND SHOOK and her heart knocked wildly inside her. For three nights, she didn't sleep. She'd always heard from her nephews at Christmas, her nieces a little more often. But this was unexpected. Maurice, her favourite, was coming to the island.

I, along with my new wife, Edith, will stay at The Occidental on Yates Street.

She knew immediately that she must go, though the prospect made her ill and absent-minded, with frequent trips to the outhouse and supper badly burned.

Agda had not been to the city since her visit to pregnant Lily, three years previous, when the sun had scorched her back and dried the ground to fine dust. When the paper-wrapped calico dress she'd carried left a sweat mark on her side. All these same nervous ailments struck her then as well. She'd stood in Lily's room, feeling the wall behind her, to be sure she remained upright.

Agda had thought often of the girl since then, wondering how she'd fared after losing the baby. She sent small packets for Lily with James—a shawl, a jar of blackberry preserves, a packet of bluebell seeds. They were, after all, both grieving. Perhaps she would visit Lily once more while in the city, bring her some small comfort. The night before she left, Agda wrapped a round of goat cheese and filled a handkerchief with plums.

In the morning, she saddled the horse and left early, while the trail was still deep in shadow and the singing birds hidden. She felt sick to her stomach and had to stop and dismount three times. James had been away and didn't know of her plans. She wondered what he would say if she ran into him. He would think she was bold or unhinged. Perhaps he wouldn't recognize her at all against the backdrop of a city. Just another woman on a horse. The thought made her mouth twitch, but the terror of city streets still clung to her, burrowed deep and gnawing at her gut.

She stabled the horse near The Occidental, a long blue building with lace curtains and a wide plank breezeway. The lobby was cool and darkly panelled, with tall palms in the corners. She stood near one of these and pretended to adjust the cuff of her sleeve. The man behind the desk watched her with patient curiosity.

"I'm looking for my nephew," Agda said, peeking around a wide, glossy frond. "Maurice Blom and his wife, Edith."

"Oh, yes. The Bloms. They rented a skiff and went for a picnic. They said they'd likely be back at four o'clock. I'm to show you your room." With a kind smile, he held out his hand, indicating the wide staircase. "If that suits you?"

The stairs were carpeted, silent and pillowy under each step. The man carried her bag, looking back to be sure she followed. "A chilly day!" he said, and Agda nodded.

In her room, she rested atop the bed's coverlet. Everything shone in the light from the tall window. A gleaming brass headboard. A polished dresser. A print of a ship at sea, behind glass. A shining porcelain doorknob, like a glossy egg.

Restless, she went to the window, parted the drapes, and looked down. A busy street, the people as varied as pebbles on the ground. A man shouted, another walked with a load of wool on his back. A woman dragged along her two crying children. No sign of her nephew, Maurice. Agda pulled the drapes shut.

Though she'd been a quiet child herself, she was a good caregiver to all her younger siblings, and later on, to her nieces and nephews. She thought she would live that way forever—moving from one brother's house to another's, helping their wives and putting their children to bed. Watching those children grow, then helping with their children, and so on, until she died. Great-aunt Agda. Great-great-aunt Agda. Her arms spread wider with each passing year.

She never had a wish to marry, and no opportunity anyway. She knew she was plain, and her shyness—not the desirable kind, but the frozen, staring kind—put men off further. But she'd had no need for a man and only a churning sort of horror for what happened in their beds.

But when the youngest children started school, her family decided to be helpful. It was noted that James, a distant cousin she'd never met, needed a wife. James wrote not to her, but to her brother. They exchanged three letters before Agda was called into the sitting room.

"I have some very good news, sister."

She preferred not to think of it now—the ease with which she was discarded.

Agda opened the curtain and looked at the street once more. She scanned the crowd for a young man with his wife, but her eyes landed instead on a woman in braids. Agda gasped. It was Lily.

She looked much the same as the last time Agda had seen her, if perhaps a little less cared for—her hair unwashed, her clothes untidy. Just a young thing, still, leaning against the harbour rail.

Beside Lily was a man who seemed quite taken with her—his mouth parted in a smile, red blotches on his cheeks. Lily stretched out her arms and said something that caused him to throw his head back in laughter.

This was no grieving mother.

Lily stepped forward with a stumble, and the young man caught her. As they turned to go, she reached out to a small boy, who was standing at the rail watching the water. A shaggy-haired, dark-eyed little boy, face dirty and feet bare.

Agda's hand flew to her mouth.

She ran out of the room and down the wide stairs, out into the sun's cold glare. The three of them had walked farther down the street, and Agda followed. All the way to the Brown Jug, a rough establishment run by James's brother, Connie. She stood a short distance away as the man held the door for Lily and the boy. When he took a step back to spit off the walkway, Agda approached him.

"*Excusez-moi,* who is that child?"

The man sized her up. "Lily's boy, there?" He nodded at the door. "That's Con Maclean's grandson, Jabe."

He went into the pub and Agda leaned against the outside wall, holding her palm to her chest and struggling to breathe.

"Aunt Agda?"

For a moment, she failed to recognize her nephew, Maurice. He peered at her and gently touched her elbow.

"Are you unwell? We were calling to you."

"Oh." She felt her damp forehead. "I was suddenly tired," she said.

Maurice and his wife took her to the restaurant attached to The Occidental, where they ordered her lemonade and a tomato sandwich. He took her hand. He was tall now, but still so young. His cheeks full and pink, his moustache soft.

"Where were you going, Auntie?" he said, his eyebrows knit into a frown. "Are you here alone?"

He thought her senile, she read it in his concern. She held his hand to her cheek to reassure him, though her mind rocked to and fro. "I am fine," she said. "Truly."

He nodded and looked at his wife, a stout and pretty English girl. Hearty, people would say.

"I've heard so many nice things," she said to Agda, her smile warm, showing a dimple on one sun-bronzed cheek. "He still has the sweater you knitted for him when he was small—the green one?"

"Oh?" Agda looked out the window, her gaze flitting along each passerby.

"He says you sang to him at bedtime. He remembers it fondly."

A child's tender feet would bruise without shoes. Without a sweater, he would catch cold this near the chilly sea. For three years she thought he was dead. For three years she had grieved.

"Oh yes," Agda said. "All the children liked to sing."

Maurice and his wife ate well and Agda tried. They told her things she barely heard, their life brightly filled, an endless ladder of happy plans. The small bakery they would run together, the house they would build for all the children they would have, the garden, the cow, the Sunday picnics with their church. And roses. Edith was known for her buttercream roses.

"You must visit us, Auntie," said Maurice. "We will have a room just for you."

"Oh yes." Agda nodded. "Yes, thank you."

"And how is James?"

Agda had the sense that she was hearing the question long after it was asked, as Maurice's face was expectant but slightly fallen. He and his pretty wife both held their forks over their plates and leaned forward, just slightly.

"Yes," Agda said. "Very good. Always working. I believe he is at one of these islands now." She gestured out the window.

"I would have liked to meet him," said Maurice.

"Yes, it's too bad." Why had James told her the lie? So wretched, so strange, and told with such pained conviction. She remembered his trembling hand at his neck, his eyes filled with horror, as if he'd witnessed every dreadful detail himself.

She'd thought: here is a man capable of deep feeling. Of sorrow. That night when they lay in bed together, he had patted her hand and she'd squeezed his in return. The next morning, he'd made her tea. She had taken comfort in these small acts of kindness.

What a fine actor he was.

"Auntie, did you hear Edith? She is asking if you have help out at your farm. When James is away?"

"I don't need help." Her smile felt foolish to her, for the effort it took to hold it. "Though I am tired. I'm sorry."

So, they took her to her room and said good night. She lay on the bed, wide awake and still fully dressed. Maurice and Edith's voices carried through the thin wall.

Her mind is feeble now. I'm sad to see it.

Has she always been so timid?

Well yes, I suppose. She seemed frightened of everyone, really. Strange. But kind, of course.

Of course.

Perhaps she should come back with us.

And live where? With who?

John might take her. Or Bertrand.

And so on. Then, later, bedsprings. And after that, soft murmurings. Then, finally, silence.

In the morning, they ate a quiet breakfast together, taking solace in the fine view of the harbour through the window. Afterward, Maurice carried Agda's small bag to the stable, where the old mare waited. The goodbye between them was polite and a little removed, as if they spoke to each other through thick glass.

Maurice kissed her cheek. "I will write more often, Auntie. I will send for you to visit once our home is built."

Maurice insisted on paying the stabling bill, and soon she was alone, riding through downtown. The city was just waking up and somehow less hostile than a fully awake one. Like a waking man or a waking bear—clumsy-footed and doe-eyed, placid and soft-spoken. Everything was kinder in the morning, even places like this, and for this reason, Agda turned around and rode toward the Brown Jug.

She tied her horse to the hitching rail, trying to remember which room had been Lily's when she last visited. Stepping back to look at the wide, flat wall, she scanned the windows, sure Lily had been on the third floor. That's when she saw the boy's head peek out. He looked down to the street below and her heart swelled. He must be clever and curious, she thought as she began to lift her hand in a greeting. But he pulled himself up farther, resting his belly onto the sill and craning his neck so he could look down to the street and the harbour.

"No!" she whispered, arm outstretched. But the boy wasn't looking at her. Now he lifted a knee onto the sill.

"No!" she shouted.

She ran inside and found the stairs, rushing to the top. She opened a door where two women were sleeping entwined on a small bed, then another where a man picked his teeth in front of a mirror. Finally, she found her boy. Standing in the window, half dressed and barefoot, his hand on the frame.

He looked over his shoulder at her, unafraid and uncurious. Agda held out her hand.

"Come," she said, forcing herself to smile. She took a step toward him, then another.

He watched as she approached, slowly, cautiously. When her fingertips were inches from his sleeve, his eyes fixed on hers, thoughtful and shining. He took her hand, and she grabbed him and swung him away from the window. She tried to hold him, but he squirmed out of her grasp and climbed up on the bed. Only then did Agda see that Lily was there, sleeping soundly. The boy crawled across the blankets and sat beside her, one hand on her head as he watched Agda. Lily did not stir.

The boy could have stepped right off the ledge and she would have slept through it all.

Agda had the urge to pull the blankets off the sleeping girl, to rip the pillow from under her head and rage at her for such neglect. Instead, she opened her arms to the boy and he came to her. She smelled his hair, sour. And his neck, like soil.

She found a pair of pants for him and a shirt, both too small. And boots—too large. Then she found a pencil and tore a blank page from the front of a Bible.

While you slept this Boy stood at the window and almost fell to his death. He is Not safe here. Have you forgotten you gave him to Me? Agda

"Come," she said, and the boy took her hand.

BEN

1891

HE DREAMED HIS MOTHER WAS HAPPY, SMILING AND SHIMmering like sun-flecked water. She was the sun, and Ben the dark earth, mud in his veins and pebbles for teeth.

Then sorrow, a soft and slithery worm, burrowed deep through his bones, spreading its ache like a slippery fungus.

His mother smiled. She shimmered.

You are good, she said, and he tried to say no, but his teeth fell from his mouth and scattered across the soil. The bed of his tongue sprouted dark with choking weeds, and his fingers reached through dirt, gnarled roots for knuckles. You are good, she said, and he woke, gasping for air.

The dead cow, unearthed by wolves or bears, picked clean by crows, was wasted down to leather and bone. Vetch had grown up through the ribs, and purple nettles filled the skull. Ben stared at it for some time before going to the cabin.

The door screeched when he opened it, and the inside felt like a cave, cold and damp. Mould had sprouted in patches along the edges of the window, and it grew in stiff white hairs from the top of the ash in the stove.

He already knew that Effie had been here at some point that spring. He'd seen her footprints along the muddy trail, and the places where she'd fallen. She'd left his bag on the table, which he'd forgotten at the farm after the fire. She'd also returned his mother's bowl. He touched the little staples, the cracks aged to brown.

Ben was still small when he broke it. Young enough to feel strong as he thrust the bowl to the floor, but old enough to feel immediate horror when it shattered. He'd looked quickly at his mother, but it was his father who spoke first. And his words weren't aimed at Ben.

"Why wouldn't you just let him go visit the Stenhouse kids for Chrissake, Agda? He's always asking, poor fecker, cooped up like one of them—" he batted his hand in the air "—them singing birds in the shops."

The shards had sat on the table until his father's next trip to the city, when he packed them in linen and set them in his bag. Weeks later, he returned with the bowl repaired, held together with wires.

It wasn't long after that his father took Ben to the city.

Ben cleaned out the stove and made a fire to dry the place out. The blankets were musty and damp, so he hung them on the porch railing where the low sun still shone weakly through the trees.

From here, he had a view of the whole yard, like it was a painting—everything meant to be looked at and understood. The tangle of weeds that had been a garden. His mother's grave, hidden in the tall grass. The apple trees, gnarled and black, their dry leaves curled like spotted trumpets.

The leaning cowshed was leaning more. The henhouse had fallen in from the weight of snow, now melted. And the dead cow was no longer of interest to the crows. He went down the cellar and stood in a murky shaft of light, his boots in two inches of water. It was a sort of dream, being back here and once more counting cabbages, all of them lined up on straw like pale heads.

The apples in the barrel were rotten. The onions were soft and black. Only the carrots in their bucket of sand were still edible.

Making his way around the property, he came to the weedy area where the old shed had been. He stepped down the wild green grass and kicked the charred timbers. There were bits of glass in the weeds, a buckled pail. And somewhere, he figured, the snake's blackened spine.

These last months he would have said, if asked, that he had no home. But that wasn't entirely true.

That terrible winter day, after the butter girls confirmed that they had not seen a short-haired woman in a blue dress, the preacher had taken Ben into the city in the badly painted wagon.

The new owners of Gus's butcher shop hadn't seen Lily either, but they promised to write Gus to see if he had.

Oland at the Brown Jug had teared up in worry, and customers sadly shook their heads. Shop owners were sympathetic or unsurprised—a few asked for debts to be paid, and all offered to keep an eye out.

Ben found Mae at her apartment, where he stayed the night. He slept on a chair while she shared the bed with her sick mother, a woman swollen up to a tight gloss. Her eyes were open all through the night, seeming to wander invisible pathways in the air.

"I'll pray for Lily every day," Mae whispered, sleepy and warm. "Remember the sparrow?"

He nodded, but Mae prayed to a distant god, visible only through a lens of water and quite helpless to feed hungry birds on His own. That night, he kept the fire lit and watched its flames curl and sway while she quietly slept.

After looking for Lily in the city, Ben made the long trek to West Cane Lake. He turned down the trail by the school and fought his way through the snowy brush to Connie's cabin. There, nestled in a tin cup, he found the wooden baby wrapped in Penny's lace. He looked at it for some time, as someone might look upon a corpse, his mind turned to dark questions.

Careful to protect the delicate lace, he held the baby in his palm. It looked startled with its misshapen face, its strange eyes that were too large and too blue, its mouth too red.

As much as he tried, he could not remember—did Lily leave it before they walked away? Or had she returned to the cabin alone and placed it on the table for him to find? Each possible answer meant something different. Each was troubling in its own way.

With no sign of Lily, Ben ended up back at the creamery. She could turn up in her funny way, in her own time, as Lily had always done. And the preacher was happy for the extra set of hands. He offered Ben a job helping replace the small log springhouse with a larger one made of stone. Charlie, who had known Ben's father—*stete, álkem*—joined in the build when he was around. And the preacher worked alongside as well, always sorting through the conflicts of his mind in preparation for the next sermon.

"How do you reconcile," he said, wrenching up a rotten timber, "a God of three parts?" And later: "How does a perfect creator create sin?"

Then, as they put away their tools for the day, "Where does God reside, if not here with us as we suffer?"

And so on. The preacher paused often when he spoke out these concerns, his wide smile faltering. Ben and Charlie could only shrug, both feeling helpless in advising on matters of the spirit.

At the creamery, the days were long, the meals hearty, and the nights astir, never quite settling into silence. From his pallet next to the stove, Ben would hear the butter girls whispering in their shared room above.

They stepped over him in the early hours on their way to the outhouse, and the preacher, when he was restless, would heat a cup of milk, his stockinged feet inches from Ben's face. When Charlie stayed nights, he slept next to Ben, speaking Lekwungen in his sleep.

Ben took a book from the preacher's collection to read, *The Royal Natural History,* volume IV. A tough chew but a distraction from things he preferred not to think about—the thoughts that kept him weighted to the pallet, like stones were piled on his chest.

On days off, Ben went into the city. Still no one had seen Lily. But finally, Gus's cousin received a reply.

> *Now what's Lily gone and done? I tell you if she makes it out my way I will promptly put her back on the Boat and give her a good Tongue Lashing while I'm at it.*

And there were other thoughts troubling his mind. Ben knew nothing of Will and how he fared in his illness, or Effie, who he'd last seen in the little barn, angry and exposed by lamplight. And Mr. Stenhouse. He would see Ben differently now. *A bad egg,* he might mumble under his moustache. *A sorry character, turns out.*

Time rolled on, and winter turned to spring. Everyone at the creamery worked until late, then shared noisy meals at the long table. The butter girls drank beer and laughed and cursed and talked over each other. They teased Ben and taught him to braid hair, and patch his clothes, and grind rosehips for tea.

Sometimes they fought and sometimes Ben heard them love each other. He became used to it all.

On Sundays, they rode in the wagon to church and listened to the preacher's red-faced recitations. On one of those days, after the snow melted, Ben watched as Mae was baptized again—and again, she pulled him into the trees afterward.

Grass turned green, and tender shoots reached up through the wintery soil. The pocked girl, Gertrude, gave birth to a baby boy, named Obadiah. Martha, the sullen cook, also became pregnant—and more sullen. Young Patience became ill, her cheeks flared red and her feet swelled. Then she recovered. Aggie ran off with a married man.

Calves were born and one died. The gardens were planted and the birds ate the seeds, after which the butter girls built a scarecrow woman in a pale yellow dress, then replanted.

Ben and Charlie got to know each other. When Charlie wasn't at the creamery, he sold herring, dried and smoked, and he delivered the post to lighthouses in his grandfather's dugout canoe. Every fall he travelled with his cousins, aunts, and uncles to Washington State to pick hops, returning with full pockets and, for some of them, Lummi wives.

Charlie often returned to the reservation. A childless place now. The quiet was strange, Charlie said. The village felt old, and therefore dying. When he was home, his mother would hold his face in both her hands. She called him *hemu*—pigeon.

In reply, Ben had told Charlie about his own mothers. The one who raised him and the one who was lost to him. He spoke of his father, whose very nature made him unable to understand love.

"Huh. That doesn't sound right," Charlie said.

"You met him."

"I didn't like him. But he seemed lonely to me."

Ben shook his head. "That's how he liked it. Alone. Did you know he killed a man?"

"That doesn't sound right either. Cowards don't kill, they run."

Ben continued to work his way through the preacher's book. He found himself enamoured of hummingbirds, nightjars, and green painted pigeons. Sometimes he would go back to the beginning, just to re-read the introduction.

> *To an ordinary observer there would seem but little in common between a scaled lizard or snake, a cuirassed crocodile, and a carapaced tortoise, on the one hand, and a feathered bird on the other. Nevertheless, the connection between Reptiles and Birds is exceedingly intimate...*

One night, when Charlie crawled onto the pallet next to his, Ben read this to him.

"Huh. Guess they all have yellow eyes." Charlie shrugged. "Hunting eyes."

Later, when Ben read it to the preacher, he said, "Well now, Ben, if I thought long enough about it, I could find much in common between myself and this rock. Or this rock and that hat on your head. Boil us down to our elements and we're all made of the same stuff, eh?"

In all this time, Ben didn't once dream of his mother. Rather, he had the usual sorts of dreams—ordinary and bizarre at once, as dreams go. A man plated in shimmery scales asking after the weather. A tree without end. A woman undressed and partly hidden behind the weeping branches of a willow—a thigh, a soft belly, a tongue dripping honey. Her fingers ran through the drizzling green leaves, revealing flashes of skin.

Summer washed in, marked by quiet changes—the slowing of the creek, the emergence of swollen green fruit on plants. The sun's blazing intrusion on night.

Finally, slowly, strangely, there came word of Lily. Or the idea of her, anyway. Seen on a steamboat in Puget Sound with a toothless captain. Seen drunk in a roadside inn. Seen chopping potatoes in a logging camp kitchen. Up north, arm in arm with a fine-looking woman (with whom she was showing all manner of shocking affection). Seen and seen, but never heard from. Not yet.

Ben still stopped his work whenever someone came down the long drive to the creamery. He was always looking for her blue skirts, dragging in the dust.

The creamery did have visitors—people who came to trade with the preacher or sit at their table. From these, Ben learned that Mr. Stenhouse had finally shot the cougar that had tormented his family. Ben had been smoothing mortar when he heard a visitor tell the preacher about it.

"Stripped the hide off and nailed it up next to the door of his house," the man said. "He's happy to show it to anyone who stops by. Tells you the whole story too."

But Ben thought of Effie. Facing that poor cougar's hide every time she entered the house, feeling its eyeless gaze at her back as she left it. That night, Ben dreamt that Effie stood before the wildcat. Plucked it from the wall and set it down on the ground, where it stood up on its four legs, gave its spine a shake, and walked off.

In midsummer, Mae showed up at the creamery. She was given a pink dress of her own and a job milking cows with her calloused seamstress fingers. Her mother was with God now, she told Ben. In heaven, where her face was once again bright and her mind a catalogue of every memory, as it used to be.

"She could tell you about any day of her life. What she ate and what the weather was and everything. She could quote any Bible verse by book and number."

* * *

Summer began to ease, nights became cooler. Leaves turned brown, while fruit took on new colour. Everyone at the creamery, save Ben, took to swimming in the evenings in the pool near the springhouse, after long, sweaty days of work. Ben turned down all offers and pleas to join in, instead placing himself in charge of building the large fire where, after dark, they cooked fish over the flames in damp clothes. When things went from raucous to quiet, the butter girls headed off to their beds above the kitchen, lanterns bobbing in the black like tiny boats at sea. Mae went along with them, unless she joined the preacher in his room or, on the best nights, joined Ben on his pallet by the stove.

One night, after the others had left, the preacher stayed with Ben at the fire. Orange sparks soared and died against the night sky.

"The springhouse is nearly done, Ben. But I sure would love to have you stay on permanent. You like it here, I think?"

Ben straightened his hat, then looked at the buildings, black shapes at odd angles, now familiar.

"I do like it here."

The preacher leaned forward and looked at him steadily. "What I can offer is a bed in the kitchen, or the room above the springhouse if you prefer the quiet. I can give you two dollars for a full week's work. If we have it, that is." He smiled wide, palms up. "But always, we will keep you well fed. I can promise you that."

"Thank you, preacher." Beneath the flames, and beneath the crackling logs, the coals flickered brilliantly, a tiny city lit up with fiery lanterns. "Can I think about it?"

That night, near the warm stove, with the whole house whispering and snoring, Ben didn't read. Instead, he thought about his past few months at the creamery. He'd grown used to the preacher's method of management, that is to say no method at all. The preacher had no grand plan, only small and fleeting ones, and every idea brought to him was treated as greatly inspired. The creamery, Ben learned, made little money, and no one seemed too much concerned. The congregation itself was unsteady in numbers—as though the little stone building breathed, filling and then emptying, so that at times only the butter girls and Ben sat in the pews. The preacher took this in stride as well. His only doubts lay within—the midnight walks down by the creek, the unanswerable questions, and, though rare, the days spent in his room, while the butter girls cast knowing glances. Sick in spirit, they'd whisper. But he always returned as he was—a friend, and a ready talker and listener.

The preacher was opposite to Mr. Stenhouse in near every way, and the creamery entirely different from the Stenhouse farm.

He did like his pallet in the kitchen of this full and busy house.

But thoughts of the farm brought thoughts of Will, who he hoped had recovered. And Effie, who he missed.

And so, on the morning after they'd finished building the springhouse above the creek, Ben woke early and looked out the window that showed a lavender sky. He felt the pull, from deep within, like a fishhook had plunged in his belly and tugged.

He rose in the dim and quiet kitchen and put on his boots, then leaned over to Charlie on the pallet next to his.

"Charlie." Ben gently shook his shoulder. "Tell the preacher I'll be back soon."

Charlie grunted but didn't move.

"You'll tell him?"

With a moan, he mumbled into his pillow, "I said yes."

At the road, Ben did not turn toward the city but toward Ash Mountain. Near midday, he passed Petrenko's, where the windows were dark and a moustached man sat in the open door. The two said hello, and Ben continued. When he reached the Stenhouse farm, he left the road but, instead of walking up their drive, went into the trees and out of sight all the way to the yard. From the bush, he studied the buildings and the corrals, the black spot where the small barn had burned. The women were in the garden. Mr. Stenhouse was in the field working alongside another farmhand, a stranger. In front of the house, the twins were sitting on the steps plucking chickens, and behind them, next to the kitchen door, hung the cougar's hide. And there was Will. Sleeping on the porch in his father's chair, chin to chest, a blanket across his lap.

Ben slipped back into the forest. Without planning to do it, he turned back and took the trail to the cabin.

AGDA

1882

FOR YEARS, MOTHER AND SON LIVED WELL TOGETHER. THEY had little at their homestead, but it was a contented life with James away. A quiet plot, a few goats, two pigs, a bordered garden with mature apple trees. They worked hard and there was kindness between them.

But as Ben grew, this calm slowly changed. Beginning with tiny rebellions, and becoming bolder, more disruptive, until Agda watched her boy of eight depart, walking behind James, following his footsteps in the mud.

He didn't understand, of course, the nature of people. How darkness spread from one to the next like a blistering fever.

Before he disappeared into the trees that day, Ben had looked back and waved. She had smiled but, when he vanished, she leaned back against the doorframe, palms holding her stomach.

On the second day after Ben left, Agda took the same path as far as Petrenko's Dry Goods & Post. She brought with her a round of goat cheese wrapped in chestnut leaves, a small loaf of bread, and four apples tied in a kerchief. Along the walk, she watched for Ben's footprints, either behind or inside James's large ones.

The Howland dog joined her halfway, creeping through the trees. He was a bristly, bony thing with large pointed ears and long legs, a solitary creature that still wanted to be near people, but not too near. Agda felt a kinship with the beast, but also found him unsettling. She wondered: *Is this how others see me? Lurking and quiet. Watchful and strange.*

At the store, Mrs. Petrenko came from behind the counter to greet her.

"Oh, Agda, it's lovely to see you." She poked her head out the door and waved her arm at the dog, then smiled broadly. "I'll tell you what, if I ever see old Joe Howland again, I'll have a word or two for him."

"He's a good dog, really," said Agda. "He only follows."

"Well, my customers don't like it." Mrs. Petrenko poured them tea at the little barrel stove. "I'm sure you know, but I saw your boy not two days ago."

"Yes. James wanted his help."

"An adventure for a boy, going into the city. You've raised a sweet soul, Mrs. Maclean."

Agda discussed polite topics with Mrs. Petrenko—the dry spring, the unusual thunderstorm that had swept through, an early aphid infestation on Agda's apple tree. A customer came in and Agda watched as he purchased coffee, lye, and dried herring. When he left, she finally asked it.

"And how is Mr. Petrenko?"

Mrs. Petrenko led her to the back room, where the midday sun was sending slivers of light through the Garry oak branches into the window. Ed lay in bed, propped on two pillows. His mouth hung wide and his eyes were unblinking and unfocused.

Agda crossed from the door to his bedside. She was looking at something forever changed—the place where a tree stood only a day before, or a pleasant home now burned to a hollow shell.

Mrs. Petrenko pushed a chair next to the bed and Agda sat.

"He appreciates a quiet visit, I'm sure, Agda. Poor fellow must be tired of my gabbing."

Agda kept her hands clasped in her lap as Mrs. Petrenko poured more tea and talked of their son, now out in Ontario with a fine young wife.

"A grandchild soon to come, and won't Ed be proud."

"Yes," said Agda, though it splintered her heart. The man had no idea of anything at all. He wasn't even here in this room with the two women who loved him.

On one of his visits, a day in early summer, Ed had brought his strong cider, which they drank after picking aphids off the apple tree. It was Agda's fondest memory of him, or nearly—drinking to giddiness near the fire while Ben slept behind the curtain. When he said goodbye, he swept aside a strand of her hair, kissed the blue vein at her temple. She thought then, next time he will come into my bed. Next time I will welcome him. And she did, and so it continued all through that summer while James was away. Until he stopped coming and she learned, from Mrs. Stenhouse, that "Poor old Ed Petrenko went and had a stroke. Talked nonsense, then slid off his chair like a bag of buckwheat."

Agda had to clamp her hand to her mouth to keep from crying out. She knew enough to understand the natural consequences of things, and felt the immediate weight of their secret wrongdoing.

Now, in this room with him, she wanted to take his hand. Tell him she was sorry he had suffered this punishment and not her.

Mrs. Petrenko was watching, so Agda straightened and met her steady look.

"I should go. Thank you for the tea."

"I know," Mrs. Petrenko said, "that the two of you were dear friends to each other."

Agda couldn't move, couldn't even look away from Mrs. Petrenko's sensible gaze.

"We've been married these thirty years, Mrs. Maclean. Nothing is secret under a roof shared so long."

And without willing it or thinking it, Agda said, "Yes. And perhaps he was as lonely here with you as I was with James." She pressed her hand to her mouth, felt the scrape of her teeth on her palm.

Mrs. Petrenko smiled as her eyes filled with tears. "Well, it is not news to me that we were an odd pairing."

"I shouldn't have—"

She waved it away. "No. It's why, I suppose, I can be an unreachable friend. I'm a good old sport, Mrs. Maclean, and it makes me a little tough to chew. I see why he longed for softness." She thumped her hand on her chest. "I mean, softness of feeling. I myself have a rather thick shell."

"It's not at all how I see you."

"I'm sure you both knew that somehow I'd rally. And here we are."

Agda walked quickly in the mud and the chill, still carrying the bundle of gifts. Behind her, she heard the stirring of leaves and saw that the Howland dog was following. She stopped and turned to the dog, her eyes blurry with tears.

"Go!" she shouted, pointing. "Get!"

She stomped her feet at it and, as she did, the dog lowered its head. The fur on its neck bristled and a rumble came from its throat. She reached in her bag and pulled out the loaf of bread, then held it out to the dog. For a moment, everything was quiet.

Then the dog lifted its lip and showed a pointed yellow tooth. With the bread held firm, Agda swooped her arm high to throw it into the trees. And the dog lunged.

Agda didn't scream as she fell—there was no time. The dog bit her ankle and ran off into the woods, carrying the loaf of bread like a pup.

* * *

The sun was low when she reached the creek that ran beside the path. Here she sat, breathing heavily, her hands shaking as she lifted her skirts. The blood was scant. Four puncture wounds, tidy black marks on her pale skin.

But the pain was like fire in her bones.

She dipped her ankle into the cold water. It eased the burn as her foot went numb, thin ribbons of blood washing away. Breathing deeply, she looked into the trees where buds had formed along the slender branches. She felt a peculiar lifting, a solace at this small hurt. The permanent mark of it. Now, finally, all was in balance.

At home, she cleaned the wound and dressed it, then lay in bed alone.

Her boy would be home soon, so she allowed herself one last grieving of her dear friend, one last guilt and sorrow. Then she tucked it away where she might one day forget, or at least think less about it.

In the morning she put on a pair of James's trousers and washed her muddy dress. She pinned it to the line and went to work, digging ashes into her garden.

BEN

1890

BEN HAD FALLEN ASLEEP OUTSIDE. HE BLINKED, BRINGING into clear focus the rough and rotting porch boards beneath his cheek, then the spray of colour that spotted them. He reached out and traced the tiny bits of colour on the wood—blue, orange, red, green. Paint. A thousand specks.

Sitting up, he looked at the far side of the crooked porch. There was a larger splat of brown near the railing.

It didn't take him long to find Effie's things in the back of the cupboard. Two paintings and a small satchel of paints, a nightdress, a quilt, a stub of candle, and a near-empty jar of plum preserves. He nodded, nearly smiling. He liked the idea of Effie using this place for something good.

Leaning the paintings against the wall, he stood back. One picture was of the cow's skeleton with a black crow on its skull. The other was unfinished—a strip of grey surrounded by billowing shades of green, which he took to be the shaded creek behind the farmhouse.

He put them back in the cupboard, then checked his bag that Effie had returned. She'd filled it with coffee, a can of peaches, hard cheese, pickled whitefish, bread gone mouldy, and a jar of milk, now separated into a briny base and a thick, curdled top. Also his mother's bowl, in which she'd placed a stack of notes.

Again I come to find your place Empty. Anyway, you'll want to know that Will walked the yard today…

His breath left him. He took the bag outside and sat on the steps with the can of peaches and the letters.

Ben,

You won't be surprised to hear that Eli spilled the beans about you making Will sick. That is entirely my fawlt when I said those things on the night of the fire. I do wonder if you'll forgive me. He spun a fine tale about that, Eli did. In its essentials he was attempting to finish the roof repairs by lamplight (The Angel!) and you showed up, ready to fight. I'll tell you, my Father was skeptical. I knew by the old twitch of the moustache. Anyway, later when my Father found my burnt up boots he set them in front of me without a word. What could I say? There is no sensible reason for my boots to be in the barn in the middle of the night while it burned.

So. I'll tread carefully until Rudy leaves for a wife or a better job. I'll speak for you again when the time is right,

Effie.

PS. Eli hasn't been around since. He fears me now and what an odd feeling that is. In truth I enjoy it.

Ben.

Here I am again in your bleak little cabin. Where are you?

I should come out and say it more plainly. I was harsh when last we spoke. I suppose you think I blame you for Will and I suppose I treated you terrible for walking into the barn. First off, you were right to go to a friend when sick. What else? No one with a speck of brains would blame you for that. I guess I said it just to be awful.

That business between Eli and myself. I'm embarrassed by it. He's terrible isn't he? So why would I go with him to the barn? I don't have much of an answer only that I wanted to know things. You're clever enough to catch my meaning. I went hoping Eli would show a side of himself that was surprising. Well he didn't.

Sarah, silly girl, expects her wedding night to be full of delights and I of course can't warn her that with Eli it will be nothing whatever to do with her at all. For the first time I want to take her hand and tell her how good she is, poor old pretty Sarah.

Dinners are quiet affairs now. No ideas or arguments from Will. No Eli and Sarah to pester. And you my friend aren't there either to nudge me with a sharp elbow when I misbehave. Rudy of course only agrees with everything and my Father says nothing at all.

Ben,
Might as well not get your hopes up about living here. Rudy went and married some giggling sort from church and Father's already replaced him with an imbecile named Mal, if you've ever heard the like. I said, what about Ben? He made a mistake but he's a good worker, and my Father looked at me straight, chewing his tobacco, then he spit on the ground and said Effie do not advise on matters not your own. So there you have it. I am formally banned from all plain speaking and you poor fellow are out of a job.

Ben set the letters down and looked at the pile of them. Effie was making near-daily visits to the cabin since he'd last seen her. Which meant she'd return soon enough.

He lay on the porch and looked at the sky. Time slowed when a person was alone. The *tok-tok* of crows in the day's heat. Shadows crawling across the yard. The rumble in his stomach getting louder.

He let his thoughts fall away. There was only himself and the wide sky, and he began to feel like he was not looking up but down. His back clung to the earth as he looked deep and down into the blue. He became dizzy, thinking *What if the earth lets me go? What if I fall like an acorn through the bottomless sky?*

That's when his mother said, *Get up.*

But when he refocused his eyes, it was Effie standing over him. From this angle, she looked like an eagle, sharp-eyed and ready. And something else. Ben shielded his eyes to get a better look. She was in tears.

"Where have you been?" she said.

"Just working. At a creamery."

"Well." She sniffed and shook her head, glancing at the yard, then back. "You look different. Filled out or something."

He sat up and moved over so there was a spot on the step for her, though she hesitated before sitting.

"I was hoping I'd see you," he said.

"You read my letters?"

"Yeah."

"Well?"

"I know you, Effie," he said. "I'm not angry with you. And I knew I'd lost the job with your father. It's all right."

He felt her relax next to him.

"How's Will?" he asked.

"On the mend."

"Better?"

"On the mend, as I say. But he's weak. Shriveled lungs. Would you believe I'm a gentle nurse?"

He looked at her, squinting into the sun.

"Well," she said, "perhaps not entirely gentle. He's morose and I'm stubborn. Anyway, I've developed a certain patience."

"He's stronger than me," Ben said. "He'll recover, I think."

"Like I did?" She held his gaze, then looked away. "No. It's not as bad as that. When Father went back to working till dark, I knew we were done worrying. You should have seen him pacing the hall though. Listening at the door while mother prayed."

"Are they angry at me?"

"They don't talk about you, Ben."

He leaned forward and set his elbows on his knees, staring at his dusty boots.

"It's funny," she said. "I never figured you to be a fighter."

"I'm not."

"No, I suppose not. But you have a ready temper, don't you?"

"Not usually."

"Well, if anyone can dig one up in a person, it's Eli."

"What does your father think of you coming here?"

"The first time I came, he showed up to get me, without a word. He tired of that and sent Mal. After that, no one came at all." She shrugged. "Now I do what I want. Sometimes I sleep here."

"I knew you did." He didn't mention the paintings.

"So. What now?"

"I don't know. I just wanted to"—he shrugged—"see everything. I wanted to see how you were. And Will. This place."

"Well. After a while, I thought I was writing to no one."

He smiled. "You're nicer in your letters."

"Ha. Maybe so." She looked at the yard. "Let's pick blackberries and have lunch."

In the cabin, he grabbed his mother's bowl and they took it to the tangled patch out at the sunny edge of the yard. They worked quietly.

Effie's face was turned away from Ben, her scalp burned pink where the hair parted. The berries were fat and glossy, and the bushes were wild with the sound of insects.

When the bowl was half full, Effie poured them each a tin cup of brandy she kept in the cupboard. They drank it on the step, along with a picnic of cold chicken, bread, yellow plums, and blackberries, their fingers stained purple, their bare and dusty feet out for cooling.

Leaning back on her elbows, Effie told him about a trip she took to help her aunt with sick children. She was loose and at ease with sweet brandy in her veins, skirts hiked up to her knees, where tiny gold hairs caught the evening light.

"Lord," she said, letting her head fall back. "I've never been so glad to be barren. I think my parents hoped I'd find a husband though. They looked disappointed when I returned as I am."

"I can't see you as a farm wife, Effie."

"Ha. Well, what else to do with me?"

They drank until it grew cool and they went inside, a little clumsy. There were new sides to Effie that he was just now seeing. When she wrote letters, she opened up all of her feelings, and when she drank more than a swig of brandy, she told stories. She told one now, as he built the fire to heat blankets for her leg.

"I used to lie, you know. When I was small. Mostly to my father."

"Yeah?" He looked over at her, where she slouched in his father's chair, her eyes lit up in mischief.

"I'd tell him Mrs. Lamb came to visit when she didn't, or that I named a kitten Pansy when really I'd named it Roberta. Things like that."

"You need better lies."

"I know. Wasn't I strange?"

"Maybe you just wanted something to say."

"One time, I told him a wolf prowled nearby, so off he went with his gun. He was gone all day. Had to work late that night to finish chores."

Ben closed the door on the stove and sat in his chair. He looked again at Effie, whose brightness had faded.

"I don't know why you'd do that," he said. "Other than being angry at him."

She leaned back again, chewing her thumbnail, her good leg over the arm of the chair and her head against the wing.

"I wrote another letter. You want to read it? I think you'll be surprised."

"Yeah, I'll read it."

She dug through her bag and brought out a slip of paper, then held it up and out of his reach. "Don't think about going back to that creamery just yet," she said. "Just put that from your head for a moment."

"All right."

He took the letter and leaned toward the fire to see it well. The words swam on the page, the firelight turning the paper to gold.

Well Ben,

Who knows if you'll ever read any of these letters? Or if all this time I'm talking nonsense to myself. I do hope you'll return because I have quite an idea that might serve us both fine. Mrs. Petrenko has put her store up for sale. You know she was all funny in the head and now her son's come out from Ontario. Mother said he found her in her nightdress knee deep in the lake looking for Mr. Petrenko. She didn't know her own son and treated him badly when he tried to get her on dry land—

"She's as bad as that?" Ben asked. "There's nothing to help her?"

"I don't know. I don't think so. Keep reading."

As you know, Father wants your land and he wants it for the price he offered you. You also know I'm good at keeping accounts. Better than Will, though no one sees it. I've helped Mrs. P over the years, and her son has offered to train whoever buys the place. You know I'm a quick learner, and I have ideas to increase profits—fishing supplies, portraits taken, cured meats. And being the only store at Ash Mountain, it'll never want for customers...

Ben set the letter down in his lap, his head floating as he looked into the fire. He imagined it—Effie keeping ledgers, ordering stock, dealing with customers in her cool, quick way.

"What I'm thinking, Ben, is we could do this together."

He looked up. Effie hadn't moved. Her body seemed heavy with sleep, but her eyes were bright and focused on him.

"We'd be good," she said. "You know. Good together."

And before he could form a thought about it, she undid the buttons of her dress, exposing her breast to him as simply as someone exposes their head when they remove their hat.

For only a blink, Ben glanced to the letter in his lap, but it was long enough that her face had hardened when he looked back at her.

She quickly did the buttons back up.

"Effie—"

"It doesn't matter."

Her cheeks were red and her chin tight. But he knew better than to say anything more, so he got up and added more wood to the stove, taking his time crouched before the fire and blowing on the flame.

"I'm slower at figuring things than you, Effie," he said.

The rest of the evening was passed in quiet, and they went to bed early. From the sofa in the lean-to, he watched her undo her long braid. With the lamp on the other side, he saw her in profile—the straight line of her nose, her hair falling forward. She slipped her dress off over her head and hung it on the bedpost, bare arms reaching to the side table. When she blew out the lamp, all was black.

In the morning, Effie rose while it was dark—he heard the ropes of the bed, then the hinges and clasps of her brace. He looked out the window at the purple dawn, then turned on his side to watch her. She was sitting with her back to him, buttoning her dress.

He made her coffee before she left, which she drank down quickly.

"I hope you don't get strange now," she said, bending to tie her bag. "It was the brandy, that's all."

"I won't get strange—"

"And I hope you'll still consider my plan." She looked up at him, her eyes pale as ice in the morning light. "To stay?"

"Stay?" He shook his head, running through his muddled memory of the night before. Effie's open dress had replaced all thought of the letter.

"You need a place, right? A job?" She lifted her bag over her shoulder and looked at him straight.

"I know nothing about running a store, Effie."

"Well, I do. Read that letter again. You're confused."

He walked with her to the door and waited as she moved carefully down the steps.

"Effie," he said. She turned around. "You should know I like it at the creamery. I already agreed to work there."

The moment between them felt long. The yard was cool and dewy, the first birds calling.

"That's fine. It was only an idea."

"But Effie, you could run it. I know you could. And I don't need the money."

He held up his hand for her to wait, then went inside and dug the deed from the small cabinet. But when he returned to the porch, he saw only the back of her, a slip of brown dress, a flash in the trees, and then gone.

* * *

That morning, his last in the cabin, Ben read Effie's letter again. She detailed accounts and additions, new services offered and modern products brought in. It was a life he knew she'd live well, and he tried to imagine himself as part of it—a shadowy figure, quietly in place, always on the inside looking out that front window to the road and the lake beyond it. Not long ago, he would have wanted that, much like he'd wanted a life at the Stenhouse farm. A cool room at the back of their barn. A quiet seat at their table.

He put the deed and Effie's letters in his bag, then remembered his mother's bowl and placed it on top. He stepped down the broken step, past the blackened apple trees, dripping with rotten fruit. Past the burned cowshed.

On the trail, Mrs. Stenhouse's words came back to him—mothers want nothing more than to watch their sons walk strongly away.

As he'd done when he was eight, and again after his father died. As he was doing right now. Once more and finally.

JAMES

1875

AFTER JAMES TOLD AGDA THE BABY HAD DIED, SHE DRIFTED about like a beaten woman. And he'd never once struck her. That was his father's way, not his. Would his father have made a cup of tea for a weeping woman? Would he have cut a hole in the wall so sunlight could come in? Ha! Imagine it.

What James worried about most was what she would do in his absence, and so he went less often to the city and abandoned the whisky runs. Then he had Connie's wrath to contend with.

"Would you have another situation?" James asked him, meaning their mother's situation. "Con. Would you have her, you know… afflicted?" As their mother was afflicted, with a deep and disturbed melancholy.

"Your frail wife is not my problem," Connie said. "If you don't want this job, I'll give it to someone else."

So James worked, but it was nearly a year before he again took the long trips through the islands, and it was during one of these that Agda went to the city and stole the boy.

He found out about it when he came home after two weeks away, expecting a hot meal and a sad but dutiful wife. Instead, she met him in the yard and dealt him the news like a hammer to the skull.

"You can't just take a baby, woman!" He threw his hands in the air. "Tell her to tend better to him, that's all!"

But Agda was hard as steel. "I'll do nothing you say," she whispered fiercely. "You are full of dark lies." And, stepping nearer, he saw the blue vein at her temple throbbing. "Why did you tell me he died, James? Something so awful as that?"

His hands dropped to his sides and he stood foolish before her. A stupid man undone by a sharp-tongued wife. When did that happen?

He followed her inside, where the boy was sitting at the table. James looked down and the boy looked up, big, wet eyes black as molasses.

"Well," James said, "why doesn't he say something?"

She went to the boy and pulled him near. "You are frightening him. That's why."

It was true. The boy looked ready to burst into tears.

James shook his head. "What've you gone and done, woman?"

Having a child in the house took getting used to. James felt twitchy and confounded each time he laid eyes him, so he worked longer outside. At night, he slept with his face to the wall while Agda tried to calm the boy to sleep.

James had seen him plenty of times at The Jug, but never like this—crying, kicking, throwing his food on the floor.

What was he supposed to do about it? Why was he caught up in this mess of baby-stealing? Either way, he had a sad woman on his hands.

On James's first trip back to the city after Agda stole the boy, he spent the whole walk turning it over in his mind. What would he say to Lily? Finally, his decision was this: say nothing at all. It happened, it was done. No sense going on about it.

Stepping into The Jug, his eyes landed immediately on his niece. She stood by a table where a man sat—Eustace, swollen and red as any drunkard. Lily's foot was up on the chair next to him, her skirts hiked to the knee to reveal a dirty stocking.

When she saw James, she smiled wide.

"We play a game, Uncle. Eustace has guessed I have twelve stripes on my stockings. If he's right, I buy the next drink." She raised her skirt a couple more inches, revealing another stripe.

"Ten!" Eustace shouted.

James walked up to him and kicked his chair. "Get out of here, you nit!"

The man stood and adjusted his suspenders—an attempt at dignity—then walked, heavy-footed, toward the door. Lily's eyes hadn't left James.

"You're a father now, as I understand it," she said. "How does it suit you?"

"It suits me nothing. I asked for none of this and want no part." He took off his hat and waved it at her. "What are you doing drunk in the day? What's wrong with you?"

Lily sat down in Eustace's chair and leaned back. "Did you know she planned to take my baby?"

"She told me he was hungry and undressed."

"Did you know she takes what isn't hers?"

"It's nothing to do with me."

"You don't like thieving, Uncle. You fire men for it."

"You already gave her that baby. So maybe it's you who thieved when you took off with it to the camp."

"Oh dear. Imagine stealing what's already yours." She called to Eustace, who'd been struggling with his coat by the door. "Eustace, be careful not to thieve your own head when you leave. I'll come after you for it since I've decided it's mine."

Eustace laughed and started toward their table, but James waved him off as if he was furiously swatting a bee.

"It's Merritt you should take issue with," he said to her.

"We were fine, me and Jabe." She pressed her ribs with both palms as if squeezing out the air. "I can't sleep now we're apart."

"You slept fine while he stood in the window. Agda said he would have stepped out to his death if she hadn't come by." He saw by the slow blink of Lily's eyes that he'd hurt her. He pointed at the window to add weight to the matter. "Dead in the street. Like your Penny."

Lily's eyes fluttered shut. James pulled his hat back on and bent forward to get a better view of her face.

"I'm done talking about it," he said. "Take it up with Agda if you like."

"I can tell it troubles you, Uncle. I can tell you know she did wrong."

"I said I'm done!"

"Anyway." She pushed her thumbnail along the woodgrain of the table. "Talking about it makes me all—" Her voice caught as she turned to the window.

"That's what I'm saying," said James. "No need to talk about it."

She nodded, still turned from him, her face red and crumpled.

"Well now, Lily, Agda'll be a good mother to the boy. She'll raise him right."

"And you will too?"

"Sure, but—"

"You'll keep him safe, Uncle?"

"I will. Of course."

She wiped each cheek roughly with her sleeve, then looked at him. "And Merritt too?"

"Bloody Merritt! I—"

"Deliver your temper elsewhere, is what I mean. Not on Merritt and not on Jabe. Will you do that for me?"

"You think me violent?"

She smiled, her face still wet. "If you want that point made, you oughtn't to make fists when you say it."

James looked down at his clenched hands. He stormed out to load the wagon, and Eustace returned to count Lily's stripes.

JAMES

1880

THE BOY WAS GONE, AND SO WAS THE CANOE. JAMES'S EYES followed the ragged trail that ran through the pebbles, where the boat had been pushed back into the water. Confounded, he peered out into the fog that hovered over the channel, but he could see nothing but gulls disappearing and reappearing, screaming like maniacs.

"What'd he go and do?" he muttered, dumbfounded. And then, "Lengnick!" He hurried up the steep path to the old shack, where he found the man passed out in his muddy yard.

"You scare him off, Lengnick?" He kicked him in the shin. "He wouldn't run off for no reason, would he?"

Lengnick slowly rose, then stumbled, then set his hands on his knees like he was going to be sick. But James had no patience for men like this. He badgered and shoved, getting only grunting responses, until he finally put together the gist of the situation. His boy had failed to deliver the whisky, then took off with the cans in the canoe, alone. It seemed impossible. His mind couldn't accept it.

So James demanded that Lengnick row him across the channel in his skiff, with a promise of free whisky on the other side. They clambered down to the beach, and Lengnick rowed through sluggish fog. Throngs of jellyfish hung suspended beneath their boat as James scanned the waters, his anger gathering like smoke in a plugged stove.

But when they reached the small beach, he was faced with the mystery before him, and his anger dissolved. An empty wagon, the nervous horse still tied. No canoe, no boys, and only what whisky was left in the wagon's bed. And, strangest of all, one can sat on the shore, with seawater pooled in its lid. There was no sense to any of it.

"The devil!" James shouted it into the silence, hoarse from the cold. He grabbed two of the cans left in the wagon and handed them to Lengnick, who then rowed off, clumsy and sloshing.

Some evil work was at hand. He knew it. Some dark thievery. Merritt. A stealer of whisky and canoes. A niece snatcher. A thief of quiet sons. When they first met, James knew Merritt would be trouble, but he didn't know he'd be forced to clean up after him. First, paying for Lily's room after Merritt knocked her up, then seeing Agda through three years of misery when Merritt stole off with Lily and the baby to some godforsaken camp. And again, paying for the butcher's place when Merritt abandoned Lily, as James knew he would. Most of all, James had provided for the boy all these years because he knew Merritt wouldn't bother to.

And now. The boy was gone, and Merritt was behind it.

What would he tell Agda?

James paced the beach, scratching his jowls, kicking stones into the water. With a wordless roar, he threw the largest rock to hand into an eddy. In so doing, he saw it, under the low-reaching branches of an arbutus: the paddle. He grabbed it and pushed aside the foliage, eyes scanning the trees in the darkening light, and sure, there lay the canoe as well, washed ashore with the tide, wedged into the tangle of growth.

He wandered farther, not wanting to consider what he was searching for: a young man and a boy. He looked across the strip of sea between the two shores, reading the water like one would read a book, eyes scanning across one way, and back, and across again.

And he spotted it—farther out, barely seen—a strangeness on the water's surface. Small like a floating black dinner plate. Something not of the sea.

James grabbed the torch from the wagonbed and lit it. He righted the canoe, pushed it out, and jumped in, sliding out over the water. The incoming tide splashed against the sides.

If that boy's lost to us, James thought, Agda will wither into her grave. He mumbled it aloud, or some of it. His thoughts often flew unbidden from his mouth.

As he neared the shifting black spot, his stomach gave way. He steadied himself to keep from being sick, then reached out. His hand hovered flat over the feathery black spill before he slowly dipped it into the icy water. He felt hair, slick and soft.

He jerked back, his heart lurching, then carefully he reached in again, fully submerging his arm. He touched a chest, a neck, a stubbled chin. Merritt! Unable to think, James found the collar and pulled, but the body was held tight, anchored in the sea. He yanked with more force and lost his grip, his fingers slipping along cold teeth, a spongy tongue.

He fell back into the canoe, panting and wild-eyed, then looked quickly around himself through the fog and deepening darkness. The torch showed murky depths and floating weeds, but no sign of the boy. He called his name and continued calling as he paddled along the edges and farther out—any which way without order or thought.

His splashing and thrashing disturbed the jellyfish in the dark, and they lit clear and green, their light passing onto his paddle and into the water, but not enough to show a boy by his hair alone.

James searched until it was too dark. Then he pulled the canoe on shore and sat leaning against it, listening to the gentle lapping of water on the pebbled beach, watching the moon's light twist and writhe along the surface of the sea.

He didn't sleep but spent the night puzzling out what had happened. At first light, he hopped back in the canoe. He passed by Merritt, who'd sunk like a man crouching, waving gently with the current. His body no doubt marked the whisky cans he was attempting to steal. No doubt his feet rested on them now like a lifeless dancer on a tin floor. Brought to justice by the strong arm of a kelp plant. Thief!

All day he looked for the boy. When he thought he saw something unusual on the sea floor, he stopped and dove in. But all he found was a shredded woman's coat, an elongated rock, and a rusted metal box. By the end, he was a wet and whimpering man, shivering and blue-nosed. He thought he might die like this, frozen, wretched, alone.

And even that would be better than facing Agda. Or Connie, who already thought him an idiot, unable to complete a simple job. Or Lily, who would lose her baby twice—first by thieving and then by drowning. The boy he'd promised to care for, the one who looked at him with those big black eyes. Better to die here now, thought James, than to face all this.

But as he stood on the shore hugging himself, teeth clattering, the image of Agda came to him. As real as if he were standing in their cabin, smelling her soap smell, and the yeast bread rising in the painted bowl. He saw her so clearly. Sitting by the window. Waiting. Hands twisted together in worry—always worry with that woman.

So he hitched the horse and climbed up in the wagon, where all of Merritt's clothes, he saw now, were draped across the back of the seat, still damp and icy. Hands shaking, he dried himself with the shirt. When he grabbed the rest of the clothes, he felt something inside Merritt's vest. He fumbled in the pocket and brought out a fat roll of money.

Well, there you have it! A thief and a liar, as he'd tried to warn Connie. But who listens to James Maclean?

He tossed the clothes in the trees and stuffed the money into his shirt pocket. Lily's money now. And he left.

EFFIE

1890

EVEN THE BIRDS WERE QUIET IN THIS HEAT. EFFIE HAD LEFT the farmhouse and walked past her sisters, ignoring their questions. She went to the river behind the house, to the place where the deepest pool formed. Her cheeks were flushed, the shorter hairs beside her face were damp and curled. The air was heavy with heat. It exhaled from everything around her—trees, soil, grass. She felt it rise from her body like steam from a kettle.

But down near the river, in the shade of tall trees, the air moved with the water, cooled by the streams that frothed and rolled over mossy rocks. Her dress clung to her sticky skin as she pulled it over her head. She unlaced her boots and unhooked her brace then peeled off each stocking. She plunged in her feet, pale green against the smooth, cinnamon-coloured rocks.

These past nights she had been restless in bed. Embarrassed and angry and unable to sleep. She should have known to keep her buttons fastened and her letters unwritten. She should have accepted what she'd always understood to be true. She was a sharp, hardened girl, and men liked them soft and sweet.

A trickle of sweat ran down her spine. Still in her cotton underwear, she lowered herself into the water, cool and pulsing around her waist. She cupped it onto her arms and neck, then slipped all the way back and under. Like this, she was stretched out in a bed of water, anchoring herself with her hands on the polished rocks beneath her. Above, the world was broken up, but below, everything was clean and dark and cool. It hummed in her ears.

She rose to the surface and took a breath, then moved to the rocks, where the water rushed around her, forming new pathways in the shape of her, pushing and fluttering the thin cotton of her drawers like fish gills.

Her eyes closed and her pores opened, inviting the river—she was a fish. The water sliding along every bit of her skin, where a shiver crept, on down and surprising. Her neck softened and her chin tilted up, eyes drawn to the branches.

With a gasp, she thrust forward, palms pressed into the mossy rock in front of her, face hovering over the brilliant green. Loamy water seeped between her clenched fingers, and a brown spider, the size of a freckle, disappeared into the tiny fronds.

The next morning, she woke in a bed to herself. With Sarah married, she could stretch wide, hands and feet to the four corners, face to the full morning sun while the twins still dreamed. Then, quickly, she got up and put on her brace, hearing her own excited breath. She went downstairs where her father was just heading outside and her mother was at the stove making some comment about Effie sleeping late.

At her father's desk in the sitting room, Effie took out a sheet of paper and envelope and began her last letter to Ben.

Ben, I have decided I will accept your offer. Here is what I propose…

BEN

1891

BEN LEFT THE CREAMERY BEFORE THE SUN ROSE AND ARrived at Effie's store by mid-morning. It sat cool under the firs and oaks on the side of the road, where the grass was still wet from the morning's dew. A fine mist rose off the lake on the other side.

Inside, he found Effie standing on a chair. She was arranging Birmingham reels along the top shelf—little brown boxes in a tidy row. She glanced quickly at him over her shoulder.

"Oh good. I have a job for you. Out at the old Balodis place. Do you remember it?"

"Hello to you too, Effie."

She blew hair from her eyes. "Hello, Ben. Are we in need of cordialities now? Like strangers?"

"Are you cordial with strangers?"

"Ha. Cordial enough."

Ben took off his hat and helped her down. It had been a month since he'd seen her, and now she avoided his look, as she did every month until she warmed to him once more.

He nodded to the reels. "Are they selling?"

"Yes. I knew they would. That's my second order, which means more money for you."

She went to her ledger and turned to the last page, running her finger along Ben's earnings. Never much, but this was the first thing she did whenever he arrived. Early on, he'd argued about taking it, because the money only sat in the tin in his bag. But he'd learned that paying Ben was part of what Effie wanted and what made her feel right around him.

"Who lives at the Balodis place now?"

"A young couple—Mr. and Mrs. Foster. With a baby. But mostly it's about the house. It's newly painted. They want the whole place in the picture."

He went to gather his camera equipment. Effie kept it neatly stored in the back room under her bed, along with her paints and boards that she was too busy to use.

The idea of a photography service was one of the first new things she'd proposed when she bought Petrenko's store last fall. At first, he did it for Effie—reading through the three fat manuals that came with the equipment and practising on her stern-faced poses. But it wasn't long until he found himself enjoying it. He liked the trek out to the homes and meeting the families, the newlyweds, the old couples, the children, the dogs. Sometimes the dead, a somber task he handled quietly, politely.

The long process of developing images needed a fine touch, and the careful and precise magic of it soon appealed to him as well.

But the photographs themselves unsettled Ben. He felt he was looking into the eyes of someone long gone. And they were. The person in the image was no longer standing still in front of their home or stiff and wide-eyed before their hearth. By the time he lifted the photographs from the developing pan, they had moved on with their lives and that moment was behind them.

Later, when they came into the shop for pick up, he'd watch them study their own faces and see that they were unsettled too. They'd glance at their own image, quick and embarrassed, or lingering and long, then showing others. They'd go home to hang the pictures on their walls.

See there. It is us as we were. Not as we are.

Ben had no images of himself, but he had kept one of Effie, which he used to mark his place in the books he borrowed from the preacher. Effie didn't know, of course. She'd asked Ben to burn all his practice photographs of her. But he'd slipped this one into his pocket while tossing the rest in the fire. Effie as she was, looking straight at him, unguarded and honest.

Effie put the sign in the window—PHOTOGRAPHER IN—and it would remain there for the two days he stayed over. Ben hefted his pack over his shoulder, placed his tight hat back on his head, and told Effie he'd be back after his visit to the Balodis place. Come evening, they'd have some brandy by the stove, as was their custom, and Effie would finally warm to him, a little.

He'd heard the murmurs—Effie was no Mrs. Petrenko. She offered no whisky tea. She snapped her fingers at children who poked or stared, and the candies were for purchase only, not to be touched by dirty little hands. People came to Petrenko's Dry Goods & Post (she'd kept the name) because it was the only store at Ash Mountain, but they didn't linger in a chair by the stove as they used to.

And there was other talk, concerning Ben and his nights spent at Effie's on the first and second of every month. Word was, they had no plans to marry but shared a bed.

And they did. It came to pass one winter night, after their brandy. Instead of going straight to the cot, he joined her under the quilt and never again slept alone during his visits.

As Ben put away his equipment, getting ready to leave, a few schoolchildren hung around the front step, sucking the pink candies he'd passed them on the sly.

He walked by the open door, holding a stack of newly arrived glass plates, thin as new frost, and he heard one of them say, "You have to get real close or you won't see her."

Ben stopped in the doorway. "See who?"

One of the boys was on the other side of road, peering down the trail. The other children turned to Ben, quiet and unsure.

"You're not in trouble," he said.

After a bit, they gushed out their story.

"The ghost lady."

"Not a ghost, a fish."

"She walks on the bottom of the lake."

"And turns over boats—"

"That's how Karl Karlsson almost died."

"Her dress is filled with rocks. That's what holds her down."

"Her teeth are pointed— Webbed fingers— Scales on her face—"

Ben looked through the trees to the lake, where a little green boat sat lazy in the sun. He nodded toward it.

"She must be sleeping," he said.

"What's going on out there?" Effie asked from behind the counter. She was frazzled over a box of mis-ordered pomade, her cheeks flushed and her hair coming loose. "They're not talking about that woman again, are they? It puts people off."

"They're just having fun. Making up monsters."

"Nothing fun about that," she said, her eyes still on the box.

Ben took the plates to the chest in the bedroom and carefully set them in their wooden slots for safekeeping.

"Bloody pomade. I ordered twelve but I'm expected to pay for the thirty-six they sent by mistake," Effie called from the front room. "They'll pretend at ignorance, too, just watch."

Ben slid the box under the bed.

"If they don't sell, Ben, you'll have to start shining your hair to match your boots."

It was night when Ben reached the creamery. He stopped and took in the expanse of stars. The clean, distant moon. Beneath it, all was in darkness but the jumping silver flecks of light on the black creek.

He walked the bumpy trail, the water bubbling louder as he neared. Dropping his bag, he stripped down to nothing and stepped into the pool to his knees. He knew he couldn't think, just do, so he walked on to the middle where it reached his chest, and he slipped under water—cool and black and coursing. He opened his eyes. Nothing. No grasping weeds, no face of his mother.

He stood and took a breath, water streamed into his eyes and down his spine. He shook it from his ears, then he stopped. Behind him, a woman's voice cried out. He turned and looked toward the house, where Patience called down from the third-floor window.

"Ben, you old devil, swimming without us! Too good for us, you goat! Look at Ben, swimming without us, the sly dog!"

Shivering and naked, he let himself fall back under, and listened to the muffled rush and hum.

Once more he opened his eyes, and this time, with his face to the sky, he saw the shimmering moon. From under the water, it was no longer a cool and perfect pearl, impossibly distant, but a mass of broken green light. It quivered on the water's surface, alive and imperfect, and close enough to touch.

ACKNOWLEDGEMENTS

SPENDING FIVE YEARS WRITING A NOVEL WOULD NOT HAVE been possible without the endless support of my family. To John, who not only endured my new obsessions but enthusiastically encouraged them. And to Maddie, Ethan, and Lex, who cheered me on, even through my absurd secrecy.

I am deeply grateful to my patient and sharp-eyed editor, Fred Stenson. Without him, this novel would remain wordy, purple, and filled with an unusual amount of "elbow clutching." And to Roberta Mitchell Coulter, who provided the final polish that made these pages shine.

I extend my heartfelt thanks to Elizabeth Philips and the team at Thistledown Press for believing in this manuscript, for the meticulous care with which you handled it, and for your willingness to champion new voices in literature.

To my fellow writers from the Ubergroup, The Art of Story, the Humber School for Writers, and Scribophile: Who else understands the late nights and early mornings, the endless research, the struggle to keep swimming when inspiration has drained away, and the ever-present feelings of self-doubt? Without your support, understanding, encouragement, feedback, and shared ideas and resources, I truly could not have reached the finish line.

I would like to thank my mentor from the Humber School for Writers, Colin McAdam, who gave me permission to "go darker." I may have run a little too hard with that, but it was freeing nonetheless. David Adams Richards, who was there before I had much worth looking at but encouraged the bones. Duncan Murell, who helped me figure out how to structure this story with its many flashbacks and varying points of view. And Tom Jenks, an early teacher whose wisdom I still draw upon, and who generously published the first chapter in *Narrative.*

Lastly, I am extraordinarily grateful for the financial support I received from the Canada Council for the Arts, the BC Arts Council, and the Humber School for Writers. Not only did this allow me the time I needed to focus on difficult elements in the novel, but it also gave me the confidence I needed to continue.

ANGIE ELLIS is a writer from Vancouver Island whose short fiction has appeared in *Narrative*, *Story*, *The Fiddlehead*, *Grain*, and other literary journals. Her stories have won the Masters Review Short Story Award, Best of the Net, and Best Small Fictions, and two were longlisted for the CBC Short Story Prize. She has received grants from both the Canada Council for the Arts and the BC Arts Council. A graduate of the Humber School for Writers program, she has also attended the Humber Summer Workshop. She lives in the Cowichan Valley..